"God, I'm on fire for you . . ."

Liza turned the key in the lock and pushed open the door. Eli wasted no time.

She had the briefest of moments to observe his expression before he shoved the door with his foot, braced his back against it, and pulled her into his arms.

Liza managed a slight gasp, then found herself engulfed in a storm. His kiss stole her breath. Nothing had prepared her for the intensity of it. The electricity that shimmered between them had never seemed this overwhelming. The actualization of that energy and the sensation of having his lips on hers, she realized before she lost the ability to think anything at all, swallowed her whole . . .

Other Avon Contemporary Romances by
Neesa Hart

HALFWAY TO PARADISE
A KISS TO DREAM ON

You Made Me Love You

Neesa Hart

AVON BOOKS
An Imprint of HarperCollins*Publishers*

This is a work of fiction. Names, characters, places, and incidents are products of the author's imagination or are used fictitiously and are not to be construed as real. Any resemblance to actual events, locales, organizations, or persons, living or dead, is entirely coincidental.

AVON BOOKS
An Imprint of HarperCollins*Publishers*
10 East 53rd Street
New York, New York 10022-5299

Copyright © 2000 by Neesa Hart
ISBN: 0-380-80789-0
www.avonromance.com

First Avon Books paperback printing: December 2000

Avon Trademark Reg. U.S. Pat. Off. and in Other Countries, Marca Registrada, Hecho en U.S.A.
HarperCollins® is a trademark of HarperCollins Publishers Inc.

Printed in the U.S.A.

10 9 8 7 6 5 4 3 2 1

For Dr. Ronald Childs and Dr. Kathleen French, for keeping me on my toes while I wrote this book. And for my on-line and real-time friends, my fellow Avon Ladies—thanks for answering questions of *any* sort at *any* time, day or night!

1

At least she should be thankful for missing *the tornado*.

Only Eli Liontakis, Liza mused, as she watched him wrap up a lecture to the World Health Congress, had sufficient charisma to convince the board of visitors at Breeland to allow her absence during the orientation for the summer program. That afternoon, while she sat in the cool confines of the ballroom of the Marriott Marquis, five hundred girls, ages 10 to 18, were arriving at Breeland Academy in the small town of Terrance, Georgia. The temperature there, she knew, topped 100 degrees. The humidity made it feel like 110. For years, the staff at Breeland had referred to the harrowing business of getting the students settled and oriented as *the tornado*. And here she was, the assistant administrator of the

summer program, in the plush surroundings of a
hotel ballroom, listening to the current superstar
of medical research charm an international audience of health professionals.

He was expounding on a point, explaining in
riveting terms the strides he was making in the
lab. She studied him through narrowed eyes and
pushed aside a sliver of trepidation. *Charisma*
didn't begin to describe the man's impact. Every
eye in the room studied him with avid attention.
Not, she admitted, that she could blame them. He
was positively mesmerizing. Despite the pictures
she'd seen of him, he still looked taller than she'd
expected. Too tall. His hair—shoulder length and
kept in a neat queue at his nape—was too black.
His shoulders were too broad, his face too angu-
larly attractive. The suit he wore emphasized a
lean torso and slim hips that tapered to long legs.
Despite his size, however, he moved with a grace
that her dancer's eye admired. With a sweep of a
tanned, elegant hand, or the intense look in his
leonine eyes, he had hypnotized his audience.
Was it any wonder the press had taken to calling
him *The King of the Jungle*?

Over the past year, Eli had rocketed to relative
stardom when his research on cell-life and chemical alteration began to attract global notice. If
preliminary reports proved true, Liontakis'
research would likely lead to the first major
breakthrough in cancer treatment and prevention
since the advent of radiation.

With his good looks, his personable speaking
style, and his incredible facility of framing

extremely complex scientific ideas in everyday language, his name had become a household word. Interest in science, chemistry, and pharmaceutical research was peaking in his wake. His style and energy had breathed new life into a languishing field, and his specialty, biochemical research, had started the hottest academic trend since Freud's ego and id. One well-known critic had said, "Liontakis has done for chemistry what Elvis did for the back beat."

Almost overnight, Eli and test tubes full of potential miracles had become icons. When his picture appeared on the cover of a magazine, it was a guaranteed runaway sell-out. Women everywhere seemed to adore his slight accent, his cultured manners, and the edge of barbarism that said all the attention had tamed him merely for a moment. Every talk show, news magazine, and network in America was clamoring for a piece of him. A Nobel prize nomination, and eventual award, seemed a foregone conclusion.

Liza had persuaded Breeland to invite him months before the media firestorm had begun. At the time, she'd believed that his relative youth— he was just 34—and his energetic lecture style would appeal to the students. She'd once heard him speak at a national teacher's symposium. Impressed with his accessibility and creative approach to a normally dry subject, Liza had felt he'd make an excellent addition to the summer teaching staff.

The students, she knew, would benefit from exposure to a scientist so versatile and talented.

But, and this was surprising, he accepted the invitation *after* his meteoric rise to fame had him gracing the cover of *Time* magazine.

For personal reasons he'd discussed only with Anna, he'd agreed to spend the summer at Breeland and delayed responding to offers from several major research facilities. Anna had told Liza that Liontakis' ten-year-old daughter had played a major role in the choice he'd made. He'd also insisted that Liza fly to New York to accompany him and the girl on their trip to Breeland.

As she watched him now, Liza decided it was an unqualified blessing that he'd chosen not to arrive at Breeland on orientation day. The last thing the staff or students needed during *the tornado* was another element of chaos. And Eli Liontakis, she'd learned, spread chaos like Jack Frost spread ice.

As he wrapped up his speech, Liza mentally chided herself to get a grip. She had a job to do. Eli Liontakis was Breeland's star attraction for this year's summer program. And Liza cared too much about the program, its students, and Breeland to let her personal feelings stand in the way of making him feel welcome.

The audience began to applaud, and Liza slipped out the back door for their scheduled rendezvous. She pressed a hand to her stomach as a coil of tension began to tighten. Soon, she reminded herself, he'd be at Breeland. He'd be on *her* territory. Then she'd feel in control again.

She waited in the impressive atrium while he made his way through a crowd of admirers. He stopped occasionally to extend a hand in greeting, or answer a proffered question, but he made his way steadily, inexorably toward her. When he finally reached her, he didn't even stop walking. His long fingers linked beneath her elbow and he steered her toward the door. "Ms. Kincaid?"

"Yes." She resisted the urge to wrench her elbow free of his imprisoning grip.

"Forgive me," he muttered, as he eased her into the revolving door. She stepped onto the sidewalk, where the blast of humidity shocked her skin after the chill of the hotel. He emerged behind her. "I'm not trying to hustle you."

"No?" A bellman jerked open the door of a limo, and Eli ushered her inside. She heard someone call his name from the hotel entrance, but he dived in after her.

When the door slammed shut, the bellman slapped the hood with the flat of his hand. The car glided into traffic, and Eli leaned back against the leather seat across from her with a soft sigh. "No. I'm not. But if we didn't get out of there before the crowd really broke, it would have taken the rest of the afternoon."

She felt a little disarmed by his easy grace. In the confines of the car, she was unprepared for the impact of his undivided attention. "I understand," she said quietly.

That made him laugh. "No, you don't. You think I'm a pompous ass for making you come up here."

That voice, with its slight Greek accent, Liza thought, ought to be registered as a lethal weapon, and the way he purred his "r's" lent the rich timbre of his tone a certain sensuality that women seemed to find irresistible. "Are you?" she finally blurted out.

"A pompous ass? Lord, I hope not. Maybe you'll forgive me once you've met my daughter."

Probably, she thought. "Her name is Grace," Liza said.

His smile was disarming. "Yes. You'll like her and she'll like you." He jerked at his tie until the elegant silk unknotted. "I'm counting on that."

Liza watched his fingers coil the tie and drop it into his suit pocket. He'd be a lot easier to handle if he'd wear a lab jacket and a pocket protector like any good nerd. "What makes you so sure?"

His broad shoulders lifted in a shrug. "Call it a hunch. The same kind of hunch that sends me off to the lab looking for answers." He'd opened the top two buttons of his shirt. "How much has Anna Forian told you about Grace?"

"Enough to make me agree to come here in the midst of orientation."

He had the grace to wince. "The timing was lousy, wasn't it?"

"The worst. At Breeland, we call orientation *the tornado*," she described. "Did Anna explain the difference between the summer program and our academic year schedules?"

"Yes." He rested a tanned hand on the snow white front of his shirt. "You have residential students during the usual school year, and a full-time faculty. Breeland is one of the most highly acclaimed private girls' schools in the country."

Liza nodded. "Yes."

"And during the summer, you run an enrich-ment program of sorts. You accept girls from dif-ferent social and economic backgrounds for an academic program designed to expose them to a variety of different disciplines. It's like camp for smart kids."

"Sort of." She couldn't keep the pride from her voice. Breeland's summer program tradition spanned decades. Liza always felt the weight and significance of being a part of something incredi-bly meaningful whenever she discussed it. "Our goal is to give students who may never have had this kind of opportunity an introduction to a large variety of disciplines. Because of the tight transition we have between the end of our regu-lar term and the start of the summer program, all our summer students and faculty arrive at the same time. That's why we call it *the tornado*. We have two days to get them settled into the dorms and into the program. All the stuff the girls think they can't live without goes in, and all the furni-ture in the dorms gets rearranged and reassigned to accommodate them. Two opposing forces col-lide on one hot day, and—"

"Tornado." His lips twitched into a near smile.

And at the first glimpse of it, her irritation began to evaporate. Who in the world could resist that damnably sensual smile and—did she dare call it a dimple—the slight slash at the cor-ner of his mouth? She nodded.

A couple of seconds of silence ticked between them. Liza gazed out the window of the limo as it inched its way along Park Avenue. She sensed him watching her but didn't dare meet his gaze. Finally he combed long fingers through his dark hair and broke the spell. "I'm sure you had a thousand things demanding your attention today. I hope you understand that I would never have requested that you come here had it not been for Grace."

That, she supposed, was probably as close to an apology as she was going to get. His ten-year-old daughter, she knew from her discussions with Anna, was the center of his life. Eli hoped, or so he'd told Anna, that a few months on the relatively secluded campus would help her recover from the recent death of her mother.

The raw note in his voice swayed her as little else could. She looked at him again, and saw the pain in his gaze. "Anna told me about Grace," she informed him gently. "I hope you'll find what you're looking for at Breeland."

After a brief pause, he nodded. "So do I."

He continued to watch her with disarming intensity. Liza found herself wishing she'd worn something other than the orange and red linen sundress that protected her from the heat, but not from his inspection. A full suit of armor might have been a good choice. "To tell you the truth," she said, when she could no longer stand the silence, "I'm not exactly sure what you want me to do now that I'm here."

"We won't need much of your time," he assured her. "I just want you to meet Grace and let her get the feel of you. It's going to be crucial that she trust you."

She blinked. "Excuse me?"

He inclined his head in a slight nod, worthy, she thought, of The King of the Jungle. "She has to trust you if this is going to work. Grace will be studying dance with you."

Her breath returned in a gulp. "Oh. Dance. Yes, Anna told me."

"My daughter likes to dance. You'll be her teacher while she's at Breeland."

"I'm not sure you understand, Dr. Liontakis. During the regular school year, I teach several classes, but my responsibilities are different for the summer program. Because I work with Anna as the assistant administrator, I have more general interaction with the girls."

"But you teach one class."

"Sometimes."

"This year you're going to."

She was beginning to understand why his critics called him tenacious. "It's currently on the schedule, yes, but—"

"And Grace is going to be in it."

She drew a steadying breath. "Not necessarily. I'm teaching this particular class because it gives me a more hands-on role with the students. When I took this job for the summer program, I told the board that my first love was teaching. I didn't want to spend so much time filling out state-mandated paperwork that I lost my contact with our students."

His mouth quirked up at the corner. "I feel the same way about funding applications for research. I'd rather handle the chemicals. Let someone else find the money."

The limo, she noted, had wedged itself into an impossibly tight space between a delivery truck and a taxicab. The late afternoon congestion meant their laborious trip toward Eli's apartment on Central Park could take an hour. By the time they got there, her nerves would be stripped raw. She folded her hands in her lap and continued. "But as much as I love the classroom, I do have other responsibilities. That's why there are six teachers in the department besides me. Depending on your daughter's experience, her skill level—"

He shook his head, any sign of benevolence in his expression gone. "You," he said with implacable calm. "I want you."

Oh dear. Liza swallowed. This wasn't going to be easy. This powerfully intelligent man was very used to having his own way. As was she. When two opposing forces collide, she mused . . . "We'll have to see," she said evasively.

He'd been idly playing with an air-conditioning vent, but turned the full force of his attention on her. "We'll do more than see, Ms. Kincaid. I want to be very clear on this point. I want you to teach Grace."

Liza frowned. "I'm flattered, but—"

"Don't be."

Her eyebrows lifted. "What?"

"Don't be. I didn't say it to flatter you. I said it because it's true. Grace needs you."

"I wasn't aware that—"

"I'm not going to argue about this. I'm sorry if Anna Forian didn't make this clear to you before you left Breeland, but this is an all-or-nothing deal. I want you."

"It's good to want things," she quipped. "Builds character."

Something dangerously seductive flared in his gaze—something that reminded her why women went wild over him. "You know, I've always admired women with quick tongues."

At the deliberately suggestive comment, she ground her teeth. "And I've never admired arrogant men."

"I'm not arrogant, I'm determined."

"You've got to be kidding. Aren't you the man who said, 'I will be the Albert Einstein of the twenty-first century'?"

His full lips curved in a tantalizing arc. Why in the hell, she wondered, couldn't she manage to keep her gaze from the firm contours of that mouth? "Absolutely not," he denied.

"You did too. I saw the interview where you flaunted yourself in front of sixteen million viewers."

"I said 'Louis Pasteur.' Einstein was a physicist." Abruptly, he shifted positions on the seat so his knee pressed against her thigh. "And I never flaunt."

He never flaunted. There should have been something funny about that comment. All he had to do was walk across a room to flaunt. "If you say so."

"Despite what you might think, Ms. Kincaid, I don't enjoy the media attention that comes with my job. It's necessary, but not particularly entertaining." He sounded bitter.

She had a brief memory of the chaos in the hotel lobby and felt a wince of regret. His ex-wife had died recently, leaving his daughter in a state of emotional trauma. Liza had learned most of the details, as had the rest of the country, from tabloid newspapers. She could well imagine the toll that had taken on him. "Sorry. That was uncalled for."

He shook his head. "No, it wasn't. I know my assistant, Martin Wilkins, has been in touch with you about some of my requests."

Requests, she thought wryly, was a gentle word for the list of demands Martin had faxed her. "Yes."

"He's not the most accommodating guy in the world."

"You could say that."

"It's his job to look after me—and he'd die for Grace. He can be a little demanding, but he does it because he cares about us."

That much was obvious. Even in her most heated conversations with the irascible Martin Wilkins, the man's devotion to his employer and Grace was unmistakable. "I know that."

"Still, I'm sure he's made your life difficult."

"Some."

"And I don't suppose," Eli continued, "that after months of dealing with Martin, and then having me practically summon you up here, that

I've given you any reason to think of me as anything but a scientific prima donna."

"Well, the thought did enter my mind."

He studied her for a moment. "But you suspended judgment?" he guessed.

"You had one thing in your favor."

"Only one?"

"For the moment. I got a call last night from Jennifer Conyers." She let the name register.

"The student newspaper editor," he said, his smile warm.

"Yes. She interviewed you on the phone last week."

"Bright girl."

"One of the brightest. You were very gracious with her."

"She asked great questions."

"Maybe." Liza glanced out the window at the busy avenue. "Still, I'm sure it wasn't like giving an interview to the *New York Times* science editor."

"I'll let you in on something. I've been interviewed by the *New York Times* science editor. The experience is highly overrated."

She met his gaze again. "The reporter seemed impressed enough with you."

His eyes twinkled. "Thanks for reading the article."

Liza ground her teeth. "It's part of my job to keep up with the publicity our faculty receives. You've had me up to my eyeballs in old newspaper clippings and videos since March."

"And you didn't like what you saw."

She chose to ignore that. "All I'm trying to

say is that not everyone of your stature would have been so generous with their time and attention to a high-school student from a school paper."

"I enjoyed it."

"So did Jennifer. She called me last night and asked me to thank you again."

"Duly noted. I'm looking forward to meeting her."

"She also wanted me to tell you," Liza continued, unable to resist baiting him, "that she'd decided to headline the article: KING OF THE JUNGLE IS THE PRIDE OF BREELAND."

He groaned and dropped his head back against the seat. "Oh, Lord."

"Don't worry. I talked her out of it."

"Thanks for that at least."

"I told her to call it THE EGO HAS LANDED."

His eyes popped open, and he stared at her for a long second. Then he laughed. The sound did funny things to her insides. This man was danger, but that laugh still took the edge off his presence. It made her hesitate.

And in that hesitation, she lost the game.

Amusement danced in his eyes. "Has it been that bad?"

"I don't know. Not really. It's very good for Breeland to have such a high-profile person on our faculty."

"But you'd rather it was someone else?" he guessed.

"I didn't say that." She forcibly stopped the rapid retreat of her patience. "I think that you are a brilliant scientist who may find that the educational environment we have here is a little, er, restrictive to your style."

He laughed again, blast his eyes. "You think I'm a pompous jerk who won't be able to communicate with your students."

She refused to back down. "As a matter of fact, yes, I do."

"Do I have any prayer at all of convincing you that I pontificate in interviews just to cover my insecurities?"

"Oh, give me a break. You're not just an egomaniac. You're *nuts*."

His expression turned suddenly serious. "Then will you at least believe that I'm a concerned father who's willing to go to great lengths to help his child?"

Liza hesitated a second longer. "That I'll buy. You wouldn't have agreed to come to Breeland, and you certainly wouldn't have asked me to meet you in New York, if it weren't true."

She felt the tension drain out of him. "And for what it's worth, I really didn't ask you here today to disrupt your schedule."

"No?"

He shook his head and leaned forward in the car. They'd turned into a gated parking garage, she noted. "No. I'm desperate, Liza." His hand reached for hers. "Please help me."

2

He was going to kill Martin Wilkins.

It was as simple as that.

The minute he got him alone, he was going to kill him. Martin, Eli's personal assistant and the manager of his often out-of-control universe, had deliberately allowed him to believe that Liza Kincaid was some prudish dance teacher he could simply intimidate into giving him what he wanted. So he'd commanded her to New York like some eastern potentate summoning a minion, and promptly been caught with his pants down. Figuratively.

He should have trusted his instincts. He'd seen her dance, after all. And the woman he'd watched moving across a dimly lit stage bore no resemblance to the woman Martin had described.

Eli's driver glided to a stop near the sheltered

entrance of his apartment building. Eli was out
the door before the driver had rounded the car.
Charlie shot him a dry look. "You're never going
to get used to this, Doc, are you? I'm supposed to
open the door."

Eli extended a hand to Liza and helped her out
of the car. "No way, Charlie. I'm more than happy
to let you worry about the traffic, but I can still
open my own doors."

"Whatever you say," Charlie told him. He
tipped his hat to Liza. "Nice to meet you, ma'am."

"It's Liza," she said, in the same natural,
straightforward way in which she said everything. "Nice to meet you, too."

"Do you want to come upstairs, Charlie?" Eli
asked. "You want a soda or something before you
head home?"

"No thanks, boss. If you're done with me for
now, I'd like to get going. My kid's got a soccer
game tonight."

"Of course. Go. You don't want to hit the
bridge traffic at rush hour."

Charlie glanced at Liza. "You're sure you won't
be needing me later tonight."

Liza shook her head. "My hotel is a block and a
half down the street. I'll walk."

"I'll walk with her," Eli said, before Charlie
could interrupt. "And please don't forget to pick
up Grace tomorrow morning at seven-thirty. You
know how her grandparents are about schedules."

"Not a chance I'd forget, Doc. All right, then,
see you in the morning." Charlie rounded the car

again, slid behind the driver's seat, and eased it toward the exit.

Liza gave Eli a puzzled look. "Your daughter's not home?"

"She's spending the night with her grandparents. It's a chance to say good-bye before Grace and I fly down to Georgia with you tomorrow."

"Oh." She frowned. "I thought I would be spending time with her tonight."

He'd thought so too, until his in-laws had started putting pressure on Grace. Against his better judgment, Eli had given in to their demands to spend more time with her. He'd consoled himself with the knowledge that he had the entire summer to find out what about the Paschells made his daughter so nervous, and to get her out from under the looming shadow of his ex-wife's parents. "Her grandparents wanted to say good-bye. I figured we could talk before you met Grace." He indicated the glass doors to his left. "The elevator's in there."

Liza gave him a final, slightly quelling look—the kind he suspected she gave recalcitrant students, before turning on a sandled foot to stroll toward the elevators. Eli remained several steps behind her to afford himself the best possible view of this woman he'd pinned his hopes on. In the past twenty minutes, he'd learned many things. Not the least of which was that this sexy blonde with her dancer's legs—the kind fantasies were made of—was as smart as he'd guessed. Another point scored for instincts, and another strike against poor Martin.

The soft tone of her voice had hooked him. He liked the warmth he heard, the underlying generosity and humor. He'd stolen a few appreciative glances at the way her wildly colored dress hugged her generous curves. She had the kind of figure meant for a man's hands. Her dress, an outrageous combination of red, orange, and blue, was practical, loose-fitting, and sexy as hell.

She moved with a certain unself-conscious grace that fascinated him. She didn't seem to know that her braided hair begged to be mussed, her tanned limbs asked for his hands, and her full mouth tempted. Occasionally, she'd toss her thick blond braid over her shoulder, but she had seemed unaware of his scrutiny.

Most of all, he liked the way her eyes lit when she talked about the school, its history, its summer program, and its students. Liza loved Breeland. So would Grace.

He slipped into the elevator behind her and hit the button for the penthouse. It embarrassed him somehow, this overt display of success. The car, Charlie, Martin, and now his penthouse apartment—they were concessions to the life he now led. Charlie and Martin allowed him more time for research and, more important, more time for Grace. He'd agreed to the penthouse only after his in-laws had persuaded him that asking Grace to adjust from her mother's lifestyle to his so soon after her mother's death would add undue stress to the child's already overburdened shoulders.

Still, it made him uneasy. He didn't like feeling out of place in his own home, and he couldn't shake the sensation that Liza Kincaid didn't quite approve of him. It shouldn't matter, he thought, as he watched the elevator numbers slide by. But it did.

There was an earthiness to her, a simplicity that beckoned him. He'd spent too long in the brittle artificiality of New York and its media culture. The decision to accept the offer from Breeland, to uproot Grace—especially now, when she still seemed so fragile—hadn't been easy, but he was certain he was doing the right thing.

Any doubts he'd still harbored had slipped away the instant he'd watched Liza Kincaid glide across the darkened stage of Breeland's auditorium.

Liza didn't know, of course, that he'd watched her dance. She had no idea that three weeks ago, he'd sat unnoticed among the parents and friends of her students, and watched the final recital. Nor did she know that he'd stayed within the shadows of the large room until Liza alone remained. With only the dull glow from the emergency lights to illuminate the stage, Liza had switched on a portable CD player and seduced him.

Anna had told him that the dance, always performed within the empty walls of the auditorium, was one of Liza's personal rituals. She'd done it every year since her return to teach at the academy. In those few moments when she believed no one watched, that there were no critics to answer to, and no audience to please, Liza Morland Kincaid allowed herself to let go. The sight had thoroughly bewitched him—and left him hungering for a clearer glimpse of what caused the passion and the pain he sensed in her.

A resurgence of that hunger strengthened Eli's resolve. This vibrant woman, who danced on air and felt such deep emotions, would bring his daughter back to him. She would share that passion with Grace, and Grace would heal. And lately, he'd begun to suspect that perhaps Grace wasn't the only one who needed a transfusion. The dust in his veins was beginning to choke him. Liza, he somehow knew, with her vitality, could bring him and his daughter back to life. Most people would think he was crazy if he even hinted at the depth of her effect on him. This was the first time he'd even met the woman, but he had learned long ago to trust this sense of connection. The same instinct that had led him to outrageous scientific hypotheses, and eventually to discovery, told him that he needed Liza.

The elevator finally reached the 47th floor. The well-oiled door slid soundlessly open. Eli hesitated a final time, then walked down the short hall to his apartment, leading Liza into his life. No turning back now, a voice told him.

She stood in the marble tiled foyer, taking in the opulent environment with a placid expression.

Eli dropped his keys on the small table near the door. "Home sweet home," he said, feeling like an ass.

"I'm afraid you're going to feel a little out of place at Breeland."

Damn, he thought. "I assure you, whatever you've worked out for us is fine."

"Martin was very specific about your needs," she said, following him toward the sparsely furnished living room. He'd had several of his personal pieces of furniture and art shipped to Terrance for his apartment there. Only the sterile, decorator–selected furnishings remained.

"Have a seat," he suggested.

She selected the leather wing chair. "We painted your living room to match the color here."

He shook his head at that as he dropped onto the sofa across from her. "That's the one thing in this apartment I actually like. It's calming. Grace likes the color."

"Willow," Liza said softly.

"What?"

"The color. It's Willow. I had to have it brought in from Atlanta. Sunny's Hardware in Terrance doesn't stock it."

Eli studied her for a moment, not sure if the teasing glint had returned to her gaze or not. He decided not to risk it. "It's Martin's job to make sure I get everything I want. He can be overzealous."

She searched his gaze with intelligent green eyes. "Like his boss?"

His lips twitched. "I feel strongly about things. It makes me good at what I do."

"I've heard that."

He sensed the reticence in her. "Do you want to tell me what's bothering you, or do you want to make me guess?"

She blinked. "Are you always so blunt?"

"Yes. Thank you for not denying that you find me irritating."

"I'm not trying to be rude. I didn't think I was being obvious."

"You probably aren't. I have excellent instincts."

She tipped her head to one side. "When did you decide that?"

He shrugged. "Lots of practice." He ran a hand through his hair. Lord, he felt weary. "I'd like to know, Liza," he pressed, "if we're getting off to a bad start here."

She hesitated a second longer, then drew a deep breath. "I'm—concerned. Not irritated. I think Breeland did the right thing when we decided to invite you to participate in our summer program. And I'm pleased that you decided to accept. I'm just not sure that you really understand the realities of our environment."

"Realities?"

"Our students. Anna told me she spoke with you at length about how we select them."

"Yes."

"So you know that talent and aptitude aren't the only reasons we accept students in the summer program. There are other considerations."

"It's one of the things I found most attractive about the opportunity."

She glanced around the apartment. He sensed her disapproval, and tamped down on his irritation. When Liza met his gaze again, he saw the passion in her eyes. "Breeland," she said, "has a long commitment to using the summer program to build confidence and esteem in girls who might not get many breaks in life."

"Girls like you?" he said quietly.

Her expression didn't flicker. "I see Anna told you how I came to Breeland."

"Your mother arranged for you to spend a summer there. You excelled in the dance program, and Breeland offered you a scholarship. Your mother didn't come back for you."

Liza nodded. "That's right. That's one of the reasons I have such a strong passion for the program. I was helped. I like to help others."

Satisfaction poured through him. She was everything he'd hoped she would be. "I understand why you'd feel that way."

"Do you?" She seemed to be searching his soul for something.

"Believe it or not, I haven't completely forgotten my roots." He indicated the apartment with a sweep of his hand. "My parents didn't live on Park Avenue, you know. I grew up in a struggling Greek neighborhood in South Queens. The lab at my school—if you want to call it that—consisted of a Mr. Wizard chemistry set and a plastic anatomy skeleton. My mentor was a retired pharmacist who volunteered at the YMCA."

"I read that," she admitted.

"So I have a certain commitment to fostering the development of young minds."

"That was one of the reasons I first pursued the idea of inviting you to Breeland."

"But now?" he prompted.

She searched his face. "You're used to a very

high standard of academic achievement. I'm not sure how you're going to adjust to our instructional environment."

Eli smiled. Lord, he liked this woman. Like a mother hen, she was diligently wary of a fox. He leaned forward and reached for her hand. Her fingers stiffened, but she didn't pull away from him. Deliberately he stroked his thumb over the rough texture of her knuckles. "You believe that I can't?"

"Did you really fire a lab assistant for filing a late report?"

His fingers tightened, then released her hand. He leaned back against the sofa. "Yes."

She frowned at him. "I see."

Eli shook his head. "I doubt it." Sunlight filtered through the wooden blinds of the large plate-glass windows overlooking Central Park. Particles of dust danced on the broken light beams. He tilted his head to study her in the wedge of light. "That assistant was also part of a previous project I'd directed where he'd consistently failed to document his research. The other three members of the development team had expressed their concern to me that he might not be up to the task. When he told me the report would be late, I asked him to come see me the next day. He sat in my office, nearly in tears, and explained that he couldn't grasp the complexities of my current research. He was smart, but not very experienced. Pharmaceuticals and biochemistry are extremely high-pressure fields. I arranged for him to work with a friend of mine who conducts product safety research. It's just as exacting, but not nearly as stressful. And then I released him according to the terms of his contract."

Liza blinked. "Oh."

"Did you believe I actually hurled a microscope at him?"

"No. That hardly seems your style."

"No?"

She shook her head. "Uh uh. I preferred the story where you ripped the hard drive out of his computer with your bare hands, and tossed it—and him—through a third-story window."

Eli laughed. "And I suppose your interactions with poor Martin have only fueled your reservations over the past few weeks."

She hesitated, then nodded. "He's aggressive about getting you what you want."

"I pay him to be." Eli shrugged. "And as I said, he cares deeply about Grace. He'd do anything for her."

"Oh, yes. Grace." Liza settled back in her chair. When she crossed her legs, he got a tantalizing glimpse of smooth, tanned thighs. "We might as well discuss that before I meet her. I really can't commit to you that I'll teach her until I've seen—"

Eli didn't let her finish. Instead, he leaned forward to balance his elbows on his knees. "Liza." He liked the way her name sounded on his lips. "Please, do one thing for me before you decide."

Her eyes widened. "One thing? It seems like I've spent the last two weeks doing things for you. I'm here, aren't I?"

The quip warmed him. "All right, one *more* thing."

"I'm not saying that I won't teach her, you know." She frowned at him. "It's just that I teach only the one class in the summer. It's selective, and I have to evaluate her skill level first. We want her to have the teacher who can meet her needs, and I may not be the best choice."

"You are," he told her.

"Why do you think so?"

He didn't dare tell her. Not so soon. What would she say if he admitted that he'd begun to fear there was no life left in his body until he'd watched her dance? He drew a deep, calming breath. "I told you earlier. I've just got a feeling about it. I know my daughter, and I know what she needs right now. You're it."

"Look, Eli." She stared at him. "You can't just go through life bullying everyone into giving you your way, you know."

He ignored that. "After you meet her, I don't think this will be an issue anymore."

"We'll see."

He pressed the only advantage he had. "Can we just agree to let nature take its course? It's going to be very difficult for Grace to leave New York. She's spent her entire life here. Her memories of her mother are here. That's why I insisted you come. I thought if she met you, if you met her—" He shrugged. "I hoped it would be easier."

Liza was searching his face with a probing intensity that made him nervous. "You haven't told her, have you?"

He hesitated, then shook his head. "No. Grace doesn't know we're going to Terrance—at least, not to stay."

She looked around the apartment. "What does she think you did with the furniture?"

"She hasn't asked."

"And you haven't offered. Very cowardly, Eli."

He winced as the accusation struck a nerve. "It's such a big change. I wasn't sure how to approach it."

She shook her head as she smoothed the fabric of her dress over her legs. "So you want me to break it to her? Have you always been this much of a wimp?"

"I don't think so. Since Grace came to live with me—" he shrugged—"I'm afraid of everything most of the time."

Her eyebrows lifted. "Except of making absurd propositions to women you hardly know?"

She had no idea how really absurd he'd like this particular proposition to be, he thought. He decided to play his final card. "Look, I want Grace to meet you because I know she'll love the idea of dancing with you."

"Why are you so certain?"

"I've seen you dance."

Liza went perfectly still. He felt the cessation of movement, almost as if her heart had stopped beating. "I haven't danced professionally in ten years." Her voice was dangerously quiet.

"Three weeks ago. I saw you then."

"Three weeks—" She stared at him. "The recital."

"I waited. I was in the auditorium."

"You watched me."

He couldn't decipher the note in her voice, but suspected a hint of accusation. "Yes."

"No one was supposed to be there."

"That's what made it beautiful."

She ignored the compliment. "I don't dance in public anymore."

"You should."

Her jaw squared. "That's my choice, though, isn't it? You shouldn't have spied on me."

"Probably not, but I did, and I knew." He leaned in, so close she could feel him speak. "I knew you could bring Grace back to me."

Three hours later, he slanted a look at Liza's profile. She sat across from him at an Italian restaurant down the street from his apartment. She studied the patrons with avid interest as she studiously avoided looking at him. After agreeing to meet him for dinner, she'd returned to her hotel that afternoon, where she'd changed into a pair of yellow and green trousers and a red cotton short-sleeved sweater. The outfit should have clashed. His former wife, he knew, would have looked at it with utter disdain. Liza made it work, though. It seemed to echo the current of energy that ran just beneath the surface of her skin.

Silently, he acknowledged that that energy was just one of the things that drew him to her. Her love of color—in her external and, he was beginning to believe, internal life—seemed almost incongruous to his increasingly bleak existence. That transfusion he was hoping for might not be so very far away. He had a pressing feeling that if he could simply touch her—deeply—some of that energy would flow through him.

After all, she'd come to New York. She'd agreed to meet his daughter and help her make the transition tomorrow. She'd even agreed to have dinner with him tonight. He was beginning to believe almost anything was possible.

He'd handled things badly this afternoon. Demanding that she teach Grace, struggling to impress her with his life and his success had made him look like a fool. Even the thought made his lips twitch. He probably hadn't bungled anything quite so thoroughly as this since he'd tried to ask Gloria Stefano to the seventh-grade dance. For the last few years, as his research had begun to attain international recognition, his employers had spent thousands of dollars on PR consultants who were supposed to have taught him the finer points of interpersonal communication. In his mind, he'd spent too much time out of the lab wooing potential financial backers, and not enough time conducting research. Big discoveries demanded big dollars, however, and as the pressures of his job had increased, so had his skill at playing to a crowd.

If they'd seen him in action today, they'd have concluded that he was a lost cause. He was fairly certain he couldn't have made any more mistakes had he tried.

Still, through some miraculous twist of divine

intervention, Liza hadn't told him no. For the first
time since that awful day three months ago when
his former mother-in-law had called to tell him
that Mara was dead, he felt like he'd survive this.
With unshakable conviction, he knew that the
woman across from him was going to help him,
and his daughter, put their lives back together.
When he'd seen her dance, he'd sensed a deep
reservoir of pain in her—she'd experienced
something, seen something, that had left deep
wounds on her soul. Yet somehow she'd managed to embrace that pain and turn it into a passion for life. While he—he had simply allowed
his own grief and guilt to render him emotionally
distant. She'd help him find his way back—if he
studied her, worked hard enough to unravel her
secrets, Liza would show him the way.

Liza seemed to sense his watchful gaze on her
face. She glanced at him over the top of her
menu. "Do I have something in my hair?"

"No," he said, wondering what she'd do if he
confessed that he was analyzing her like a lab
specimen. "I was trying to figure out why you're
still here."

Her lips lifted in an ironic smile. "That makes
two of us."

"I didn't handle things very well this afternoon."

"You could say that."

"I should have explained weeks ago why I
wanted you to come here today. I should have
asked you directly if you were willing to help us.
I'm sorry I pressured you."

"You should have asked me weeks ago if you could watch me dance, too. That didn't stop you."

"It was an indescribable experience." She had, he thought, the most alluring way of looking at him. "I wish you wouldn't let it make you uncomfortable."

"I can't help it. It embarrasses me to know that you were watching me."

There it was again, that unabashed honesty that seemed so rare in the world where he lived. "I understand that."

"How can you?"

He shrugged. "It's a personal thing. Science isn't so very different from art, you know? I know there are some things I do, risks I take in the lab, that I'd prefer to keep to myself. What I saw—it was intimate. Had you known I was there, you wouldn't have shown it to me."

"No. I wouldn't have."

"I'm not sorry I watched," he admitted.

"That's part of the problem." She frowned. "I'm not sure how to take that. I think you *should* be sorry, but it's hard to say when I'm not so certain that *I'm* sorry you watched. It's weird."

Eli searched her face, her eyes, for any clue that might tell him what she was thinking. She couldn't know, could she, that he'd decided that night that he wanted to have an affair with this woman? Yet—he probed the heightened flush on her cheeks—she must have known the sensual pace of the dance, the sheer pulse of the music, could have that effect. What he'd seen that night had been a vision of Liza Kincaid's fantasies, an expression of deep passion and sensuality that had left him craving a taste of her. "Liza." He leaned closer to her. "Please tell me what you're thinking."

She set the menu down and folded her hands in her lap. "You looked very sad today when you told me about Grace." Her expression turned thoughtful. "I've spent most of my adult life trying to help kids like her discover who they are, what they can do. Every child deserves to know she has something unique and special to offer the world."

"I don't know what to do for her," he admitted. "I'm at wit's end."

"I know. I also know you were telling me the truth when you said you were desperate. I couldn't resist that."

Eli let his eyes drift shut. "You can't imagine what it means to me to have someone willing to help."

"You haven't had much support, have you?"

He shook his head. "My parents are both deceased, and Mara's parents—well, let's just say that we've had a difference of opinion on what's best for my daughter."

"They want custody."

He didn't ask her how she knew that. "They haven't said that—but I sense it. Mara's mother, especially, seems to think Grace needs a woman's influence in her life."

"She probably does."

His eyes shot open. He stared at her in disbelief. "You can't believe—"

She held out her hand. "Eli, I wasn't taking sides with your mother-in-law. Children—all children—need adult role models. Grace is hurting, you know that."

"She was close to her mother."

"And because of that, I'm sure there are some things she could discuss more easily with a woman than with you. That doesn't mean she needs to live with her grandmother. If Mara's mother is committed to helping Grace, then she'll understand that your daughter needs you right now."

Eli waged a mental war for control. "I'm sure you're right."

Liza watched him with careful scrutiny. "But you're afraid?"

"I'm the first one to admit that I'm not a perfect father. There were times—too many of them—when my commitment to my work took precedence over my commitment to Grace. I wasn't always there for her. After the divorce, things got worse. I wanted to avoid Mara, and in avoiding Mara, I didn't see as much of Grace as I wanted to—as I should have. She got caught in the middle of a nasty adult situation, and that shouldn't have happened."

"You know," she said softly, "it takes an incredibly strong person to admit they've made a mistake." She paused. "A person strong enough," she added, "to help his child recover from a terrible trauma."

"I won't lose her." The resolution hung in the

air between them—seemed to shimmer in the candlelight.

Liza gave him a slight smile. "Keep feeling that way, Eli. It's crucial—for you and Grace."

Slowly, he nodded. He let several seconds of silence pass before he met her gaze again. "Will you answer another question?"

A smile touched her lips. "Sure."

"Your decision to have dinner with me tonight. Why?"

Her lips twitched. "I have to eat, don't I?"

He decided to ignore that. "Can you tell me it had nothing to do with the fact that I connected with you when I saw you dance?"

"I barely know you." Her voice had dropped to a low whisper. The sudden rush of color in her face confirmed his suspicions. She'd known exactly how that dance would affect him.

He gave her a piercing look. "Really? I know you," he assured her. "I saw everything I needed to see when I watched you."

Her discomfort was palpable. "I don't know," she finally admitted. "I can't explain it."

"I can." He drew a deep breath, inhaling her scent. It was citrusy and soft—like her, piquant and sweet. "You seduced me, Liza. You know it."

Her sharp intake of breath spiked his blood temperature. "This isn't fair, you know. You have the advantage."

"How do you figure that?" He could feel the heat in his own skin, now. "I'm the one who's had weeks to remember what I felt like watching you move on that stage."

"You're embarrassing me."

"Why?" he pressed. "Why should you be embarrassed that you're a deeply sensual woman? It was beautiful." He dropped his voice a notch. "It was breathtaking."

Liza gripped her hands together so tightly, her fingers turned white. "I feel like you eavesdropped on my fantasies. It makes me a little uncomfortable."

"I wouldn't take it back even if I could."

"Do you have to taunt me about it?" she asked, her voice sharp.

"I'm not," he assured her. "I'm trying to be honest with you. What I saw that night—" He shook his head. "I wanted that woman, Liza. I want her now."

Her eyes clenched shut. "This is crazy."

"Probably," he concurred. "But it's been keeping me up nights thinking about it."

Liza shook her head. "I am not the kind of woman who sends men into spirals of unfulfilled longing. Why are you doing this to me?"

"Most men haven't seen you dance," he said. "If they had, you'd have this conversation more often."

She finally opened her eyes. They had turned a cloudy green—the same color, he thought, they'd turn when he made love to her. "Have you always been this blunt?" she asked him.

"Yes. I like people who know what they want. I don't see any reason to understate the obvious."

"Is that why people call you a mad scientist?"

"Probably," he said, without a hint of humor.

"Unless I miss my guess, you're thinking I'm a little crazy right now. Aren't you?"

He saw the response spring to her lips. It hovered there for a moment, but then she shook her head. "No. I—I actually have something to tell you."

Another point in her favor, he noted. This was a woman who would never balk at the truth—not even for the easy way out. "You do?"

"I saw you deliver a lecture," she said carefully. "Before today. A while ago, actually—before your research started to attract so much attention. It was a symposium for private school educators, and you were speaking on the importance of making science entertaining and applicable in the classroom."

He searched his memory for a minute, then nodded. "I remember that. It was one of the earlier events the administrators at my lab asked me to attend. I think it was a trial run to see how I would do talking to an audience instead of a room full of lab rats."

"You were—compelling." She held his gaze, and he adored her for it. "I decided then that I wanted you."

The statement set off a bomb in his gut. He blinked, fighting down a blinding desire to lean across the table and cover her firm lips with his. Dragging in a much-needed breath, he said, "You wanted me to teach at Breeland, you mean?"

She didn't back down. "Yes—"

He didn't miss the open-ended meaning of the word. "Ah," he said.

Liza's eyes twinkled. "That's sort of the way I felt about it."

"Are you trying to make me crazy?"

"From what I've heard, you're halfway there already."

"If I wasn't, I am now." He leaned back in his seat and dropped his gaze to the flickering candle on their table. If he looked at her a moment longer, he'd probably do something he shouldn't. "Just so we understand exactly what we're dealing with here, I want you to know that what I want from you is a hell of a lot more than a teacher for my daughter."

Liza's breathing stilled. He felt it. "Duly noted."

He looked at her again. "I'm not trying to intimidate you. I just wanted you to know where we stood."

"I understand."

"So, I don't suppose there's any chance—"

She shook her head. "Before you start, you should know that just because I've admitted I feel a certain, er, attraction to you, doesn't mean I'm ready to jump into anything complicated. We have to spend the next three months together. Don't you think a little caution seems prudent here?"

"I hate caution."

"I've heard that." Liza narrowed her gaze at him. "Doesn't it ever bother you that people say you're crazy or obsessive about things?"

He sensed there was a deeper meaning to the question, something he couldn't quite pin down, so he chose his next words carefully. "I never thought about it. I did what I did because it came naturally to me. I lived in a world where speculation and outside influences weren't very important." He studied his hand for a moment. "When you're very committed to something, when you feel passionately about what you do, you invest a lot of yourself. There was a time when I lived for my work. All that obsession, well, it had an external and internal effect on me. It wasn't unusual for me to come out of the lab after three or four days having neither slept nor eaten. I'm pretty sure I looked a little insane in those days."

"Hair too long, eyes bloodshot, three-day-old beard," she guessed.

"I probably didn't smell that good either."

"Thanks for the word picture."

He slanted her a wry smile. "No problem. I've been told by some very high-priced PR consultants that I have a rare gift for communication."

"Let me guess. You started winning awards, and the media wanted to talk to you. All of a sudden, the lab rats who'd been paying you subsistence wages for all that research decided your image wouldn't help build their war chest full of grant dollars. They decided to bring in some pros to spiff up your image—which they didn't give a rip about until you put them on the map."

"That about sums it up."

"Jerks," she mumbled. "Where were they when you were working yourself into an early grave?"

He shrugged, his feelings less defined. "It's different now. *I'm* different."

Her gaze narrowed. "Since Grace."

He nodded. "Since Grace came to live with me," he spread his hands in an ineffectual gesture, "every day's a new challenge. I don't doubt that it's making me a little crazy. Before, everything was black and white. Research either revealed answers or it didn't. Data was quantitative. Lab results could be measured and analyzed. Now, everything's in constant flux."

Liza swept her menu and silverware aside so she could prop her elbows on the table and studied him, her expression intent. "Anna told me that one of your biggest concerns is the way Grace has withdrawn from you. You said she was in the car crash that killed her mother?"

"Yes. Grace was in the back seat, thank God. If she'd been in the passenger seat, she probably would have died, too."

"How did it happen?"

"I'm not sure, exactly. They were headed out of town—on the way to see Mara's fiancé. Mara lost control of the car and smashed into a parked tractor trailer. The front end of her car was demolished."

"Mara died at the scene."

"Yes." He closed his eyes. "At least, that's what the paramedics told me. The truck had broken down, so the driver had left it on the roadside and gone for help. It was late. As far as I know, no one stopped to help for at least an hour."

"Oh, Eli."

"The truck driver returned with a tow truck and discovered the wreck. Grace was conscious and in shock, and Mara was dead. I have no idea what Grace experienced in the interval between the accident and the truck driver's return. She won't discuss it."

"Poor thing. I can't imagine."

"Neither can I," he admitted. "And she's lost. I look at her, and I know she's lost. Grace used to be the happiest child in the world. I loved being with her." He felt a familiar burning in his throat. "We had a unique bond. Grace is the greatest miracle in my life. I lived for her smile."

"What about now?" Liza prompted.

"She quit smiling." He shook his head. "She quit laughing. She's almost quit talking to me. At times, I think she quit living."

"That accident had to have a terrible effect, Eli. I know it's hard to be patient, but it's going to take time for her to recover from that."

"I know. And I wish I knew exactly what happened that night. Grace won't talk about it with anyone."

"Wounds that deep are slow to heal. I know it sounds clichéd—and I wish it didn't. But you know it's true."

"It doesn't make me any less frustrated."

"I know. I wasn't being trite."

He flashed her a slight smile. "Sorry. I didn't mean to snap."

"You didn't." Liza's eyes registered a warm

sympathy that encouraged him to give up his secrets.

He wiped a hand over his face. "And I know it doesn't help any that Grace has lived with her mother since our divorce. As if the grief of losing her mother wasn't enough to cope with, she's having to adjust to living with me."

"It's an adjustment for both of you, I'm sure."

He nodded. "It is. I'm not used to being this accountable for where I am, and what I'm doing. I'm having to adjust to Grace's insecurities about living with me."

"It's not just you, Eli," Liza assured him, "any child who has lost a parent fears losing the other. It's normal for her to cling to you a little."

He'd give his soul to feel like Grace was clinging to him rather than pushing him away. "I'd do anything for Grace, but I've run out of plans. I'm counting on Breeland to give her a fresh start. It's my hope that if we can get out of the city for a while, and away from the memories, maybe she'll start to open up a little. I can give her more time while we're down there. I've taken a three-month leave of absence from the lab. They're not even supposed to call me down there." He gave Liza a piercing look. "This is my last hope. I'm counting on it, and I'm counting on you."

She didn't look away. Instead, she laid her hand on his shirt sleeve. "Since I'm going to meet her in the morning, why don't you tell me about her," she prompted.

He looked at her fingers for a second, then covered them with his own. "Because I'm not sure I know her."

Liza's fingers fluttered beneath his, but she didn't withdraw her hand. "I think you might surprise yourself, Eli."

3

And he had, he thought, as he paced the floor of his apartment the following morning. Responding to her gentle prompting, he'd managed to tell Liza all about Grace. Her favorite color. The dress she liked to wear for fancy occasions. How she liked to get up and pour cereal for both of them on Sunday mornings. The name of her stuffed elephant. The way she twirled the curl at her left ear whenever she felt nervous or apprehensive.

Which, he noted, she was doing now. She sat at the dining room table, with her thin legs crossed at the ankles, and watched him pace. With her perfectly combed hair and unnatural stillness, the twitching of her index finger on that curl gave the only sign of her agitation. Eli forced himself to relax.

He smiled at her. "Did you have fun with your grandparents?" She'd been asleep when he'd picked her up the night before.

She nodded—that solemn, polite nod he had grown to hate. "Yes, sir."

"Grandmother was going to take you shopping at Bergdorf's. Did she?"

"Yes, sir."

"Did you buy anything new?"

"No, sir." She twirled the curl again.

Eli exhaled a long breath. He crossed the room in a few quick strides to sit next to her. "Sweetheart." He cupped her face in his hand. She tensed, but didn't pull away. He considered that an excellent sign. Once, she had flown easily into his arms, but since her mother's death, she'd developed an aversion to being touched. "Someone's going to come by this morning. I'd like you to meet her."

Grace's eyes widened. "She's not another doctor, is she?"

He winced. In his desperation, he'd dragged Grace all over the city from specialist to specialist, looking for anything, anyone, who would help him find the child he remembered. He'd gladly give ten years of his life just to hear her laugh again. "No," he said. "She's a friend of mine."

Grace's eyes narrowed. He could see her processing the information. "What kind of friend?"

Interesting question, he thought. "A good friend. A nice friend."

"I don't know any of your friends."

The statement made his chest hurt. In the months since Grace had come to live with him, he'd had no idea how to fit her into his life. And she'd noticed. He had a strong feeling she didn't like it, either. "I thought you'd like to meet this one. Her name is Liza."

"Oh." Grace hesitated for a long moment. "Do you like her?"

Eli nodded. "Very much."

"Then I'll try to like her, too, Father."

He resisted the urge to try to hug her. She'd rebuff him anyway. She always did, now. He had never realized how thoroughly he could miss a person until Grace had withdrawn from him. "I don't think you'll have to try," he assured her. "She's very—" The buzzer rang from the lobby. Eli had already phoned downstairs to tell the doorman to let Liza up. He shrugged. "She's here."

"Martin's not here to let her in," Grace informed him, in a voice way too old for her ten years. "Today's his day off."

"I know. So why don't we go meet the elevator?"

She hesitated, then slid out of her chair. "Yes, sir."

Eli resisted the urge to fidget while he waited for the elevator to arrive. He had not, he realized, been nervous about anything since the day he'd delivered his first scientific lecture to a room full of his colleagues. In two days, Liza and Grace had turned him into a wreck. When the elevator doors slid open, his chest tightened again. Liza, clad in yellow jeans and a bright blue tee-shirt, smiled at him. "Hi."

He nearly drowned in his relief. He had half believed that he'd imagined the effect she had on him. During the night, he'd even begun to question his own sanity. "Hi," he said. "Sleep well?"

She gave him a wry look. He'd left her at the door of her hotel room with a kiss that had sent steam shooting out his ears. If she'd been half as affected as he, she'd been up most of the night. "Yes," she said, "although I spent most of the evening on the phone with the faculty at Breeland. I'm afraid your phone bill will be atrocious."

"I think I can handle it."

"I hope so. I'm certainly not paying for it." She turned her attention to Grace. "Hi," she said, sticking out her hand the same way she'd greeted Charlie the day before. "I'm Liza."

Grace edged closer to Eli. After several long seconds, she took Liza's hand. "I'm Grace."

"Nice to meet you." Liza pointed to Grace's shoes. "Hey, cool shoes. I've never seen purple ones."

Grace glanced at her feet. "Oh, my father bought them. I'm not sure where he got them."

"He's got good taste."

Grace glanced at Eli. The uncertainty in her gaze threatened to undo him. He indicated the door. "Why don't we go in? It'll give us a chance to talk. Would you like something to eat, Liza?"

Grace led the way down the hall. Liza gave him a dry look. "Are you kidding? They brought me a twenty-five-course breakfast at the hotel. I usually just eat cereal."

Grace had pushed open the door to the apartment when she turned to look at Liza. Liza seemed to sense the importance of keeping the conversation going. "The truth is, I'm a sugar freak," she continued. "Actually, I'm a Froot Loops girl, but I'll settle for Captain Crunch in a pinch."

Grace's eyes widened. She seemed captivated by the idea of an adult consuming anything so frivolous. Eli didn't doubt it. Mara had lived on yogurt and tofu, while he lived on frozen dinners and shredded wheat. Grace leaned slightly closer to Liza. "I like Lucky Charms," she whispered.

Liza tilted her head in apparent thought. "The cereal part, or the marshmallows?"

"Definitely the marshmallows," Grace confessed. "I just eat the cereal because I have to."

"Me, too." Liza eased her way into the apartment, with Grace close on her heels. Eli stood at the door an instant longer and considered the very real possibility that he was going to fall on the floor in gratitude. He watched Liza set her bag on the coffee table, then sink onto the leather sofa. Grace, who continued to watch her with a mixture of caution and fascination, slid onto the cushion next to her.

"Anyway," Liza was saying, "I had heard, forever, that I should be eating something really healthy, but I just decided one day that there was no point in denying myself Froot Loops. And," she leaned closer to Grace, "when I eat Lucky

Charms, I don't even eat the cereal at all. Just the marshmallows. I throw the rest away."

Grace glanced at Eli. She was playing with her curl again, he noted. He strode across the room to sit on the coffee table facing them. "Grace," he said quietly, "I don't think I told you that Liza is a dancer."

Her fingers stopped twitching. "You are?" she asked Liza.

Liza nodded. "Yes. Your father tells me that you are, too."

Eli kept his gaze trained on his daughter. She rubbed her palms on the legs of her jeans as she thought about Liza's comment. "Sometimes," she said quietly.

"Are you very good?" Liza asked.

Grace looked like she might panic. "I don't know. I guess so. A little, maybe."

"Hmm." Liza leaned back against the sofa. "I don't know if I'm very good either." Eli gave her a sharp look, but she continued to focus on Grace. "I used to think it really mattered whether or not I was good at it."

"Of course it matters," Grace insisted. "Why wouldn't it matter?"

"That's what I thought. Everyone said it mattered, so I believed them."

Grace shook her head. "I bet you're really good at it."

"Maybe." Liza lifted one shoulder. "Some people say I am. But that's not what counts."

Grace frowned. She was looking at Liza like she had a screw loose. "Of course it counts."

"No, it doesn't. What counts is whether or not I like it." She leaned closer to Grace. "Do *you* like it?" she prompted.

Grace hesitated. "I don't know."

"You don't know? Really?" Liza looked at her intently.

Grace looked at her hands. "I suppose I do," she confessed.

"Me, too." Liza drummed her fingers on the end of her knee. "What do you like about it? The most, I mean."

Grace thought it over. "I like the way the music makes me feel." She frowned as she concentrated. "I like to move when the music makes me move. It flows through me, you know. Sometimes," she paused. "Sometimes, I feel like I'm flying."

Liza smiled at her. "So do I."

"Really?" Grace raised anxious eyes to hers.

"Really. I feel better when I'm dancing than when I do anything else."

Grace leaned back against the couch. "Me, too."

Eli held his breath. Liza nodded. "That's why I like to teach people to do it."

"You're a dance teacher?"

"Yes. I work at a school in Georgia. I teach girls to dance there."

Grace started fiddling with her hair again. She looked at Eli. "Did you know that Liza taught people to dance?" she asked.

"Yes," he said.

Grace's breathing seemed too shallow. She turned her attention back to Liza. "Could you teach me?"

"Would you like me to?" Liza asked.

Grace paused, then nodded. "Yes."

"Are you willing to come to my school?" Grace drew in a sharp breath, but Liza laid a hand on her small knee. The child didn't flinch, Eli noted. "Your father could come with you."

Grace looked at him again. "Would you?"

He nodded. "Yes."

"I'm starting a new class in a couple of days," Liza told her. "Do you think you could make it by then?"

Grace continued to watch Eli. "I don't think it would be a problem," he said.

"Will there be kids my age?" Grace asked.

"Lots of them," Liza assured her. "And most have never had a dance lesson."

Grace met her gaze again. "I think I'd really like to learn ballet. I like it best."

"I teach that," Liza assured her.

Grace chewed on her lip as she seemed to consider the information. "Would I get to wear toe shoes?"

"We'll go get them today," Eli told her. His voice sounded hoarse.

Grace wavered a second longer, then nodded. "I think I'd like to go if it's okay with my father."

Liza smiled at her. "Then we'd like to have you."

Eli saw what he thought, miraculously, was the hint of a smile ghost across Grace's lips. He glanced at Liza, but she was absorbed in something Grace was telling her. So he let the thrill of that slight victory fill him.

* * *

The outdoor temperature neared 100. Even in the air-conditioned room, a blanket of humidity choked out most of the oxygen. Liza adjusted her navy tank top and tried not to squirm in her chair. Though she understood the necessity for it, she hated this part of orientation. She'd arrived in Terrance with Eli and his daughter just in time to catch the welcome speech from the president of the alumnae association. She'd hoped their flight from New York would get in late, sparing her the rhetoric, but fortune hadn't been so kind.

Instead, she'd made it back to campus with sufficient time to change and make it to the lecture hall for the final speech of the day. A quick scan of the room told her the students were as bored as she was.

Trickles of sweat traced sinuous paths down her back beneath her tank top. The air conditioner couldn't compete with too many hot bodies in a too small space. The group in this room was the sixth and last to hear the welcome speech and administrative details. The oldest students in the program, they were here to serve as mentors to the younger girls, and their maturity level helped them through the laborious welcome speeches. Liza listened to the chairman drone about the golden days of Breeland while she scanned the room.

Eli Liontakis, looking like a poster boy for the island of male models—that place where men don't sweat, their clothes don't wrinkle, their

hair always has enough wave to make women
want to touch it—strolled into the back of the
room.

Blast his eyes.

He'd had her seriously off kilter since last night
and he knew it. She'd managed to distract herself
today by paying close attention to Grace, but
always lurking at the back of her mind was the
memory of the way he'd looked at her outside
the door of her hotel room.

And then he'd kissed her.

It had been easily the most thorough, mind-
stealing kiss of her life. Liza felt her temperature
rising to match the heat of the room at the memory. He had incredible lips, which did unbeliev-
ably sensual things. Those hands, long and
elegant, had swept up her back, and when he'd
buried them in her hair, she'd almost melted into
the floor. Her blood had started to sing by the
time he ended the kiss. A devilish smile had
played across his mouth, then he'd set her away
from him and strode away without so much as a
good-night-sorry-to-get-you-so-worked-up-and-
then-leave-you-hanging farewell speech.

And he had the nerve, she'd noted, both this
morning and now, to look completely unruffled
by the entire thing. With his hair clipped neatly at
his nape, and black clothes draping his too-
powerful frame, he looked every bit as daunting
as his reputation. After spending two days with
him, Liza guessed that the media called him *The
King of the Jungle* for reasons other than the obvi-

ous play on his surname. He *commanded* attention, and he seemed to know it.

"Liza?" She started when she heard her name. Anna Forian, Breeland's summer program administrator, chairman of the academy's board of visitors, and Liza's mentor and dearest friend had somehow managed to wrest control of the microphone from Edna Prentiss, president of the alumnae association. Anna stood at the podium, looking at her expectantly.

Liza shook her head to clear it. "I'm sorry. I—"

With a knowing smile, the older woman indicated the audience. "One of our students has some questions about Mr. Liontakis."

She didn't doubt it. From the moment Breeland had announced that they'd procured him as their summer chemistry instructor, interest in the school, and its programs, had skyrocketed. Eli Liontakis, it seemed, was the most fascinating figure to hit the scientific world since Louis Pasteur started playing with bread mold. Liza glanced at him. His expression didn't flicker.

Anna indicated the room with a sweep of her well-manicured hand. "I think you can answer those questions better than I can, Liza." To the students she explained, "Most of you know that Miss Kincaid teaches dance here at Breeland during the regular term, but you may not know that she assists me with the scheduling and staffing for the summer program. She's responsible for Mr. Liontakis."

Liza shot her a dry look as she edged her way to

the front of the platform. "I doubt that," she muttered to Anna, then faced the sea of expectant faces. Eli leaned against the back wall, staying in the shadow of the door. The students wouldn't see him unless they turned to look. "As you all know, we're very fortunate to have a man of Mr. Liontakis' stature and achievement to lecture here."

"When do we meet him?" a girl called out.

Liza remembered her from the previous summer. "Welcome back, Christine. Mr. Liontakis is already on campus." She glanced at him over the heads of her audience, finding silent amusement in his growing discomfort.

Another girl squirmed to the front of her chair. "I just can't believe you got him. I mean, *Liontakis*. He's unbelievable."

He certainly was, Liza thought as she saw a sparkle enter his eyes. Her students lapsed into a casual discussion of his appeal while she watched him. His only reaction to the somewhat ribald course of her students' comments was a slight lift of his eyebrows. Liza sensed that the conversation was about to spin dangerously out of her control. Tearing her gaze from Eli's, she forcibly dragged her concentration back to the students. "I'm sure the next couple of weeks will give you all a chance to ask Mr. Liontakis about his career," she said. "Those of you in the science program will be working with him directly."

"*I* certainly want to work with him directly," one of her students was saying. "I'm hoping for some one-on-one instruction."

"Oh, *as if*?" Lindsay, one of Liza's best dance students from the regular term, chimed in. "Like he's going to be tutoring you in the table of elements. I mean, geez, the guy is going to win the Nobel prize."

"Yeah," Christine answered. "Did you see that picture of him on *Time* magazine? He is too-hot."

His lips twitched. Liza thoughtfully tapped a finger on the podium. "This isn't getting us anywhere."

"No," one of the girls drawled, "but it's doing a lot for my visualization skills."

"Is it really?" Liza slanted Eli a dry look. He'd had her on edge since the night before. She couldn't quite resist the urge to turn the tables. Just how, she wondered, would The King of the Jungle cope with a room full of hormonal teenaged girls? Stifling a smug smile, she gave a shrill whistle. The girls fell silent. "I can see you're all far more interested in Mr. Liontakis than you are in administration."

"We'll *find* the dining hall," Lindsay assured her.

"Well, then—" Liza shot Anna and the alumnae association president an apologetic look. "I'll just turn over the podium to the man of the hour." She indicated the back of the room with a wave of her hand.

With a collective murmur of confusion, her students turned to face him. If she hadn't known better, she'd have sworn the color she saw in his face was a blush. "Mr. Liontakis," she said, "since you've decided to join us tonight, this will give you a chance to meet some of your students."

He gave her a knowing look. She'd trapped him like a rat, and he knew it. With the fifty girls watching him in rapt attention, he had two choices. He could follow her lead and take the podium, or, he could look like a fool by turning to leave. Liza waited patiently while he weighed his options.

No surprise, he rose to the occasion. He shot her what she could only define as a look of admiration, then he strode toward the front of the room. He walked, her dancer's eye noted, with the same feline grace as his namesake. "You win this hand," he said for her ears only as he reached her, "but not the game."

Liza ignored him. "I'm sure you'll have no trouble convincing the girls to stay while you tell them your plans for the next few weeks."

From the looks on the girls' faces, he'd have to toss them out of the room before they let him leave. She met Anna's amused gaze and indicated the door with a tilt of her head. "Ms. Forian and I," she told the class, "have to finish getting everyone settled in." She indicated Edna with a sweep of her hand. "If you have any questions, I'm sure Edna can help you."

Liza started for the door. Anna rose to follow.

"You're leaving?"

"Yes. After being gone for the past two days, I've got over two-hundred-fifty other girls to check on."

"I see." He glanced quickly at the audience, then back at her. "When can I see you again, Liza?"

Damn him. The question was deliberately provocative and he knew it. The wide-eyed looks on the girls' faces told Liza all she needed to know. By that evening, the gossip line would be abuzz with speculation. "At the faculty meeting the day after tomorrow," she shot back. "My schedule's packed between now and then."

The girls, sensing the challenge, turned in tandem to look at him. He leaned one hip on the edge of the lecture table, then tilted slightly toward her. "Mine is too. I'll call you later. Don't worry. We'll work it out."

She thought about responding, then decided against it. Anything she said would just make the situation worse. Might as well leave him to deal with the questions while she made a strategic retreat to the sanctity of her office. "Fine." She turned to go.

"Liza?"

Liza hesitated, then faced him a final time. "Yes?"

"Tonight. I'll call you tonight."

The rake. Liza heard Anna's laugh, and in spite of herself, choked out one of her own. With an innocent expression on his face worthy of a Shakespearean actor, he disarmed her. She shook her head. "Welcome to Breeland, Mr. Liontakis."

Liza slipped into her office with a quiet sigh of relief. It felt good to be home. The trip to New York had taken its toll.

Anna, looking frustratingly unflustered, sat in

the chair across from her desk. Well into her seventies, Anna Forian had the perfectly composed look of a southern matriarch. Beneath the gentle facade, however, Liza knew there lay an iron will and a survivor's instinct. Liza frowned at her. "How do you manage to look so cool when I feel like I've been in the sauna? We have got to have the HVAC checked in that building"

Anna tapped her manicured fingernails on the arm of the chair. "I didn't just spend the last ten minutes squirming, either."

"I wasn't squirming."

Anna's gray eyebrows lifted. "If you say so."

"I wasn't. Want something to drink?"

"Water." Liza pulled two bottles of water from the cool interior, then handed one to Anna.

"Are you going to tell me about New York?" Anna finally asked.

Liza cringed. *What's to tell?* she thought. I'm wiped out. He blew me away. I'm still crazy, and I don't know why you thought otherwise? She took a sip of her water as she looked for a place to begin. "Eli told you that he hadn't seen a lot of his daughter in the five years since his divorce?"

"Yes. We discussed that in our initial interview."

"Evidently, she's been withdrawn and sullen since she came to live with him. She's definitely hurting. That much is obvious."

"He's willing to do whatever's necessary to help her," Anna assured her. "I knew that right away."

Liza studied the expression on Anna's face. In

the years she'd known the older woman, she'd developed a deep respect for her insight and discernment. "You like him, don't you?"

"Very much. You will too, when you know him better."

"I'm trying."

"Seeing him in New York didn't help?"

"New York didn't help," she admitted.

"Ah." Anna drank some of her water. "Did you go to Joshua's grave?"

The mention of her infant son sliced a wide gash in Liza's heart. "Yes." Her voice thickened.

"I'm sorry you went alone."

"I always go alone."

"I'm sorry for that, too."

"I know." She twirled her water bottle. "I keep thinking it will get easier."

"You don't just get over something like that."

Liza nodded. "I suppose not."

"But I had hoped it would give you a special sensitivity to what Eli's going through with Grace. You know what it's like to lose a child, Liza. Can you imagine losing one that's still alive and will accept nothing from you?"

"I'm sure it's very hard."

"But you still don't trust him?"

"I trust him. I just have serious concerns about how well he's going to fit in here."

"I don't."

"So you've said."

"And if you don't trust him, at least trust me. I've been running this program for a long time. I know what I'm talking about."

Liza hesitated. "He's very—charming," she said quietly.

Anna's laugh—an amazingly young sound—reminded Liza of wind chimes. "Good heavens," she said. "I'm seventy-three years old. You don't think he bowled me over, do you?"

Liza winced. "No. It's not that."

"I'm not a muddle-headed old woman, you know?"

"I know. And I didn't mean to insinuate that I don't trust your judgment."

"But you don't want him here?" Anna insisted.

"Let's not forget that it was my idea to bring him here in the first place."

"Which you started to regret almost the minute you saw him start popping up on the news every night."

Liza resisted the urge to cringe. If she'd had reservations before she'd met him yesterday, she now had stark terror. How was she supposed to explain the effect he had on her? "I just don't want him to disrupt what we have here. Since this is the first year Breeland's had a male on the faculty, I know everyone's going to be watching. To make matters worse, his presence is going to bring the press down on our heads. I liked it when we had nice, quiet summers."

"Our budget didn't like it."

Liza nodded. "I know. I know this is good for business and good for the program. We're much higher profile with him here."

"But you couldn't resist playing that little trick on him this afternoon."

"What trick?"

Anna laughed. "I might be old, but I'm not that old. You deliberately baited those girls, then tossed that man into shark-infested waters. What did he do to you in New York to deserve that?"

Kissed me senseless and left me to founder, she thought. "Nothing."

Anna looked at her skeptically. "Really?"

"Of course really. I told you, I went to the lecture. I went to his apartment. We had dinner. I met his daughter. We flew here. That's the whole trip in a nutshell."

"I think you're leaving out the highlights."

"There are no highlights," she lied.

"If you say so."

"I do."

Anna shook her head. "So you weren't getting revenge just now."

"Of course not. You saw how curious the girls were. I thought he'd like to answer their questions."

Anna's expression told her she wasn't buying it, but she didn't press her. "How do you think he's doing?" Anna asked.

A tiny smile played at the corner of her mouth. "I'm sure he's charming their bobby socks off."

"I don't doubt it." Anna glanced beyond Liza's shoulder through the small window that overlooked the hub of the campus. "Best I can tell, he's drawing a crowd. Looks to me like word is spreading across campus like wildfire."

Liza followed her gaze. A steady stream of students and faculty were hurrying across the lawn toward the academic building. Several girls stood outside the window of the lecture hall, straining on tiptoes for a peek at the genius. "Great. I can't get eighty percent attendance for a scheduled session, and all he has to do is walk down the hall to have the masses fall at his feet." A clamoring noise from the corridor captured her attention.

"Good grief." Anna glanced over her shoulder. "What's going on out there?"

"I think the King of the Jungle is inciting the natives to riot."

The door of her office flung open. Eli, trailed by several members of the faculty, edged his way in, then shut the door on the din. He gave Liza a piercing look. "Well, that was just charming, Liza. Thanks."

"Anytime," she purred.

Eli glowered at her, then his gaze turned to Anna. Liza saw the instant warming of his expression. "It's very nice to see you again, Anna."

Anna beamed at him. "It's good to see you, too." Her blue eyes twinkled. "Even if you are wreaking havoc in our well-ordered world."

His gaze swung to Liza. "I'm not the one stirring up trouble."

She choked. "Excuse me? What was, 'I'll call you tonight'?" She dropped her voice to mimic his husky tone.

That won a slight chuckle from him and from Anna. Eli propped one hip on her desk. "It was payback. You set me up in there. You didn't think I'd let you get away with that, did you?"

"A girl can dream, can't she?"

The clamoring noise outside her office grew louder. Anna gave them both a knowing look. "I'd better go deal with that. What did you do to those girls, Eli?"

He shrugged. "Nothing I can think of, though that woman from the alumnae association was shooting me poisoned looks by the time I got out of there."

Anna laughed. "Oh, don't mind Edna. It's not personal. You're just too masculine. That's what got her riled up."

Liza was having trouble breathing. Eli gave her a shrewd look. "You don't say."

"Yes," Anna assured him. "You're shaking things up around here, Eli. You know it, but you don't have to act like you're enjoying it so thoroughly." She slipped out the door to deal with the din in the hallway.

Eli leaned closer to Liza and twined a strand of her hair around his index finger. "Oh, but I am enjoying it," he said, his voice a dark whisper. She wouldn't be surprised if the windows in her office fogged over. "I'm enjoying the hell out of it."

4

Liza winced as she felt the pull of an underused muscle. "Stretch high over your head," she prompted her class, leading them in a cool-down exercise. "You don't want to let your muscles tighten up."

"Too late," Lindsay quipped from her left. One of the older students who helped teach the class, Lindsay had been taking summer dance lessons from Liza for over eight years.

Liza sent her a wry smile as she adjusted the stretch. "I know the feeling. I've been doing too much paperwork lately and not enough dancing." And too many sleepless nights, she mused, and not enough rest. Eli had persuaded her to have dinner with him and Grace last night. She'd been delighted to answer Grace's questions about her classes, the school, and the program, but had

found the pressure of Eli's constant gaze fluster-
ing. He'd walked her to the door of his tiny apartment—it seemed so much homier than his lavish
penthouse in New York—and stolen a quick kiss
while Grace was still in the other room. Too soon,
they'd been interrupted, and Liza had found herself, again, lying awake most of the night with
thoughts of leonine eyes and elegant hands.

Now, she forcibly pushed the thought from her
mind as she finished the routine, then faced her
class full of glowing, flushed girls. "Great job,
today. We did a lot for the first day."

The girls responded with nods and groans as
they moved to collect their gear. Unlike the academic track of the program, which separated the
girls into age-based classes, the fine arts classes
were segregated by skill. With her administrative
responsibilities, Liza only had time for one class
in the summer. It was easily her favorite part of
the day. She glanced at Grace, who had shown
considerable promise during the class, but who
now somberly collected her belongings. At the
back of the room, Liza noted, Anna Forian stood,
also watching the child's progress.

"Lindsay," Liza said.

The girl looked up from her gym bag. "Yeah?"

Liza indicated Grace with a slight wave of her
hand. "Let's go meet Grace."

Lindsay nodded. Liza had explained the child's
circumstances to the older girl, and believed
Lindsay could help Grace make the adjustment
to the daily routine at Breeland. "Sure, Liza."

Liza smiled at the informality. She liked everything about the summer session better than the regular academic year. They walked together to where Grace was carefully folding a towel. "Hi, Grace," Liza said.

Grace gave her a wary look. "Hello, Liza."

"You did really great today. Did you enjoy your first class?"

"Yes, ma'am." The child slipped the perfectly folded towel into her gym bag.

Anna had crossed the room to join them. "How was the first day of class?" she asked.

"We were just talking about that," Liza responded. "Grace was going to tell me how she liked it."

Grace glanced from one adult to the next, before finally settling her gaze on Liza. "You're a very good teacher. I learned a lot of new stuff."

"Did you have fun?" Lindsay prompted.

Grace nodded. "Yes, ma'am." She continued to fill her gym bag.

Liza's worried gaze slid to Anna. The older woman gave her an encouraging smile, then extended her hand to Grace. "I'm Anna. I'm glad to finally meet you, Grace. Your father has told me so much about you."

Grace paused in the act of unlacing her shoes to shake Anna's hand. "He told me about you, too."

Anna's eyes twinkled. "Did he, now?"

"Yes, ma'am. He said you're in charge of the school."

"That's an interesting theory," Liza joked. Lindsay laughed.

Anna remained focused on Grace. "Is that all he told you?"

Grace hesitated, then shook her head. "No, ma'am. He said he liked you. And that you were as old as my grandmother, but you don't act like it."

The three women laughed, and though Grace watched them, visibly unsure about the wisdom of the revelation, she finally managed a slight smile.

Anna looked at Lindsay. "Lindsay, dear, why don't you show Grace where the dining hall is so the two of you can get some lunch? I understand we're having chicken croquettes today."

"Croquettes?" Lindsay said. "Jeez, why didn't someone tell me? By the time we get there, they'll be all gone."

Liza nodded. "Word has been spreading across campus since the dining hall breakfast shift got off work."

"Crud," Lindsay said. She hoisted her gym bag higher on her shoulder. "Come on, Grace. We're going to have to shove to the front of the line if we want anything to eat. Every time Jody makes croquettes it starts a riot in the dining hall."

Grace looked to Liza for guidance. At her reassuring nod, she picked up her bag and looked at Lindsay. "What are croquettes?"

"I'll tell you on the way." Lindsay led the child from the room.

Liza released a slow breath. "Tough nut," she said quietly.

Anna nodded. "I see that. How did she do today?"

"How much of class did you observe?"

"Just the last few minutes. She seemed fine."

"She is." Liza pulled the towel from around her neck to wipe her still-flushed face. "She's quite good, actually, but Eli's right about her reserve. She doesn't want to lose control."

Laughing, Anna handed Liza a water bottle from the low table. "She came to the wrong place, then. We wouldn't know how to act if we weren't teetering on the edge of disaster."

Liza stuffed the bottle and the towel into her own bag. "No kidding. I take it you heard about the minor revolt in the dorm this morning."

"Yes. You had some problems with those kids from Westover?"

"You could say that. They wouldn't take showers."

"Any particular reason?"

Liza shrugged. "Showing their independence, I guess."

"How did you handle it?"

Her lips twitched. "You don't know?"

"No. The dorm administrator told me I should ask you."

"I set the fire hose on the lowest pressure and sprayed 'em down. They were mad at first, but they got over it. It was kind of fun, actually."

"I don't doubt it."

"By the end, most of the girls had joined in. There were soap bubbles and wet bodies everywhere. The place was a mess, but we cleaned it up." She shook her head. "I can't believe Amelia didn't tell you." Amelia Pankhurst, the dorm administrator, had failed to see the humor in the situation.

"She didn't have the same outlook on the incident as you."

"I'll bet she didn't."

"You might want to apologize."

"Amelia," Liza said pointedly, "needs to get a grip. It's *summer* camp, not boot camp."

"And you and I need the Amelias to enforce the rules so we can decide when to break them."

Liza hesitated, then slung her bag over her shoulder. "Point well taken." She tipped her head to one side. "Am I ever going to stop learning things from you?"

"I hope not." Anna's smile was warm and open, as it had always been. Liza smiled back. "I thought," Anna said, "that you and I might go over and see how our star instructor is fairing with his first day of classes."

"I'm sure he's fine." She wasn't certain she was ready to see him again.

"My guess is that nobody told him he's expected to let his class out on time when we have croquettes in the dining hall."

"I'm pretty sure that's in the orientation packet."

Anna gave her a dry look. "Very funny."

"Why don't you go check on him? I should probably find Amelia."

"Why are you avoiding him?"

"I'm not," she lied. Anna's eyebrows arched.

Liza released a slow breath. "Okay, I am."

"Why?"

"I don't know. Do I have to know?"

"I think he'd like to know how his daughter did in your class today."

"That's hitting below the belt."

"I'm thinking of retiring," Anna said, "and becoming a travel agent for guilt trips."

"You'd be prize-winning at it, I assure you."

"So are you coming or not?"

Liza mentally chided herself for acting like a fool. To a man like Eli, a few kisses and an expression of physical desire came naturally. She was the only one, she was convinced, staying up at night wondering what to do about it. "Sure," she said. "You can catch me up on all the administrative nightmares of the morning on the way to the lab."

They found Eli, holding the rapt attention of his class of twelve- and thirteen-year-olds, while he carefully placed a flowerpot on top of a lidded coffee can. "Billions of tiny, highly combustible particles of grain," he was explaining, "are generated by grain kernels rubbing together as they move along conveyor belts and shift between bins. Inside the enclosed chambers, those particles rise in a cloud."

He stuffed a small tube into a hole in the bottom of the can and began slowly pumping a plunger. "When that dust gets in with the right mixture of oxygen and then comes in contact with a spark, or even an overheated bearing on a conveyer belt, it is extremely explosive."

Liza gave Anna a wary look. Eli's class was fixedly staring at the coffee can and flower pot. He was concentrating on the demonstration, and didn't seem to notice the two women in the back of the room. He used his free hand to light the small Bunsen burner on the lab table, sending a steady current of heat to the base of the coffee can.

"Think of how quickly kernels of popcorn explode under the heat of a skillet or hot air. The dust particles are smaller pieces of the same combustible product. The finer the particle, the drier it is and the more quickly it ignites when mixed with air."

One of the girls called out, "What causes the spark?"

Eli nodded as he continued to pump the small rubber bulb. "Industrial equipment is prone to heating and sparks. Sometimes, all the grain particles need is enough heat to explode. Just like the popcorn. When you pop it in the microwave, heat alone causes it to burst. In the right conditions, grain particles will spontaneously combust with tremendous, intense heat and pressure," he said. "When that happens inside a container where you have lots of particles in a cloud, it will cause an explosion."

As if on cue, a loud *bang* came from inside the coffee can. The girls screamed. Eli grinned. The flower pot shot straight through the window. The crash of broken glass and the clang of the coffee can on the slate lab table added to the chaos.

Liza gave Anna a shrewd look. "Remind me of this the next time I suggest getting a male instructor."

Anna smiled at her. "The girls seem to be enjoying themselves." Most of them had rushed to the broken window to view the remains of the flower pot, smashed to bits on the sidewalk below.

Above the din of squeals and laughter, it was almost impossible to hear. Liza grimaced, put her fingers to her lips and let out a shrill whistle. Sixty heads turned her way—including Eli's. His eyes sparkled in quiet challenge.

Liza turned her attention to the girls. "Having fun, ladies?"

"Did you see that?" one of them asked. "He shot that thing right through the window."

"That was so cool," another girl responded. "Can we do that again?"

Eli shook his head. "It wasn't supposed to break the window. I've never had one go sideways like that."

"Well," Liza drawled, "aren't we fortunate to have experienced the miracle of scientific unpredictability?"

He shot her a dry look. "I'll clean it up."

Anna shook her head and produced a digital phone from her pocket. "Don't worry about it. I'll call maintenance. Step away from that glass, girls."

"Miss Kincaid," the girls were demanding Liza's

attention. "Did you see it explode, or did you get here after?"

"I saw it."

"Nobody ever did anything like that before." Liza recognized the speaker as one of the girls involved in the fire hose incident. She'd had quite a day.

"No, not here anyway. If Mr. Liontakis is through with you for the day, you guys can go to lunch." She sent him a questioning glance. "Any parting shots?"

"Don't try that at home," he warned the class.

They grabbed their books and gear in a flurry of laughter and excited chatter, and quickly streamed from the room. Two stayed to ask Eli some specific questions about the experiment, then raced out the door. Anna put the phone back in her pocket. "Maintenance is on their way."

"I'm very sorry about the window," Eli spread his hands in front of him. "I must have put too much dust in the can. Usually, it just shoots a couple of feet in the air."

"Quite effective," Liza quipped.

"It gets them talking anyway," he concurred. "I find that people approach a science class with the idea that it's all boring theory." The way he was scrutinizing her made Liza wish she'd taken the time to change out of her dance clothes. She felt grubby and, somehow, exposed to his searching eyes. Eli's gaze slid to Anna. "If I can show them some tangible things, they're more open to the subject."

Why did he have to look so damned attractive anyway, Liza wondered. Liza frowned at him. "So what's next? Molotov cocktails?"

Eli laughed. "This is my last explosion of the summer, I assure you." The comment was innocent enough, but the look in his eyes belied his calm facade.

Liza swallowed. "I'm taking the window out of your pay check."

"Fine." He moved a step closer. "You're the boss."

She was vaguely aware that Anna was watching the interchange with barely disguised glee, but he'd captured her gaze, and she couldn't make herself look away. "Don't you forget it either," she admonished quietly.

"Not a chance." He shifted toward her. "Am I going to get a bad evaluation for this?"

"I haven't decided yet. Do you have any more tricks up your sleeve you should warn me about?"

"Lots."

A shiver worked its way down her spine. "Are they dangerous?"

He tilted his head to one side. His eyes practically gleamed at her now. "I guess that would depend on your definition of the word."

Liza coughed, breaking the spell. She looked at Anna. The older woman was beaming at them. Liza drew several calming breaths. "You, uh, were going to suggest lunch?"

Anna nodded. "I was. I thought Eli could tell us about his first day of class, though I suspect we've seen the highlights."

"The rest was boring, I assure you." He slipped off his lab jacket. Liza wished he hadn't. He seemed more potent, somehow, clad in a dark green tee-shirt and worn jeans. Tossing the lab jacket across the slate table, he quickly arranged his papers. "We went over Bunsen burner safety today."

She crossed her arms over her breasts. "Hence the explosion?" Liza prompted, despite herself.

He flashed her a winning smile. "Naturally. What good is a safety lesson without a demonstration of potential consequences?"

Anna nodded. "And a very graphic one, at that." She folded her hands in front of her and regarded him with a benevolent look that somehow set Liza's teeth on edge. "Why don't you join us for lunch, Eli? You can tell us about your impressions of Breeland, and Liza can tell you how Grace did in class today."

His expression turned suddenly serious. The twinkle abruptly left his eyes. "How did she do?" he asked. "I hadn't realized you'd see her first."

Liza nodded. "Dance is her first class of the morning. She did fine. She's a little shy, but so are a lot of the girls at this stage."

"You think she'll be all right?"

"Yes. We have all summer to draw her out."

"I know. It's too soon to expect anything. Where is she?"

"At lunch with the girls."

The explanation obviously pleased him. "Good.

She doesn't have any girls her age at home. I think that's part of the problem."

Anna concurred. "It's always helpful for children to interact with their peers. Especially girls. They need confidantes."

A commotion at the door indicated the arrival of the maintenance crew. "Let's get out of their way. We can discuss this over lunch."

Eli quickly stuffed his papers into a worn satchel. "Good idea. On the way over there, you can explain this rumor I heard about croquettes."

Eli set his briefcase down inside the door of his temporary apartment. For a moment he didn't recognize the sound coming from the living room. He glanced around the corner to find his daughter, seated on the sofa, laughing with Anna Forian. For long seconds he savored the rare sound. "I'm home," he said at last.

Anna flashed him a welcoming smile. His daughter, he noted, didn't meet his gaze. "Hello, Eli," Anna said. "I was just asking Grace how she liked her first day of classes."

Eli waited. Grace gave him a partial smile. "Hello, Father."

"Did you have a good day today?" he prompted.

"Yes, sir."

"I thought Lindsay was going to stay with you this afternoon until I got home."

"She had to go," Grace said.

Anna nodded. "Liza needed her help with something at the office. I decided I'd much rather visit with Grace than help Liza stuff envelopes. So I persuaded Lindsay to swap job assignments with me."

"Can't blame you for that." Eli leaned against the door frame. "Grace, honey, I thought maybe we'd go out for dinner tonight. Does that sound good to you?"

She studied her green jeans with avid interest. "If you want to."

Eli slanted Anna a pained look. "Would you like to join us, Anna?"

She glanced from Grace to him. "No, I don't think so. Another time, maybe." Anna stood. "Grace." She waited until the child looked at her.

"Yes, ma'am?"

"You'll come see me like you promised? Tomorrow after classes, maybe?"

"All right."

Anna nodded, apparently satisfied. "I'll be going then." She gave Eli an encouraging smile. "I hear Solanto's has good pizza. You might want to give it a try."

He thanked her, then waited until he and Grace were alone before approaching his daughter. Carefully, he crossed the room to sit next to her on the sofa. Encouraged that she didn't move away from him, he forced himself to relax. He leaned back and pillowed his head on the cushions. "I had a pretty good day," he told her.

Grace met his gaze, but didn't respond. He tried again. "I thought my classes went okay. Well—except for the one where I shot the flowerpot through the window."

Her slight smile felt like a gift from heaven. "Lindsay told me that happened. She said there was glass all over the place."

He nodded. "Actually," he rolled his head to the side so he could grin at her, "it was kind of funny."

The smile broadened slightly. "I heard that, too."

"The best part was that Liza and Mrs. Forian were in the room when it happened."

Grace pressed a hand to her mouth to suppress a rare giggle. "Did you get in trouble for that?"

"Well, I think Anna may have let me off the hook, but I'm not sure about Liza."

Grace shook her head. "She likes you," she said seriously. "She's not going to get mad over something like a window."

He studied her closely. "What makes you think she likes me?"

"I don't know." Grace shrugged. "She just acts like it."

He looked at the sad, expressive eyes. "Can I tell you a secret?" he asked.

"Sure."

"I kind of like her, too."

Grace nodded solemnly. "I can tell."

"You can?"

"Yes."

Grace thought it over for a moment. "How much do you like her?"

"A lot."

Her forehead creased. "I see."

"You know what else?" he asked.

"What?"

"I don't like her better than I like you."

Grace blinked. Eli reached over to tuck her hair behind her ear. "Honey," he said quietly, "I love you very much."

She froze; she had rejected his efforts to embrace her in the weeks since her mother's death, but he decided he could no longer resist the urge to comfort her. He pulled his daughter into his arms and pressed her to his chest. "Ah, Grace," he said into her hair. "Do you know I would do anything for you?"

She nodded. He savored the feel of her thin arms wrapped around his neck. "Are you sure?" he prompted.

"Yes, Father."

She smelled like baby shampoo, he noted, and the thought made him nostalgic for a time when things were so much simpler. The phone started to ring. Grace wriggled away from him. "I'll get it," she announced, and raced from the room.

"Father?" she called from the doorway. "That's Martin on the phone. He wants to talk to you."

Eli glanced at his watch. "Well, why don't you tell him he'll have to call me later?" He gave her a slight smile. "I think we'd better get moving if we want to get a table at Solanto's."

Grace hesitated, then smiled at him. "Okay."

She hurried from the room, and Eli tucked the picture of her smile into his growing reservoir of hope.

5

Liza froze at the door to the lab and watched, intrigued and unwillingly enchanted. Eli, his face a mask of concentration, was explaining a complex equation to a lone student. "All right," he said, his voice patient and warm, "let's look at it another way. What's your favorite color?"

The girl eyed him warily. "Green."

"Okay, good. What two colors make green?"

"Yellow and blue."

"Right." He wrote a Y and a B on the chalkboard. "Are those the only two colors that make green?"

The girl frowned. "What do you mean?"

"I mean, what would happen if you added some red, or some purple or some black."

"Well, it would depend on how much. I used to

work in a paint store. There are lots of shades of green."

Eli looked positively elated. "Exactly." He began adding numbers to the growing equation on the board. "So fifteen parts yellow and one part blue wouldn't necessarily make a gallon of white paint turn green."

"No," she said. "It would just be a weird shade of yellow."

"Right." He scribbled another equation beneath the first one. "So lets say that the elements are like paint. When you mix them in different quantities, you get different results. The elements themselves, like pigments, don't change, but the equation you use affects the outcome."

Comprehension dawned on the girl's face. "Oh, I get it. You can mix hydrogen and oxygen and not necessarily get water."

He beamed at her. "Precisely." Over her head, he flashed Liza a bright smile that melted the soles of her shoes to the floor. "Mixing elements is the magic of chemistry."

Cretin, Liza thought. He was baiting her again, and given the almost angelic look in his eyes, she was finding it difficult to hold it against him. His student, still oblivious to Liza's presence scooped up her books and slid off the stool. "Thanks, Dr. Liontakis. I was starting to think I was just really stupid for not getting this."

"Kelly," Eli admonished, "some people have a tougher time grasping abstract concepts. Their brains aren't wired that way. It doesn't make them stupid, just different." He started to erase the equation. "Besides, I'm pretty sure I couldn't properly mix a gallon of paint if my life depended on it."

Kelly laughed and turned toward the door. "Oh, hi, Ms. Kincaid."

"Hi, Kelly. How's it going?"

The girl gave Eli a grateful look, then edged toward the door. "Better now. I think I can finally do my homework."

"Great. So I take it chemistry's not as hard as you thought it would be."

"No," the girl said, her voice filled with wonder. "It's really not. I had such a hard time with science at school last year. I didn't think I could do this."

"Surprise," Liza said with a slight smile.

"Yeah." Kelly laughed. "You know, I even think I like it a little."

"I'm glad to hear that," Liza assured her.

"Me too." Kelly looked at her watch. "I gotta go now. I was supposed to meet my friends on the east circle five minutes ago."

"Well, have a good afternoon, then."

"I will." Kelly glanced at Eli once more. "Thanks again, Dr. Liontakis."

"Anytime," he assured her.

She hurried from the room. Liza gave Eli a wry look. "No matter what their age, they can't resist you—can they?"

He laughed. "You don't seem to be having any

trouble resisting me. What was that comment you made the day I met you—something about *the ego has landed*?"

She cleared her throat. "Yes, well, I'm a few rungs higher on the evolutionary ladder of hormonal development than the average adolescent girl. And I was still trying to recover from the impact of having you appear in my world. That doesn't count."

He laughed. "Did anyone ever tell you that you have a charming kind of bluntness?"

"Not in those words, no." Liza walked into the sunlit room, studying with avid interest a complicated combination glass and steel table where colored liquids traveled from beaker to beaker. "Is this a potential life-saving experiment?" she asked.

"No." His voice was filled with amusement. "It's water and food dye."

That brought her gaze to his. "You're kidding."

"Nope. People have expectations of what they'll find in a lab—that looks both interesting and intriguing—and isn't as disgusting as cages full of rats. It makes students ask questions. I started using that in lectures about a year or so ago." His amber eyes twinkled—blast him. He was damned near irresistible when his eyes twinkled. "Frankly, I think my audiences find it far more fascinating than they find me."

She doubted that. "I have to tell you, your students are quite taken with you. You're getting rave reviews."

"I'm glad. I'm enjoying them."

He was watching her with that uncanny probing look that reminded her that he'd kissed her—
twice, and left her yearning for more. What was
worse, it reminded her, ruthlessly, that this man
had seen her dance. Though she doubted he
could possibly understand the implications of
that, she'd be far less nervous, she was certain, if
he'd seen her naked. "You're fitting in very well
here," she told him finally. "I'm sure it hasn't
been easy."

With a slight grin, he turned to erase the equation from the board. "The male/female ratio is a
bit daunting, I'll grant you."

"Most men might find it advantageous."

"I'm not most men," he said as he replaced the
eraser in the tray. When he faced her again, the
afternoon sun slashed across his face, throwing it
into stark shadow. "I like to concentrate on one
woman at a time. It's like scientific research. I can
give more of my attention to the project if I'm not
distracted by—other demands."

Liza felt the familiar tug of awareness flowing
through her blood.

She forced those thoughts aside. Digging in her
pocket, she produced the certified letter he'd
received that morning at the school office. "This
came for you about an hour ago. It seemed
important, so I thought I'd give it to you now
rather than making you wait until this afternoon
when the mail gets delivered."

He accepted it with raised eyebrows, glanced
at the return address, then tossed it, unopened,
into his briefcase. "Thanks."

"Aren't you going to read it?"

"Eventually. I know what it is." His gaze met hers, held it. "I was actually hoping I'd see you today."

"Grace is doing really well," she assured him.

"She seems to be. That's not what I wanted to talk to you about."

"No?"

"No." He moved around the desk to walk toward her, his lips curving into a smile. "You know exactly what I want to talk to you about. That's why you've been avoiding me."

That made her laugh. "Are you kidding? I don't have time to breathe, much less to figure out how to avoid you. I'm just really busy."

"Hmm." He braced his hip against one of the worktables. Why, she wondered, did he have to look so damnably attractive? In black jeans and a black shirt, he practically oozed sex appeal. Even his white lab coat failed to dull the effect. If testosterone had an odor, it would be the musky, heady scent she detected whenever she made the mistake of standing too close to him. One look across a room, even across the campus, could send her blood pressure to the moon. "So, you didn't show at the welcome reception last night because you were busy?"

"That's right. Two days in New York left me drowning in paperwork," she said.

"You were missed."

"I was sorry to miss it. I usually enjoy the event. It's a good chance to get to know the new faculty." She shook her head. "I'm many things,

Eli, but I'm not a coward. If I didn't want to see you again, I'd tell you."

"Everyone asked about you." He took a step closer. "I wanted to see you."

"Sorry."

His eyes sparkled again. Where had he learned how to switch that on and off? He must know that he could melt at least half the female population with that look. "I'm glad to hear that," he said softly. She realized, too late, that he now stood mere inches from her, "I thought maybe you were having second thoughts." He traced a finger over the curve of her upper lip. "About kissing me, I mean."

"You kissed me," she pointed out.

"You kissed back."

She wasn't about to argue with that. "To tell you the truth, I am having second thoughts. And third thoughts, and fourth thoughts."

"I can't stop thinking about it either," he assured her. "But please tell me you don't regret it."

"No," she said carefully. "I don't regret it. Reality intrudes every now and then—"

"I hope you're not listening to it."

"To reality? Well, not really. But you have to admit, this is a little complicated."

He pressed her hand closer to his chest. "Why does it have to be complicated?"

Her eyebrows lifted. "I don't think you have a very realistic idea of what we're dealing with here."

"What we're dealing with," he said, his voice a

low purr, "is a very potent attraction. I want to explore that attraction and find out where it'll take us." His gaze narrowed. "I want to make love to you."

Liza swallowed. Her blood had turned sluggish. "Eli—" she glanced over her shoulder. "Do you have any idea what kind of logistical problems—"

He pressed a finger to her lips. "If it weren't for the fact that we're in the middle of the smallest town in the world—"

"It's not the smallest," she said.

His lips kicked into a smile as he traced the curve of her mouth again. "It's small enough. And the campus is even smaller, am I right?"

"Yes." She pushed his hand away. "It might seem trite to you, but that's the way it is here. If you and I—" she drew a deep breath—"if we pursued this—"

"We're *going* to pursue it, Liza. There's no question about it."

She drew a deep breath. "When that happens, we'll become the primary focus of the gossip vine."

"So?"

Irritated, she glared at him. "So, where you're from, that might not be such a big deal, but I assure you, it's crucial around here. I don't exactly relish being the center of public speculation."

He tipped his head to one side. "That's the reason you quit dancing."

She cringed. "It's part of the reason. That's all you need to know."

He shook his head. "That's where you're wrong, Liza. There's so much more I need to understand about you. So much more I want to learn." His fingers moved over hers in a slow caress. "Have dinner with me tonight? I want to spend some time with you."

"No."

"Liza—"

"Eli, be reasonable."

"I hate being reasonable. I learned that lesson in the early days of my career. You never get anywhere by being reasonable."

"Are you always this persistent?"

"When I want something."

"Disappointment can build character, you know?"

His laugh warmed her blood. "I have all the character I need, thank you."

"Crumb," she muttered.

He took a step closer. "Have I mentioned that I adore you when you say that?"

"Stop."

"No way, babe. I'm just getting started. I want to know exactly what kind of woman uses 'crumb' for a swear word."

"The kind that lives in a very small town on a very small campus where everyone knows everyone else's business." A slight smile fleeted across her lips. "If I said 'damn' the foundations of Breeland would crumble to rubble."

He laughed, and kissed the corner of her mouth. "I want to know everything about you," he told her. "And I want to know what puts that look of terror in your eyes whenever we talk about this."

Lord, was she that obvious? She extracted her fingers from his grip. "I'm not afraid of you."

"No," he said carefully, "I don't think you are. And I also don't think you're really all that terrified of a little idle speculation. But I think you're a little afraid of yourself—a little afraid of what you're feeling."

Liza backed up a step. "This is moving kind of fast for me, that's all. I don't normally make rash decisions."

He hesitated, then shook his head. "You and me, Liza," he waved his hands between them, "it's—inevitable. It's like a chemical reaction."

The air radiated with pure sexual tension. Her body was tingling with the same kind of energy she felt in the seconds before she danced. She wasn't sure she could take much more of this without melting into the floor. "Eli, please."

"Oh, I plan to," he assured her. "I plan to please you in so many ways you'll be begging me to stop."

"Every cell in my brain is screaming that this is not a good idea," she protested. A trickle of sweat glided down her spine. "I can't think this fast."

"Then don't," he muttered.

Her eyes shot open. "Eli—"

He shook his head in frustration. "You are probably the most stubborn woman I have ever met, do you know that?"

The question made her smile. "I suppose you've grown accustomed to women who simply fall at your feet at the merest hint of your interest."

"As a matter of fact," he said, sounding arrogant enough to live up to his title as The King of the Jungle, "I have."

That made her laugh. "Then I suppose Grace isn't the only one who'll be getting an education this summer."

His curse was succinct and to the point. She shook her head in silent admonishment. "If you're feeling that frustrated," she teased, "I understand Amelia Pankhurst has expressed an, er, interest."

He gave her a look that could have curdled milk. "You're a laugh a minute, do you know that?" With a swipe of his hand, he ruffled his beautiful black hair. "If I didn't know better, I'd think you were enjoying driving me to new heights of sexual frustration."

"The feeling is mutual."

"That's not the only feeling that's mutual, and you know it."

She did—and didn't bother to deny it. Instead, she decided her nerves had stood as much close proximity to him as they could take for one day. She deftly changed the subject. "I've got to get to class," she told him. "It's been too long since I've danced this much—and if I don't spend a half-hour stretching, I'll pay for it."

"Massage is good for that, I hear. I took physiology classes in med school, you know? I could probably do a reasonable job of working out your muscle tension."

He could probably melt her bones into puddles if he set his mind to it. Deliberately, she ignored his suggestive comment. "I just stopped by to give you the letter and let you know that Anna wanted to know if you're free for dinner tonight."

"I hadn't planned on being free," he told her with pointed reference to his earlier invitation, "but it seems my plans have changed."

Liza nodded. "I'll tell her. She's having dinner with Bill Maxin. He's a member of the board of visitors and one of our biggest financial supporters."

"So I should make a good impression?"

"It wouldn't hurt."

He studied her for several seconds. "Will you be there?"

"I hadn't planned on it."

"What if I say I won't go unless you go?"

"Bill is an important financial support for Breeland. It's extremely important for us to keep him on our side."

"Then this is sort of a command performance."

"It would help, considerably, if you attended. You probably don't know this, but it wasn't particularly easy for Anna and me to persuade the board to invite a male faculty member to the summer program—even one of your reputation." Her lips twitched. "Although, if anyone is eavesdropping on this conversation, perhaps I should say *especially* one of your reputation."

"You're absolutely hilarious, you know that?"

Now serious, she added, "Look, traditions are

strong here. Bill supported us—with his vote and his money. It would be—advantageous—for you to meet your benefactor."

Eli nodded. "I understand. I haven't spent the majority of my career conducting scientific research without learning the politics of fund raising."

"Good. Then I'll tell Anna you'll be there."

"If you will," he said softly.

She glared at him. "That's not fair. I've got too much work to do to spend another evening out. I can't spare the time."

He shrugged. "I'm not particularly concerned with being fair. I'm concerned with finding out what you're hiding between all those carefully built walls you have." His gaze narrowed. "I'm concerned with making you realize that this energy you feel when we're together isn't going away." Moving a step closer, he loomed over her. "I'm concerned," he said, his voice a low whisper, "with giving you a glimpse of what it's going to be like when we're as close as we can possibly be."

"Eli—"

He snaked one hand around her waist. "And mostly, I'm concerned with learning where you hide the vibrant, passionate woman I saw on stage. I wanted her then. I want her now. Those are my terms."

Her temperature had spiked up several degrees, and her lungs felt tight and constricted. Drawing a suffocated breath, she said, "You're not giving me much choice, are you?"

"No," he said, tightening his hold on her waist. "I'm not."

She wavered on indecision, then slowly nodded. "All right. I'll be there."

The flare of heat in his eyes stole her breath. "I'll look forward to it."

Six hours later, Liza shot Anna a wry glance across the table in a local restaurant and asked herself how in the world she'd gotten sucked into this. Anna's steady refusal to meet her gaze told her Anna knew exactly what she was thinking. She was simultaneously infuriated and fascinated with The King of the Jungle. She wondered if antelope and zebra felt this way in the few moments before they became prey to a leonine hunter.

"Eli," Anna was saying, "I'm so glad you were able to join us tonight."

Eli gave Liza a knowing look. "So am I."

Anna ignored the undercurrent of tension and indicated the man on her left. "Bill was eager to meet you."

Bill Maxin, a member of Breeland's board of visitors, and one of the school's largest financial contributors, cleared his throat. "I'm sure Anna has told you how pleased we are to have you here this summer."

Eli slanted a look at Liza. His lips twitched, as if he sensed the train of her thoughts. "The pleasure's mine, I assure you. I'm glad Anna suggested this." He glanced at Liza again. "Aren't you?"

Liza resisted the urge to kick his shin under the table. Instead, she indicated the dimly lit restaurant with a sweep of her hand. "This is one of our favorite places to come when we want to get away from the dining hall." He couldn't possibly miss the chill in her voice. "Breeland is a small town. Everyone knows everyone else's business." She gave him a warning look. "I've found that it's easier not to invite speculation."

He looked amused, and, she admitted, devastatingly attractive. "It's nice here." He glanced around, this man who was used to high-ticket fundraisers and glamorous social events. "Thanks for suggesting it," he told Anna.

She nodded. "It's a nice break from the noise—which, you'll soon find, can be deafening during the first few days of the summer session."

Bill laughed. "It usually takes a week or so for us to tire all those girls out enough to get them to heed the lights out time. By then, they're hitting their bunks as early as possible."

"That explains," Eli said, "the ruckus I heard when I went to pick up Grace's sitter."

"Lindsay worked out for you?" Liza asked.

"Yes." He glanced at her. "That was a great idea on your part. Grace really likes her."

"She really likes Grace. I think they'll get on well together."

He turned back to the older couple. "I went to pick her up, and the resident director—"

"Amelia Pankhurst," Anna supplied.

Liza gave him a dry look. Eli's lips twitched. "Ms. Pankhurst was looking a little harried. I noticed the noise level was, uh, spectacular."

Bill shook his head. "Nothing in the world quite like the collective squeals of teenage girls."

"Bill," Anna told Eli, "never had the fortune of having daughters in his home. He and Charlotte had four sons."

Eli nodded thoughtfully. "I'm fairly certain I don't remember doing much squealing as a teen."

The thought was so ludicrous, Liza nearly choked on her water. Eli shot her a wry look. "All right?"

She nodded. "Just trying to picture you dreamily staring at some pin-up girl and squealing. The image got the better of me."

"Actually," he confessed, his eyes gleaming at her, "I was quite enamored with Marie Curie."

With little imagination, she could see him sitting at a dimly lit desk pouring over the writings of the Nobel prize–winning woman chemist. "I'm sure you were."

"I never could find a picture of her to hang on my wall, though."

"Since the only picture of Madame Curie I've ever seen made her look more like her husband Pierre than a pin-up model, I'm not surprised."

Eli laughed. The sound tripped a few hidden triggers in Liza's nervous system. "I'm a brain man myself. As much as my father tried to impress on me the aesthetic value of Marilyn

Monroe's attributes, I was more, er, inspired, by neural synapses."

Everyone laughed. Eli held Liza's gaze a few seconds longer, then turned to Bill and deftly changed the subject, "So tell me how you got connected with Breeland, Bill."

"Married a Breeland grad," Bill said with characteristic pride. He loved the school almost as much as he had loved his late wife. Liza felt herself relaxing. She genuinely liked Bill Maxin, and the feeling, she knew, was mutual. With characteristic insight, Anna had known that the two men would relate well. She sent her friend a shrewd look.

Anna finally met her gaze. The creases that dug deep at the corners of her eyes were crinkled in merriment. Silently, Anna lifted her glass in a slight salute. Liza shook her head at her and leaned back in her chair. At least, she mused, Bill loved to talk. She wouldn't be expected to pull much weight in the evening's conversation.

As the evening progressed, Eli impressed her with his attention to Bill's seemingly endless line of questions, his easy banter with Anna, and the almost seamless way he fitted himself into the casual atmosphere. He was accustomed, she knew, to a circle of highly sophisticated intellectuals. But he laughed a genuine laugh at Bill's jokes, responded with smooth grace to Anna's probing queries, and managed, somehow, to look relaxed and comfortable in the quaint atmosphere.

Blast him, Liza thought, taking another sip of her water. Her nerves were stretched tighter than Spandex. Worse, the knowing glances he sent her told her that he knew exactly what she was thinking.

Generally, nothing in his demeanor suggested that he felt the shimmering tension in the air between them. Then, in the space between one breath and the next, he'd give her a look that seared a path all the way to her nerve endings. The brightness she saw in his eyes told her that he not only knew, he was reveling in it.

Liza drew a calming breath and surreptitiously glanced at her watch. Another hour at most, and the torture would be over.

"Eli," Anna said as they savored dessert, "it's obvious how much you love what you do. I'd like to know what you enjoy about the process of research."

He set his glass down with a slight smile. "Chemical research is such a challenging field. Some find it boring, I know, but it's the mysterious nature of the science that attracts me. I'm as far out on the edge as it's possible to be. Sometimes it can even be dangerous, but the thrill of discovery is worth the effort. When I've unlocked the mystery, I feel simultaneously exhilarated and exhausted." He looked at Liza. "It's pure magic. I imagine you feel that way when you—dance."

She swallowed. His pause had been deliberate and suggestive, and she could cheerfully have killed him for it. With careful precision, she set down her water glass. "Actually," she said, "when I dance, I like to attack the stage. If I think of the stage as my battlefield and the choreography as my war strategy, I find that the aggression gives the art a certain energy." She met his gaze in open challenge. "I imagine that I'm annihilating the music with each step—draining the blood from it, so to speak."

Eli laughed. Anna, she noted from the corner of her gaze, looked on the verge of hysteria, while poor Bill seemed as oblivious and benevolent as usual. Liza didn't take her gaze from Eli's. "Most choreographers tell me they think twice before attempting to design a piece for me."

"I don't doubt it." His dimple was back.

She felt a surge of irritation that matched the sudden flushed feeling on the surface of her skin. She dropped her folded napkin to the table. "And speaking of choreography, I still have some work to do on a few routines. I really need to go."

She was halfway out of her chair when Eli rose and reached for the check. "Actually," he said, "I do, too." He flashed Anna and Bill a slight smile. "Thanks so much for inviting me tonight."

Anna snatched the bill from him. "No, no, it's our treat." She glanced at Liza. "Liza will tell you, we like to make our guests feel welcome."

Liza could think of several things she'd like to make him feel, and welcome wasn't one of them. She flashed Anna a wry look. "Hospitality is your strong suit, not mine."

The older woman's eyes sparkled. "But you're learning, dear. I'll see you tomorrow?"

"At three." Liza reached for her purse. "Good night, Bill. Thanks again."

"My pleasure." He nodded to Eli. "We'll have to do this again before the summer's over."

"I'd like that." Eli looped his fingers beneath her elbow as if it were the most natural thing in the world. "We'll see you both later."

Before she could respond, he was ushering her from the restaurant. She waited until they reached the sidewalk before she freed her elbow from his grip. "I should kill you."

He gave her a deceptively innocent look. "What?"

She scowled at him and made an expressive gesture with her hands. "You know exactly what I'm talking about. Those looks you were giving me, well, you practically steamed the water in my glass."

His mouth quirked into a slight smile. "You noticed."

"You don't have to sound so pleased with yourself." She stalked several paces away from him, pacing the sidewalk in agitation. "Damn it, Eli, it's one thing for you to play this game with me when we're alone—"

"It's not a game, Liza."

She chose to ignore that. "It's another thing entirely for you to do it in public."

"Is that why you told me dancing is like terrorism?"

"I said warfare, not terrorism."

He was laughing at her. She could see it in his eyes. "My mistake." Tilting his head to one side, he crossed his arms across his chest. He looked, she noted in quiet disgust, absolutely beautiful tonight. In a pristine white shirt and perfectly fitted black jeans, he oozed sex appeal—and she was the one getting slimed. "Why are you so agitated?"

At that, she stopped pacing. "Why am I—" She stopped before she started sputtering. Stalking across the few paces between them, she said in a low voice, "You tried to seduce me in front of my boss, a member of my board, and a restaurant full of people."

He didn't blink. "Did it work?"

The knot of frustration in her belly was giving way to humor. "You aren't even going to deny it, are you?"

"No." He gently toyed with one of her earrings. The warmth of his hand spread goosebumps along her flesh. "Are you?"

Distracted, she realized, by the feel of his hand, she'd lost the thread of the conversation. "Am I what?"

"Going to deny what's going on here." His voice was casually amused. He knew exactly what he was doing to her.

"What's going on here," she said quietly, "is that you've completely lost your mind. Eli, you can't keep doing this to me."

"Frustrating you?" he asked. "Believe me, that's not my plan. I'm hoping to get to the satisfaction part of this relationship just as soon as possible."

"And everyone in there knew it, too." She

hoped the dim light from the street lamp would sufficiently disguise the flush on her skin.

His gaze turned thoughtful. "Would I have had the same response if I'd done it in private, or would you have taken the bait?"

"That's not the point."

"Sure about that?"

"Eli." Liza reached for her patience—a valiant effort to be sure when he had her teetering so completely off balance. "Did you listen to a word I said earlier today?"

"All of 'em. And I decided to disregard your very practical advice that we have a logistical nightmare on our hands. Why don't you leave that up to me?"

"You have got to be kidding."

"Uh uh. I'm trying to seduce you into thinking of what's between us as more than a battle of wills." He moved an almost imperceptible distance closer. "I want you to feel the heat and like it. I like it."

Liza threw up her hands. "I don't suppose it's occurred to you that you barely know me—and I barely know you?"

His beautiful lips moved closer to hers. "I *know* you, Liza. I've known since I watched you dance. It's just as I said—we're like a volatile chemical combination. Given the right environment, the results are going to be spectacular."

The breath froze in her lungs. "Or disastrous. Look, you're in a very difficult time in your life. I can understand why you might think that this—"

"Stop that." He frowned at her. "This doesn't

have a damned thing to do with my former wife."

"She just died, Eli. Surely you know—"

"I know that whatever feelings I had for Mara died years before she did. Don't talk yourself into believing that what I feel for you is even remotely related to some latent sense of longing for Mara. It's not." He wiped a hand over his face. "Mara died, and it's a tragedy that her life ended so early, but I'd be lying to you and to myself if I told you I felt anything for her other than pity."

"Oh."

"So now that we've dispatched with that, do you have any more objections you want to offer."

She drew a calming breath. "It's not that I'm objecting, exactly." At the flare of heat in his eyes, she backed up a step. "Don't get any ideas."

"Honey, you can't make a comment like that and not expect me to get ideas."

"The point I'm making," she said through gritted teeth, "is that I think we should spend some time getting to know one another before we jump into something we might both regret."

"I'm not going to regret a moment I spend with you." He looked amused, now, and it irritated her.

"Just because you live in a world where actions have no consequences doesn't mean—"

He had the gall to laugh. "You know, you sounded just like a schoolteacher when you said that."

"I am a schoolteacher, and I'd appreciate it if you wouldn't laugh at me."

His expression sobered. "I'm not laughing, Liza. I'm just trying to keep from pouncing on you."

"Eli—"

"Look." He held out his hand in silent entreaty. "I'm not totally insensitive to what you're trying to tell me."

"But you don't think that maybe the timing is rotten?"

"As for my relationship with Mara, or lack thereof, you're going to have to take my word for that. About the other, well, what's really the harm in having the faculty and staff talking about our relationship?"

"Other than the fact that it would wreak havoc with my credibility?"

"Why? Because you're human. Because you can feel something for someone and act on those feelings?"

No, she thought, *because I made this mistake once and I pay for it almost every day of my life.* "No," she said, deliberately keeping her voice calm, "but just because I feel something doesn't mean I have to act on it, you know."

"Let's not forget that chemistry is my strong suit. I happen to be one of the world's leading experts on uncontrolled reactions."

"And modest, too," she quipped. "How did I get so lucky?"

"I was wondering when you were going to realize that—the lucky part, I mean."

"You mean you don't seduce every woman you meet?"

"No." He drew the word out until it caressed her tingling nerve endings. "Just the ones I really want." Moving closer, he blocked her view of everything but his wide chest and impossibly dynamic face. "The ones who seduce me first."

Liza's eyes drifted shut. "Would it do me any good at all to launch into a lecture on the merits of self-restraint?"

His laugh made her tremble. "None."

"I suppose you didn't go to a Catholic school?"

"Public."

"Darn. The nuns would have instilled a little self-control in you."

"You got yours from Breeland?" he guessed.

"Yes."

"Ever lost control, Liza? Ever lost control and liked it?"

Once. Once, and the consequences nearly killed me. "That's not what—"

He interrupted her by sweeping his thumb over her sensitive skin. "I can't help myself. The elements are already mixed. We just have to wait and see what kind of reaction we're going to get."

"You can't imagine what you're asking from me."

He tipped her chin up with his hand, waited for her to meet his gaze. "It'll be magic, Liza. Don't be afraid of it."

She trembled. "You're not being fair."

"I don't have time." He raised her hand and pressed a soft kiss to her wrist. "And unless I miss my guess, neither do you."

6

"**A**bsolutely not," Eli told Martin Wilkins. "I'm not doing it." It was Sunday afternoon, and he and Martin were having their weekly briefing on the demands for Eli's time and professional expertise.

"Eli, listen to me. The Paschells just want to visit down there. They say they're worried about Grace, and they want to check on her. Don't be so antagonistic."

"I hate to break this to you, but my in-laws never do anything for altruistic reasons. If they want to come down here, it's not because they're worried about my daughter."

Martin made a slightly disgusted sound that conveyed a world of disapproval. "I know that, but they're starting to talk about custody, Eli. You have got to pay attention."

He was having trouble breathing. "Did they say that?"

"Not in so many words, no."

"They better not, either. I'm not letting them take her away from me."

"Then don't be so belligerent about this. What's the harm in allowing them a visit?"

"Grace is just starting to get settled here," Eli explained. "I don't want to upset the balance." He didn't want them anywhere near her, was the real story, but he kept that to himself. Martin would figure it out on his own.

"I understand that, but I think you need to give this serious thought. If they start pushing you for custody, your reputation could suffer."

"To hell with my reputation." Eli knotted the phone cord in his fist.

"The administrators at the lab might feel differently than you about that."

"Then screw them," he said. "I don't think it's a good idea right now, Martin. That has to be enough."

"It is," Martin said, his voice so soothing it grated Eli's nerves. "All I'm saying is, perception is important. Your research on the Kelsen Project is drawing incredible speculation. You're a public figure now, and your private life is part of the equation."

"I understand that."

"At least let me tell the Paschells you'll consider a visit when things are more settled. It will keep them calm."

"They're not coming down here," Eli insisted.

"I'll tell them you're thinking about it."

Eli swore at him. Martin's sigh was long-suffering. "Did you even *read* the press clippings I sent you?"

"Yes," Eli said irritably. "Certified mail, Martin? What's next, a singing telegram."

"I was hoping to convey a sense of urgency."

"What you conveyed was melodrama." The clippings had detailed a few challenges from some prominent research scientists to his research. He leaned against the wall in his kitchen and wiped a hand through his hair. "Look. Do what you think is best. If you want to issue a statement about the research, fine. If you want to try and appease the Paschells, that's fine, too. But I don't want them here. Not right now."

"I understand." Martin's tone softened. "How is Grace?"

"Better, I think."

"I'm glad to hear it." Martin paused. "Anything you want me to tell your bosses at the lab?"

Eli released a harsh breath, his frustration steadily tying a knot in his gut. "Tell them we're doing fine, and Georgia isn't the backwater capital of America."

"I'll see if I can dress that up a bit."

"That's what I pay you for, Martin."

The other man laughed. "You pay me to keep your butt out of trouble."

"My point exactly."

"All right, Eli. I'll stall the lab. I'll stall your in-laws, and I'll find a way to notify the media and the world scientific community that you are alive and kicking despite evidence to the contrary. Any other dirty work you want me to take care of?"

Eli shook his head with a slight smile. "That covers it, Martin—oh, one more thing. Grace will have a dance recital at the end of the summer. I'm sure you'll want to be here."

"Wouldn't miss it," Martin assured him.

"I knew you wouldn't. I'll get the dates to you so you can buy your plane ticket. Thanks, Martin." Eli said his good-byes, then hung up the phone.

"Father?" The voice came from the doorway.

Eli spun to face her. "Hi, honey. I thought you were spending the afternoon with Beth today."

She shrugged. "I was." Entering the room, she dumped her backpack on the table. "We finished practicing our dance routine. Liza gave me a ride home."

But didn't come in, he noted. "I see."

Grace studied him for long seconds. "Are you mad at Martin?"

"No."

"You sounded like you were mad."

He shook his head as he moved toward her. "I was frustrated, but not with Martin. He's taking care of something for me."

"Is it a lawsuit?"

Eli ground his teeth. There was no lawsuit— not yet, anyway. And if Grace thought there was, he'd bet his right arm she'd gotten the information from her grandparents. "There is no lawsuit," he told her. He spun a chair around so he could straddle it. "Martin is handling some press releases and some publicity from the lab for me, so I don't have to worry about it while we're here."

She frowned. "Are you—" Grace bit off the question.

"Am I what?"

Her face was a mask of worry. "Are you going to go to jail?"

Eli stared incredulously at her. "No," he said harshly. "No." God, what had Mara's mother told her? "Honey, come here." He indicated the chair in front of him. "Grace, tell me what's going on."

Grace slipped into the chair. "I heard Martin on the phone with your lawyers. Everyone was yelling. Then Grandfather said something about your legal problems, and I thought—"

"You thought what?"

"Grandfather made it sound like you were in trouble."

"Well, I'm not."

"And you're not going to jail?"

"No." He drew a deep breath. "That's not even a remote possibility." Eli tucked a strand of hair behind her ear. "I don't want you to worry about that."

"Why is Martin so worried, then?"

"The Nobel prize nomination has brought a lot of scrutiny and attention to some of my research. There are some doctors who are trying to disclaim what I proved in the lab."

Grace's eyebrows knit together. "That's stupid. If you proved it, you proved it. What are they trying to claim?"

"That I didn't do my research right and my results are wrong."

"But they aren't," she insisted.

He gave her a wry smile. "Thanks for your support. The point is, my bosses at the lab are nervous about it. They want me to go back to New York to defend myself."

She swung her feet back and forth beneath the chair. "Why can't you just tell them to mind their own business?"

Eli laughed. "Sometimes adults fight over stupid stuff, Grace."

"Like you and Mama?"

He caught his breath. "Some of the stuff your mother and I fought over was stupid, yes."

"Like me?" she asked quietly.

His hands tightened on the back of the chair. Had his mother-in-law been present at the moment, he wasn't sure he could have kept from applying the same force to her throat. "No. I know you heard some of the arguments your mother and I had about you, but I want you to understand that we had those arguments because we both loved you. Both of us wanted what we thought was best for you. We just didn't always agree on what that was." He fought back a wave of guilt as he realized, again, just how much of a toll his ill-fated relationship with Mara had taken on his child. "In fact," he added, "I can honestly say that no matter what we argued about, or how often we argued, I was always really grateful to your mother for giving you to me."

"Are you sure?" she said softly.

The disbelief in her voice lacerated him. "Absolutely sure," he answered, his voice rough. "I'm so happy to have you living with me, Grace. Never doubt it."

Grace hesitated, then nodded. "Okay."

His heart rate began to return to normal. "What do you want to do for dinner?"

"Pizza?" she said hopefully.

He groaned. "We've had pizza for the last three nights."

"It's better than your cooking."

Her expression was so serious, he couldn't tell whether she was making a joke or not. He stared at her. Grace stared back. "Are you teasing me?"

Grace shook her head. "No. You're a terrible cook. Martin is much better."

"Well, Martin isn't here."

"I suppose we'll starve before the summer is over."

He searched her expression. A hint of humor lurked in her clear blue eyes—eyes so like her mother's. The spark took him by such surprise, he probed it, trying to burn it into his memory. "You *are* teasing me."

Her lips twitched. She'd gotten that expression from him. "So can we get pizza?"

Eli laughed. "No. We can't get pizza. How about tacos?"

"Can I have mine without lettuce?"

"Yes."

"Okay," she agreed. "Even Mama could make

tacos, and she cooked even worse than you do."
Grace slid off her chair. "Will you help me with
my homework after dinner?"

"Sure."

Picking up her backpack, she slung it on her
shoulder. "Then maybe I can help you figure out
how to get Liza to go out with you."

She hurried from the room, and Eli buried his
head in his hands. Nothing, not his greatest
accomplishments in the lab, not his career
achievements, not even the knowledge that the
work he conducted saved lives and helped millions of people had ever given him this rare feeling of euphoria.

Liza had fled the sidewalk after dinner that night
with a mixed sense of dread and anticipation.
The weekend passed, as did the next three days
of classes, with little or no contact with him, and
her nerves had finally begun to settle. Looking at
herself in the bathroom mirror near her cramped
office in the administration building, she scrutinized her every feature. It was an okay face—it
probably wouldn't stop traffic, but she was mod-
erately attractive. If she could fix one thing about
it, she'd narrow her nose a little. She'd always
longed for the patrician nose of a super model.

Irritated, she dabbed powder on her face to cut
the shine. Even if her nose were pencil-thin, she
still wouldn't have the kind of face that sent men
tumbling into fantasy land. No, no matter what
he said, Eli had been taunting her—playing at the

sophisticated kind of flirtation he was probably used to. In her more honest moments, she admitted to herself that she felt the connection between them, but neither of them had the simple, unencumbered life that allowed for spur-of-the-moment decisions. He had his daughter to consider, and she had her own reasons for caution.

And if the last week were any indication, reality had finally set in. Even if they agreed to pursue their relationship—she pulled a brush through her hair—the logistics would be next to impossible. Evidently, he was finally starting to realize that. In a town as small as Terrance, on a campus as small as Breeland, privacy was unheard of. She was busy, he was busy, and the chances of them finding time for a conversation, much less anything else, were next to nil.

When she'd realized that, she'd started to feel—safer. Another word to wince at, she admitted, as she dropped her compact and brush back into her purse. Safe, predictable, comforting. That had been her preferred status for years. Why, now, did it seem so disheartening to picture herself in that role for the long term.

One look at The King of the Jungle, she mused, and she'd heard the call of the wild. For the past week, she'd been firmly lecturing herself on what had happened the last time she'd answered that call. It had ruined her life. Almost for good.

Fortunately, the lecture was easier to swallow when Eli wasn't tempting her with his golden eyes and his firm lips. The man had, she admitted, just about the sexiest lips she'd ever seen. She remembered focusing on them the first time she'd seen him lecture. Full and firm, they begged to be touched. Just the thought of stroking them, *kissing* them, made her shiver. It was no wonder she felt precariously close to tumbling over a cliff when he was taunting her.

So she should, she told herself, feel extremely grateful that except for faculty meetings, and across the width of the dining hall, she hadn't seen him since their dinner with Bill and Anna. Anna gave her glowing reports about his progress with his classes. As far as Liza could tell, the girls were enjoying his lecture style. She'd had no additional spectacular reports of exploding flower pots, but as the second week drew to a close, the general consensus was that Eli Liontakis had taken Breeland by storm and won them with effortless charm and grace. Amelia Pankhurst, she thought with a dry smile, seemed particularly intrigued by the presence of such an eminently eligible bachelor.

Liza looked at her reflection and frowned. When, she wondered, had she become such a stick in the mud? Here she was, well into what appeared to be a phenomenally successful summer program, and her mood was as sour as three-month-old milk. With a slight sigh, she pushed a blonde curl behind her ear. "Oh, get a grip, Liza," she muttered and reached for the door handle.

She pulled it open to find Lindsay, looking

strained, pacing in the hallway. "Hey, Lindsay. What's up?"

"Oh, thank God." Lindsay grabbed her hand and started pulling her toward her office. "One more minute, and I was coming in after you."

"What's going on?"

"You have visitors. Mrs. Forian told me to come find you."

"Visitors?" Liza's eyebrows lifted.

"Yes. They claim they're Grace's grandparents."

A chill coursed through her. She wasn't precisely certain why, but she just knew that Eli wasn't going to like this. "Okay." She shook her hand free. "I'll handle it. You go get Dr. Liontakis. He'll want to see them."

Lindsay gave her a concerned look. "He's in class."

"Tell him to let his class out early. The girls will appreciate it."

"All right." Lindsay hesitated. "Liza—is something—wrong?"

Liza studied her closely. "I don't think so. Why do you ask?"

"I don't like those people," the girl admitted. "They're weird."

As far as Liza could tell, Eli didn't care for them either. "It'll be all right, Lindsay. I promise."

"Are they going to take Grace away from here? Because she's just sort of coming around. I don't think that would be a good thing."

Liza sighed. "Me either. And, no, they aren't.

Eli's her father and guardian. She's not going anywhere he doesn't want her to."

Lindsay exhaled an audible sigh of relief. "Oh, good. I like her."

"I like her, too. Go get Dr. Liontakis, Lindsay, okay."

"Got it." She hurried off in the opposite direction. Liza took a deep breath and shoved open the door to her office. The scene that greeted her made her feel oddly violated. The tiny, cramped space—strewn with books and paperwork—had been her personal sanctum for years. Now, it felt invaded by something almost repugnant.

Only Anna, seated behind the desk, looking perfectly composed, assured Liza that the other two occupants of the tight space hadn't rummaged through her desk. A formidable looking woman, with expertly coifed hair more white than brown, wearing a tailored mauve silk suit sat perched on the front of the battered leather visitor's chair. Liza's gaze darted quickly to the corner where a tall, scowling man who looked as though he hadn't spent more than five minutes outdoors in the last twenty years, leaned with one shoulder braced against the rickety bookcase.

She looked quickly at Anna, who gave her a slight nod. Liza dropped her bag on the cluttered table by the door and walked into the room. "Hi. I'm Liza Kincaid."

The woman fixed her with a glacial stare. "We are Grace Liontakis' grandparents. We've come to see how she's getting along here."

Not to see her, Liza noted. "Well, you'll be very

happy to know she's doing extremely well." She moved behind the desk to stand next to Anna. A show of unity seemed prudent. "And I'm sorry, I didn't catch your names."

Grace's grandmother gave her a withering look. This was not the type of woman, Liza suspected, who generally got asked for ID. Her husband cleared his throat. "I'm Leonard Paschell, and this is my wife, Doris."

Liza nodded. "Grace speaks of you often." She didn't bother claiming it was nice to meet them.

Doris Paschell moved closer to the edge of her seat. She looked, Liza thought, like a vulture perched over rotting prey. "We've been talking with Martin, and I'm quite concerned about Grace being here. I'm sure I don't have to tell you—"

Liza cut her off with a wave of her hand. "I'm not sure what Martin has told you, but I can assure you that you have nothing to worry about. Grace is fitting in very well."

Anna nodded. "She's enjoying her dance classes, making new friends, generally seems to be taking to the program like a duck to water."

Doris's expression soured further. "It is my understanding," she said through partially clenched dentures, "that the children at this school are chosen from among, er, less-advantaged applicants."

Liza ground her teeth. Anna leaned back in the desk chair and continued to assess Doris Paschell with cool disdain. "Many of them, yes."

"Then you'll understand, of course, why we

feel a certain anxiety about Grace's interaction with them while she's still so vulnerable after her mother's death."

"We were always careful," Leonard interjected, "about the friends we chose for Grace."

"Sometimes," Liza countered, unable to keep the frost from her voice, "children like to choose their own friends."

"And sometimes," Doris's expression was condescending, "children don't know what's best for them. That's why they have adults in their lives."

Liza could feel her anger peaking. She hoped Eli got here soon before she deprived him of the pleasure of strangling these people. "And Grace is fortunate to have her father. He cares about her very much."

Doris's lips compressed into a line so tight, her upper lip all but disappeared. Anna shot Liza a warning glance. Leonard cleared his throat again. "Yes, well, you can understand why we want to have an active role in our granddaughter's life. Mara was our only child."

"Naturally," Anna assured them. "That's why I've arranged for you to tour the campus. You'll be able to see the buildings where Grace has her classes, as well as our dining hall and gymnasium."

Doris, Liza noted, looked ready to pop a cylinder. "We have a limited amount of time here. We'd like to spend that time with Grace."

"And we'll be happy to arrange that," Liza assured her, "as soon as we have Dr. Liontakis' permission for a visit."

Doris sputtered. "His permiss—"

"Now, see here," Leonard took a menacing step forward. "We don't need his permission to see Grace. We've been taking care of her for years."

Liza rocked back and forth on the balls of her feet, genuinely enjoying herself now. "I understand, but of course you realize that we can't simply authorize visits with our students without guardian or parental permission. It's state law. We have to put our students first, you know."

Doris's nostrils flared as she studied Liza with glittering eyes. "I'll have you know—"

"I'm here." Eli shoved open the door and charged into the small room with the finesse of a class five hurricane.

"Eli." Anna greeted him with a bright smile. "Grace's grandparents decided to come by and see Breeland for themselves. I've arranged for a tour of campus."

"What's going on here, Eli?" Doris demanded.

He leveled a glacial look at her. Liza took careful note of that look, and marveled that Doris Paschell, evidently, didn't have enough sense to heed its warning. "That's what I'd like to know," he said with careful control. "I wasn't aware you were planning to come for a visit."

"We spoke with Martin yesterday," Leonard told him. "Doris was concerned."

"Really?" Eli turned on him. "About Grace? About her reputation? About my reputation? Which is it?"

"Don't be crass," Doris snapped. "You know

how we feel about this." She leaned back in the chair. "These children are not appropriate play-mates for our grandchild."

Eli clenched his teeth so tightly, Liza could see the effect along the ridge of his jaw. She wouldn't be surprised if he cracked the enamel on his teeth. "Look, Doris. I went over this with you when I accepted the job here. I am Grace's father, and this is what I felt would be best for both of us."

Doris glared at him. "As if you'd know. You had almost nothing to do with the child for the past four years."

"I'm not going to even bother to respond to that." The tension in him shimmered in the small room. "The point is, it was my decision to make, and I made it."

"And I have the right to know," Doris told him, "that your *decision* isn't harming my grandchild."

"That's right." Leonard nodded. "We want to see Grace."

"And you will," Anna assured him as she punched a button on Liza's phone with a well-manicured nail. "But she's in class just now, so you might as well see the grounds."

The intercom crackled. "Yes?"

"Connie," Anna asked the receptionist. "Is Bill here yet?"

"Just arrived," Connie assured her.

"Excellent. We'll be right out." Anna stood and indicated the door with a sweep of her hand. "If you'll follow me, I'll introduce you to Bill Maxin. He's a member of our board of visitors, and he'll be delighted to show you around the campus. I thought I'd go along." She gave Liza a meaningful look. "In case you have any questions I can answer."

Trapped between blatant rudeness and Anna's iron-hard will, the Paschells looked first at each other, then at Eli. "We will discuss this later," Leonard told him.

"There's nothing to discuss."

Doris rose from her chair with a sigh of disgust. "You're not going to win this battle, Eli. The sooner you accept that, the better. Grace belongs with us. We've known her longer. We've been closer to her than you ever have. Mara would have wanted it this way."

"Then Mara should have stated that in her will."

Doris gasped. Liza winced. Leonard looked like he might bury his fist down Eli's throat. Anna wisely pulled open the door. "Ah, Bill," she said to Bill Maxin who stood just outside. "Perfect timing." She gave Doris Paschell a bland look. "Shall we go? It will take a while to see the entire campus."

Doris spared Eli a final glare as she glided from the room. Leonard, too, stalked by. Anna gave Liza and Eli a knowing look, then silently shut the door behind her.

Liza's breath drained from her body. She hadn't realized she'd been holding it. Eli started swearing the moment the door clicked shut. She let him rage for a full twenty seconds before she crossed the room to wrap her arms around his waist. "Sorry," she muttered into the soft denim of his shirt. "I would have spared you, but I didn't think it was wise."

He crushed her to him with stunning force. "No, I needed to be here. What did they say before I arrived?"

"Nothing important. Doris, er, hinted that she thinks the girls at Breeland aren't what she might call 'her kind of people.' "

That won a harsh laugh. "You could say that. Doris's kind of people are heartless bastards who like to screw up other people's lives."

"I'm sure it was hard on them when Mara died."

He sighed. "In their own way, I guess. Still, I'm not going to play this cat and mouse game with them. They want to take Grace from me, and it isn't going to happen. That's all there is to it."

"Are they suing you for custody?"

"Not yet. For now, they'd just like to bully me into giving it to them."

Liza tipped her head back so she could meet his glittering gaze. "Do you want them to see Grace while they're here?"

"Hell, no," he admitted. "But I don't suppose I can avoid it."

"Does she like them?"

He considered that for a minute, then shrugged. "It's hard to say. She doesn't seem to loath their company, although to my knowledge, she's never actually asked to visit with them."

"How often does she see them?"

"As seldom as possible. I'm not really sure what Doris and Leonard tell Grace about me, or about my relationship with Mara, but I get indications that I wouldn't like it if I had all the facts."

Unable to resist, Liza smoothed the frown from between his eyebrows with her index finger. "Grace hasn't told you?"

"She hardly talks about it. The other day, though," he shook his head, "I'm having some PR problems—it's really more of an annoyance than anything. But I was on the phone with Martin about it, and by the time I hung up, Grace was asking me if I was going to go to prison over it." His scowl deepened. "I'm sure she got that fear straight from Doris."

A niggling worry began to amplify in the back of Liza's mind. "Have you—considered—that the Paschells might try that to take Grace from you?"

"Hell, yes, I've considered it."

"What are you doing about it?"

He frowned at her. "What do you mean?"

"You can't just ignore it, Eli. You have to respond."

"You sound like Martin."

"God help us."

"Look." He looked exasperated. "There's a researcher—Dr. Jonathan Dally—who is challenging some of my research. This type of thing happens all the time in the scientific community. One scientist beats another to the finish line, and the next thing you know, someone's crying foul. It's not a big deal."

"But the publicity is bad."

"It's annoying," he clarified. "Not bad. He

doesn't have a lot of support, but it's a very high-profile situation."

"Which is exactly my point," she told him. "It's high profile enough that the Paschells can use it against you." She drummed her fingers on his chest. "Have you even bothered to defend yourself?"

His lips twitched. "How do you know I'm right and he's wrong?"

"Oh, don't be an ass. Of course you're right."

"Thanks for that."

"My point is, that if you continue to ignore this, the publicity is going to get worse. You'll look like you're hiding something if you don't respond."

"I know," he assured her. "And I'm going to. I just wanted to get Grace settled in here without worrying about all that."

"But she's been concerned. You said so yourself."

"I didn't think she even knew about it until she brought it up."

"Parenthood 101, Eli. Children know just about everything that's going on in their home."

"I'm learning that."

"Did you talk to her about it?"

"Yes."

"Did she seem okay with it after you discussed it?"

"I think so, yes."

Liza nodded. "Then it's going to be all right, Eli. We'll handle the Paschells."

He searched her face for long seconds, then his

fierce expression began to register subtle changes. "Do you think so?"

"Yes. You don't even need to worry about it."

He rubbed his hand down her back. "How long is this tour that Bill and Anna just led them on?"

"Oh, it'll take at least two hours. Three if Bill gets really wound up with stories about the history of Breeland. Anna will make sure Doris has quarter-sized blisters on her heels from walking on the brick paths in those pumps."

She could practically feel the tension draining from him. "Lord," he groaned as he leaned his head back. "They make me crazy."

"I can certainly understand that."

He met her gaze again, and this time, a subtle awareness glowed in his eyes. "And speaking of crazy—" his hands molded her to him, "do you realize this is the first time I didn't have to manipulate you into my arms."

"Eli—"

He shook his head. "Don't, Liza. Not now. We're alone. Finally. My heart is still pumping a hundred miles an hour from finding out Doris and Leonard are here." He shifted against her, a slight, alluring motion meant to seduce. "I don't want to argue. I haven't got the energy."

Her hesitation fled in the path of a gripping need that spiked her temperature several degrees. Clad in a denim shirt, he looked devastating. Her heart missed a beat. "You have friends, now, Eli. You don't have to do this by yourself."

He lowered his forehead to hers. "I know.

Thanks for heading them off at the pass. I'm not sure how Grace would have reacted if they'd swooped into one of her classes.

"Like any normal kid would if her grandparents suddenly showed up at camp. She would have died from embarrassment." She smoothed a wrinkle above his shirt pocket. "And you can thank Anna. She handled it. I'm pretty sure Doris wasn't prepared for coming up against Anna's iron-spined determination."

He laughed. It sounded a little rusty, but it definitely counted as a laugh. "Probably not."

"What did you do with your class when Lindsay came for you?"

"Dismissed 'em." He gave her a wry look. "That's what my boss told me to do. Lindsay said so."

"I did."

"Does this mean we both have an afternoon off?"

She hedged. "I'm really swamped."

He tightened his hands on her back. "I haven't seen you for days."

"Of course you have. I saw you yesterday afternoon at the faculty meeting."

"Alone, Liza," he said with strained patience. "I haven't seen you alone"

"I seem to remember pointing out the challenges of that to you."

"You don't have to look so smug."

"I'm not smug. Just practical."

"I think you enjoy torturing me."

"I do not. If you wanted to see me, I've been right here."

"And always just out of reach," he murmured. "Fancy that."

Liza shrugged. "Think what you like, Eli. I warned you it would be like this."

"Don't fight me, Liza," he cajoled.

And she sank farther into his web. "It's not—"

"Please don't fight me."

His lips were a fraction of an inch from hers when a commotion outside the door arrested their attention. "He's right in there, sweetie," Connie was saying. "Go on in."

Eli's startled gaze met Liza's as she pushed away from him. A split second later, Grace walked into the office. She looked from Liza to Eli, then back again. "Lindsay told me you wanted to see me." She looked at Eli. "Hello, Father."

He gave Liza a sharp look, then his features softened. "Hi, honey. Are you done with class?"

"Yes." She looked at Liza again. "Is something wrong?"

"No." Deliberately avoiding Eli's gaze, Liza sat on the edge of the desk. With a slight wave of her hand, she indicated the battered chair where Doris had perched. "Nothing's wrong. Your dad and I just wanted to talk to you about something. Want to sit down?"

Grace's expression turned wary as she slipped onto the chair. "What's going on? Am I in trouble?"

Eli cleared his throat as he crossed the room in

three quick strides. He squatted by Grace's chair so his face was eye level with hers. "Your grandparents stopped by today," he explained quietly. "They'd like to see you."

"Oh." She stared at him. "They're here?"

When several seconds of silence passed, Eli pressed. "Would you like to see them?"

She chewed on her lip. "Do you want me to?" she asked carefully.

"Honey," he said slowly, "you can do what you want. If you want to see them, you may. If you don't want to, you don't have to." He narrowed his gaze as he studied Grace's tense expression. "Do you think I'd make you see them?"

"They're my grandparents," she said.

"Yes." He swept her dark hair from her face with the pads of his fingers, "And because of that, you need to be polite and kind to them. But if you don't want to see them for some reason, then will you at least tell me what that reason is?"

She hesitated. Liza waited with bated breath while Grace searched her father's expression. Finally, she leaned closer to him. "Are they going to make me leave?"

"Leave Breeland?"

That hesitation again. "Yes."

"No," he assured her. "I won't let them do that."

"Are you sure?"

"Absolutely." His hands, Liza noted, had turned white from his grip on the arms of the chair, but he kept his voice low. "If you don't want to leave, we won't."

"I don't," she said.

"Then it's settled."

Grace laid her hand against his cheek. "Daddy?"

His eyes drifted shut. "What, sweetheart?"

"If we eat dinner with them, can they leave right after?"

When he opened his eyes again, Liza saw the humor in them. "Want to know a secret?" he asked.

Grace nodded. Eli smiled at her. "I don't like spending time with them very much, either."

The child looked immeasurably relieved. "For real?"

"For real."

"Mama liked us to go over there a lot."

"I know."

Grace frowned in concentration. "How come I never met your parents?"

"My parents aren't alive anymore. They died before you were born."

She seemed to consider that. "Both your parents died?" He nodded. Grace's hands twisted in her lap. "When?"

"I was eighteen when my father died. Mom died three years later."

"I didn't know that. Mama never told me."

"I should have told you. I'm sorry I didn't."

"If I'd met them, would I have liked them?"

"I think so. They would have liked you, too."

She met his gaze again. Liza could see the pain on the child's face. "I don't think Grandmother likes me very much."

Eli's shoulders shuddered. "Why not?" he asked quietly.

"She wants me to be more like Mama."

And, Liza thought, *less like Eli*. Eli traced the curve of Grace's jaw with his index finger. "You don't have to be like your mother, Grace. You don't have to be like me, either. I just want you to be yourself."

She hesitated, but finally nodded. "I guess so."

"And," Eli continued, "If you want me to talk to your grandmother about it, I will."

"It's okay," she assured him. "I don't think she's really mean or anything. I just think she's really sad that Mama died."

"She is." He kissed her forehead. "And you look a little bit like your Mama. It makes it easier for your grandmother to remember your mother when she's with you."

"I know." She studied his face for a moment. "But, Daddy?"

"Yes?"

"Do I *have* to go over there every week when we're home?"

"Didn't your Mama take you every week?"

"Yes. Especially when she was with Paul. She liked to drop me off for weekends. She said she wanted me to know Grandmother and Grandfather better, but I think she just wanted to be alone with Paul."

Liza saw the flash of anger that registered on

the hard angles of Eli's face. He wrestled with it for a moment, then brought it under control. "Maybe you're right," he said. "But can we make a deal that if you don't want to go somewhere, you'll just tell me about it? Things are different for both of us, Grace. I'm learning, too. I want you to talk to me about what you think. Okay?"

Grace hesitated, then nodded. "Yes, sir."

"That's my girl."

"Daddy?"

This time, his smile was dazzling. "What?"

She framed his face with her small hands. "No matter what Grandfather says, I'm really glad you let me live with you."

Liza's breath caught. Eli looked like he might faint. Grace bussed his lips with a quick kiss. "Can I go now?"

"Yes." His voice sounded gravelly.

She slid out of the chair and dashed toward the door. "Thanks. Ms. Jordan promised me and Beth we could have free ice cream at the hop shop if we helped her with the chalkboards this afternoon."

"Don't want to miss that," he answered.

And she was gone.

Eli groaned and dropped into the chair.

"Congratulations," Liza said softly.

He met her gaze. "I don't think I've felt this good in months."

7

Liza slanted Eli a cautious glance as he drove in silence toward her apartment. When they reached the parking lot, he didn't even wait for an invitation. He rounded the car and took her elbow so he could walk with her to her door.

The evening, she knew, had exacted a high price on his temper. Anna had arranged for Liza, Eli, Grace and the Paschells to join her for dinner at Solanto's. Twice, Eli had excused himself from the table for what Liza suspected was a trip outside where the air didn't ring with Doris's barbed comments or Leonard's snide remarks. Anna had deflected the majority of the venom with her usual finesse, while Liza had spent the bulk of the evening twisting her linen napkin into knots. For her part, Grace hardly spoke until after dessert, when Eli asked her if she'd like Anna to take her home.

That suggestion had sent the child into flights of rapture. At the Paschells' protest, Liza had quickly pointed out that Grace had class in the morning. Finally, the couple had given in. No sooner had Grace and Anna left the table, however, than Doris had stripped off any semblance of civility and ripped into Eli. Angry that he'd taken Grace away from the city, angrier still that he'd done it against her objections, and furious that Grace was taking dance lessons, when, evidently, her mother had expressly forbidden them, Doris had blistered Eli with a twenty-minute harangue. Leonard's only addition had been to deliver a cold warning about the effect all these changes might be having on Grace. And then he'd said the word *custody*.

As soon as the threat was in the open, Eli tossed his napkin to the table, rose to his feet, and extended his hand to Liza. "Ready?" he'd asked her.

Silently, she'd stood. He then leveled his amber gaze on his in-laws and bit out a slicing directive that he hoped this visit ended their harassment of him and Grace. Without further comment, he'd led Liza from the restaurant. He'd left the bill, she noted with sadistic glee, to his in-laws.

Once in his car, she'd tried to cajole him out of his brooding silence, but her attempts were met with monosyllabic answers and terse silence.

Now, as she fumbled with her key, she cast a cautious glance at his profile. He looked—she considered it for a moment—predatory. She'd seen a nature special once that had studied lions, and the changes in their behavior immediately before and immediately following a hunt. Eli had that before-the-hunt look.

Quickly, she turned the key in the lock and pushed open the door. He wasted no time.

She had the briefest of moments to observe that his expression had altered from glittering rage to glittering something else before he shoved the door shut with his foot, braced his back against it, and pulled her into his arms. "Damn it," he said as his head bent to hers.

Liza managed a slight gasp, then found herself engulfed in a storm. Overwhelmingly intense, his kiss stole her breath. Nothing had prepared her for the fire of it. The electricity that shimmered between them had never seemed this forceful—this overwhelming. The actualization of that energy, and the sensation of having his lips on hers, she realized before she lost the ability to think of anything at all, swallowed her whole.

Eli circled her waist with one arm as he eased her steadily between his outstretched legs. At a flick of his hand, her purse tumbled to the floor. He guided her arms around his neck, then settled his remaining hand at her waist. Her fingers threaded into his hair. She tugged until it slid loose from the leather band that held the queue in place. Warm and silky, she couldn't stop sifting it through her hands.

With his large palms pressed to her spine, his

thighs anchored against her hips, and his mouth moving over hers with silken promise, he wove his magic until her knees buckled. Liza found herself clinging to his shoulders. She'd never considered herself the clinging type, but then, Eli had a way of turning her into a puddle.

When he finally lifted his head, she had trouble focusing her eyes. She pressed her face to his throat. "Eli, the other day, when I told you the timing had to be right for us—"

He trailed a line of kisses along the cord of her neck. "Hmm."

The slight grunt sounded so arrogantly male, she smiled. "I think maybe it's right."

He went perfectly still. "Liza—" he breathed her name against her ear. His breath felt hot and sensual.

"You can't stay the night," she said quietly. She wasn't sure if that was merely a warning or an argument.

"I know." He still hadn't moved.

She drew a deep breath. "Take me to bed, Eli."

His groan ricocheted off her sensitized nerves. He kissed her again, slanting his mouth over hers until she felt her equilibrium shatter. "Tell me what pleases you," he muttered as he swung her into his arms. "I want to know what turns you on."

She released a shuddering breath. "You do."

He carried her down the hallway. His every touch sent heat coursing through her. The way he looked at her had her trembling. He seemed fascinated by the goosebumps on her flesh. He touched her, and caressed her, and made her feel indescribably beautiful.

Neither of them spoke as they peeled away clothing and inhibitions. She sensed his urgency, and surrendered to it. His nerves, she knew, had been laid bare that day, and at least she could give him these few moments of oblivion.

When they stood naked, lit only by the shaft of moonlight streaming in through her windows, she led him to the bed—where he took her to paradise. He didn't take his eyes off her when he retrieved the foil packet from his wallet—nor when he readied himself to protect her.

When he joined their bodies and visited indescribable pleasure on her, she felt her mind slipping away. He called her name at the last—when Liza was clinging to him, their breath and their heartbeats were so close they were indistinguishable.

Afterward, she lay panting against his chest, feeling the same breathless exhilaration she felt after she danced—only better. The feeling frightened her a little, but she refused to give in to that fear. Instead, she traced a lazy pattern on his bare chest, listening to the rapid beat of his heart. A few seconds more, she promised herself. Just a few seconds more.

Eli's hands slid over her naked skin, as if he couldn't stop touching her. She tried to cling to the pleasure for as long as she could, but the insistent voice in her head grew louder. Don't get too close, it warned. Whatever you do, don't get too close.

With a heavy sigh, she released her fragile grip on the peaceful contentment, and watched it slip away like leaves on the wind. Her eyes drifted shut in a moment of regret, before she took a firm hold of herself and forced levity into her tone. "How do you *do* this to me?" she asked, taking heavy breaths of his clean scent.

"It's not me." His palms slid up her spine. "It's us."

Liza summoned the energy to push away from him. He let her ease back a couple of inches, but kept his hands firmly locked on her back. She frowned, but didn't struggle. "I don't think so. I think it's you."

"Uh uh." His grin was devilish. "Chemistry, remember?"

"I flunked chemistry." She couldn't keep the irritation from her voice.

"You'll pass it this time." He kissed her again, more softly, breathtakingly sweet. "I'm going to give you private lessons."

"The last time I took a chemistry class, I set the lab on fire."

Amusement sparkled in his amber eyes. "So far, you're batting a thousand, then, babe— because you set me on fire every time you look at me."

She gave him a disgruntled look and pulled free of his arms. "Very funny."

"Personally," he assured her, his tone cautious. "I find it hilarious." He paused. "Is something wrong?"

Liza deliberately turned away from him and swung her feet over the side of the bed. "Of course not. Do you want something to drink before you go home?"

"Very subtle," he muttered. "You're acting weird."

"Sorry. One of my moods, I guess." She reached for her robe. "Grace is waiting for you—or did you forget that?"

That same anger she'd sensed in him briefly flared in his gaze. "Damn it, Liza, I just spent an entire evening defending my right to be a father to my own child. You don't have to remind me of my responsibilities."

The harsh note in his voice melted her as little else could. Filled with remorse, she leaned across the bed and softly kissed him. "I shouldn't have said that."

He crushed her to him. They lay in silence for several moments while he drew comfort from her presence. "I'm sorry I snapped at you."

"It's been an emotional kind of day," she admitted. "I understand."

His hands molded her to him. "I don't want to leave."

"You have to. I understand, Eli. Don't worry about it."

He studied her through narrowed eyes. "You're sure you're all right."

"I'm fine." She could see the doubt in his eyes, so she shook her head. "Really," she assured him. "I'm fine. We both knew it would be like this."

"I want to wake up with you tomorrow."

"And you can't. Neither can I, for that matter." She couldn't define the strange feelings roiling through her, but she didn't like them. She felt betrayed, irrationally, by the very truth she'd felt compelled to point out to him. She wondered if he'd always have the power to do this to her—to send her normally steady emotional well-being into orbit.

"I suppose," he said finally, "that I should at least be grateful to the Paschells for this."

He was teasing and she knew it. But it stung. She looked away to mask her hurt. "I suppose so."

"You *are* upset," he said.

"No. I think you should go now."

He swore again. "You know if it weren't for Grace—"

"I know."

"She has to come first, Liza."

She did know that, and she felt like a jerk. She also felt like having a good cry and didn't know why. "I'm the one who pointed out that it was time for you to go, remember."

He studied her a moment longer, then rolled from the bed. She watched him put on his trousers and shirt. He dropped to the side of the bed to slide on his socks and shoes. "She'll be wondering where I am."

"I'm sure she will."

He glanced at her over his shoulder. "And you're sure you're all right."

"Fabulous."

He frowned at that. "Why do I think I'm going to regret this by tomorrow?"

"I don't know."

"I have a very sick feeling that I'm screwing this up as surely as I screw up every conversation I try to have with my child." A rare note of uncertainty laced his tone.

Liza deliberately put aside her misgivings and focused on him. "You're a wonderful parent," she assured him. "Grace loves you very much. It's obvious."

"I can't lose her," he said—his voice gruff.

"I know. You won't."

He finished putting on his shoes, then leaned over the bed to kiss her a final time. "Thanks for tonight."

She frowned. "Don't mention it."

He watched her for several seconds, that same puzzled look in his eyes, then stood. "Why don't you get some sleep? I'll see myself out."

"Okay."

He nodded once, then strode from the room. She leaned back against the pillows, fighting a wave of unexpected anger. What had she expected anyway?

She heard him shut her apartment door, and she leapt from the bed, pulling the belt of her robe tighter as she ran. When she ripped open the door, he was standing at the end of the hall near the elevator. "Oh, by the way," she called. "In case you were wondering—it was good for me."

His eyes widened in shock. "Liza."

"Thanks for asking. Have a nice night, Eli."

She slammed the door shut only to have him pound on it seconds later. "Damn it, Liza. Open the door."

"No," she told him. "You have to go home now."

He swore. "We're drawing a crowd out here, do you know that?"

Her neighbors and colleagues, she imagined, were enjoying the hell out of this. "I'm not the one banging on the door in the middle of the night."

He swore again. "Are you going to let me in or not?"

"Not tonight," she assured him.

She could practically feel his frustration through the door. "I'm going home now."

"Have a nice evening." This time, his curses were more colorful. "And watch your language," she chided. "You're supposed to be setting an example for the students."

"We will discuss this tomorrow," he promised.

She didn't answer, and seconds later, heard him stalk away.

"What did you say," Anna asked her at six the next morning. "Specifically?"

Liza's eyes drifted shut. She should have expected this, she supposed. After the scene she'd caused last night, it shouldn't have surprised her that Anna, and evidently the rest of the campus, already knew what had happened. These things never took long. "Who told you?"

Anna's leather desk chair creaked as she leaned

back in it. They were enjoying their six A.M. morning ritual of coffee and campus gossip. They'd been meeting at this time for years—having long ago learned that the early morning quiet was the best time for undisturbed conversation. Anna answered, "He did."

Liza's eyes shot open. "Eli?"

"Yes. I was waiting at his apartment with Grace, you'll remember. He was a bit, uh, agitated when he came in."

She smiled slightly. "I'll bet."

"What did you say to him, Liza?"

"I don't think it was what I said—I think it was the moment of delivery that mattered."

"You slept with him," Anna said. It wasn't a question.

"We made love," Liza admitted. "There wasn't any sleeping involved."

"You're angry."

Liza frowned. "Not really. It just knocked me off balance a little. I'd been telling him for days that he didn't really have a grasp of how difficult this would be." She picked up her coffee cup and took a sip. "You should have told me that he watched me dance."

"You would have been uncomfortable."

"Yes."

Anna studied her, probing. "Why is that?"

"You know why. No one watches me perform. Not since—well, I quit that."

"It's not right, Liza."

"It's my choice," she said firmly. "And you shouldn't have told him."

"I like to meddle. You'll have to forgive me." The twinkle in the older woman's eyes belied the humility of the answer.

Liza couldn't suppress a laugh. "You're impossible, do you know that?"

"So everyone's been telling me." Anna drank some of her coffee. "May I take this to mean that you aren't going to tell me what happened last night?"

"You may."

"Are you angry at him?"

"No."

"He thinks so."

"I'm not. I'm just annoyed that things are so—frustrating. And that he's so cavalier about it. He could at least *try* to act like it bothers him a little."

"What are you going to do about it?"

"I don't know. There's not much to do."

"I don't think he's going to let the matter go, Liza."

She winced. "I was kind of afraid of that."

"And you might as well prepare yourself for the third degree from your neighbors."

"You don't think they'd dare ask me to my face, do you?"

"Depends," Anna said, "on how much you piqued their curiosity."

"Oh, it's piqued all right."

Anna's eyebrows lifted to disappear behind her fringe of bangs. "I can see I should have pumped Eli for more information."

"You're not getting it from me."

"I'll wheedle it out of him."

"I don't doubt it."

With a nod, Anna put down her cup. "All right, let's go over this report before we run out of time. Since you're not going to assuage me, you might as well brief me on this afternoon's faculty meeting."

Eli stood in the narrow corridor outside Liza's rehearsal room and wrestled with his temper—and, if he were honest with himself, a growing sense of anxiety. He'd used her last night.

And she'd known it. He'd been tense and angry after the confrontation with his in-laws, and he'd used Liza to work off his frustration. He'd taken women to bed for less honorable reasons, he supposed, but somehow, it hadn't seemed to matter before.

Today, he felt low as a snake.

After a mostly sleepless night when he'd had ample time to think about what she'd said, how she'd acted, and how he'd reacted, he'd awakened feeling irritable and stressed—and an uncomfortable twinge of guilt had been eating at him all morning.

Sure, she'd known from the start that he wanted her. He'd been playing from an open deck. But that didn't change the simple fact that he'd taken advantage of a very tense situation last night—and she knew it.

The door of Liza's classroom opened, and her students began to file into the hall. This was her last class of the day. If he caught her now, he could have her all to himself. Enough time, he thought grimly, to grovel.

Several of the girls greeted him as they walked past. He chatted with them, keeping a careful eye on the door. When Liza finally appeared, the small crowd of students seemed to sense the importance of the moment. They stopped talking. Liza met his gaze over their heads. She looked tired, he noted, but oh so incredibly touchable. With a fine sheen of sweat still glistening on her forehead, and her red leotard casting a rosy hue on her skin, she looked very much like she had when he'd slid out of bed the night before. She held his gaze a second longer, then turned to shut and lock the door behind her with careful precision.

He gave her students a reassuring look, and dismissed them with a slight nod of his head. They hurried off, their giggling and chatter fading as they disappeared around the corner.

When Liza faced him again, they were alone. He had nothing to say, so he simply stared at her. She stared back. Several moments passed before she made the first move. With a muffled exclamation, she walked straight into his arms.

Relief exploded inside him. Somehow, he hadn't managed to screw this up completely. Even years later, the fights with Mara, her charges of his insensitivity and selfishness still rang in his ears. He'd survived his failed marriage, but not without his share of scars. "I'm sorry," he mumbled. "I shouldn't have done that last night."

Liza shook her head. "It's not your fault."

"Yes, it is." He took long seconds to absorb the feel of her pressed against him. "I acted like a jerk."

"Sort of," she concurred.

"Only sort of?"

"I knew you had to leave," she explained. "I shouldn't have held that against you."

"I didn't have to leave without making you understand what that meant to me. It was selfish."

He heard her chuckle, and the rest of his anxiety washed away. "Well," she said, tipping her head back to meet his gaze, "now that you mention it—"

He shook his head. "Are you going to torture me about this for the rest of the day?"

"Will it do me any good."

"Probably."

"Really?"

"And you don't have to look so damned amused."

"I can't help it. It's vaguely satisfying."

Eli's eyes sparkled. "Well, if you're going to torture me, can we at least go somewhere less public?"

"Depends," she told him. "What are your intentions?"

He blinked. "Are you kidding?"

Liza laughed. "Besides *that*, I mean."

"Oh. We need to have the conversation we should have had last night."

"Would that be the conversation we should have had before or after you carried me past the transcendental plane of existential bliss?"

A smile tugged at his mouth. "The what?"

"I learned that in Mrs. Petrie's English class."

"Doesn't Grace have her for creative writing?" he asked.

Liza nodded "She's been teaching here a very long time."

"Should I be checking my daughter's homework for creative euphemisms for, er, existential bliss?"

"Oh, definitely. The *Rubaiyat of Omar Khayyam* is one of Mrs. Petrie's favorite books."

"Great. My daughter's reading smutty Persian poetry."

"Don't worry. I think Mrs. Petrie sticks to animal stories for the younger grades. It's the high schoolers you have to keep an eye on."

"I'll remember that." He kissed her softly. "Are you done for the day? Anna said you probably would be."

"I am. Are you?"

"Yes. I have labs only every other day—so I've got some time. Your office?"

She hesitated, then shook her head. "No. How about your apartment?"

His eyebrows lifted. "Really?"

"Yes."

"Honor demands that I point out to you that there's a bed at my apartment—and that my concentration might be somewhat fractured, given the obvious conclusions I'm bound to draw from this proposal."

Liza laughed, and it warmed him. "Well, I certainly hope so."

He kissed her, hard and long and hungrily until he felt sure she understood all the things he'd left unsaid the night before. "Do you want me to drive?" he asked.

"I'll have to meet you there." He adored the husky note in her voice. "I have to stop by the office first."

"Twenty minutes," he told her. "I'll be waiting."

8

"Eli—" she gasped forty-five minutes later. "This is too much—" her voice threaded, as he bit gently on her earlobe.

He raised his head to give her a wicked grin. She'd knocked on his door twenty minutes ago, and they hadn't even made it to the bedroom. He had her ready for him in seconds as the passion between them flared to new heights. "I know," he assured her.

He took a second to prepare himself, then put himself right where he wanted to be. The feeling was every bit as mind-stealing as it had been the night before. Liza clutched at him, and he traveled with her all the way to the stars.

Moments later, they lay, replete and exhausted, reaching for breath and for sanity. He kissed her gently on the lips. "Thanks for coming," he told her.

She giggled. "My pleasure."

In his nerve-numb state, it took him several seconds to catch the pun. When he did, he laughed. "And thanks for giving me a second chance."

She stretched, a lazy dancer's stretch that gave him an oh-so-tempting view of her many assets. "It was my fault, too. I'm sorry I let you leave like that. I was feeling a little shattered, and it was strange having you walk out on me."

"We'll work harder at that next time."

Her gaze strayed to the clock. "How much time do we have?"

"Grace should be home in an hour."

Liza nodded and reached for her shirt. "And I've got to be at a meeting by six. Want some coffee before I go?"

He sighed. "I guess. I hate this."

She pulled on her shirt, then her jeans. "It's the best we've got, Doc. Take it or leave it."

"I'll take it." He dressed, too, so he could trail after her to the kitchen.

She pulled open a cabinet. "Where's your coffee stuff?"

"Bottom left. I'll do it." He brushed past her.

"Fill the pot, I'll make the coffee. I don't trust anyone to make coffee for me."

He poured the water into the coffee maker, then stepped back to let her finish the job. He braced one hip against the counter and studied her as she moved comfortably around his kitchen. It felt uncommonly good to have her there—better, probably, than it should to have her doing something as simple for him as making a pot of coffee.

Shaking off the odd feeling, he grabbed two mugs from the rack and set them on the counter.

Liza gave him a thankful smile. "It'll be several minutes until this is done. While we wait, you can tell me what that visit from your in-laws really meant last night." She paused. "Or would you rather not?"

His euphoria evaporated. He pushed away from the counter in sudden agitation. "I don't know," he admitted. "I've been wrestling with this almost every day since Mara died. I didn't have much peace from it until Grace and I got down here."

"They're really determined, Eli. I think you should give some serious thought to what you're going to do if they make a legal move for custody."

"What I want to do is to strangle the Paschells and get them out of my life."

"I know the feeling. They're pretty rotten."

"I'm sorry," he said, meeting her gaze suddenly, "for the things they insinuated about you and the program here."

"You mean the 'dancers have questionable morals' comment?"

He winced. "Did she say that?"

"Yes. You were outside slamming your head against the brick wall."

"How'd you know?"

"You had lumps on your forehead when you returned to the table."

He managed a slight laugh. "I wouldn't doubt it. Anyway, you didn't have to take that."

Liza shrugged. "It's okay. I'm way past the stage in my life where everyone's opinion counts." The coffee pot had started to gurgle. "I think it was hard on Grace, though."

"I'm sure it was. She looked miserable."

"Do you think they're like that when she's alone with them, or was that just a show to impress us?"

"I don't know, but I'm going to ask her. I'm not sending her over there anymore if she hates it."

"It would be hard," she said carefully, "to take her out of their lives completely."

"Not if we didn't live in New York," he said.

Liza's eyebrows lifted. "Is that a possibility?"

"Hell, I don't know." He finally stopped pacing and dropped into a chair. "I'm not sure of anything anymore, except that I'm not going to let Mara's parents destroy what I have with Grace."

Liza waited for the coffee pot to finish, then poured two cups. "Cream and sugar?" she asked him.

"Black."

She set the two cups on the table and took the seat across from him. "Did Mara name you as Grace's guardian in her will?"

"That's part of the problem." He picked up his mug. "Mara didn't have a will, but according to the divorce settlement, we had joint custody. When she died, I became Grace's sole guardian."

"Sounds airtight."

"It is—mostly. But if the Paschells can persuade the court that the conditions which existed at the time of my divorce no longer stand, then they might have a case. When Mara and I split, I rarely traveled. Now that I'm on the road so much, Grace's grandparents could argue that it's bad for Grace." He took a tentative sip of his coffee, winced as it slid down his throat.

Liza toyed with her mug. "So you think they might try to convince a judge that your commitment to your work at the lab would prevent you from properly caring for Grace?"

"That—or that I'm reckless with my research and my career is about to go down the tubes."

"Oh, that's ridiculous," she scoffed.

"Some judges are—easily influenced."

"And the Paschells are in a position to exert significant pressure."

"Yes."

"But so are you," she argued.

"Yes. And I won't hesitate to do it if I have to. I was trying to spare Grace, and me, the messy reality of a publicity deluge. It's hard to make people understand how common this really is. All the pharmaceutical firms are looking for the same types of drugs—everything from weight-loss aids to cures for cancer.

"I know of five other scientists who are working on some of the same research we are right now. Generally, it's a civil business. We're in this together—fighting diseases that are common enemies. I wouldn't hesitate to share some research with one of my colleagues if it meant we could get to an answer more quickly. Every mystery we solve unlocks the door to thousands of other secrets."

"But it's not always like that?" she prompted.

"There's a lot of money involved. Greed is part of it. Sometimes, one guy gets to the answer quicker—usually because he's lucky—and when that happens, his sponsors make money. Lots of money." Eli shrugged. "Generally, the rest of us recognize that whatever strides were made benefit all of us in some way. But the field has its share of bastards."

"Like Jonathan Dally?"

"He's their king," he said with a slight smile. "And he's been bitter about me since we first worked together ten years ago. I got a grant he wanted, and that grant led to some groundbreaking strides in virus control. He never got over that."

"And now he's making you pay for it," she guessed.

"That's the way he sees it. He's getting some attention, anyway. If it hadn't been for the Nobel nomination, no one would have cared. He maybe would have gotten some coverage in some medical journals, but that's about it. Now, I'm stuck. If I make a public statement about Dally's accusations, the interview demands will start pouring in. First, it'll be print media. Before long, the morning shows will call. Everyone's going to want a piece of me, and I only have so many pieces to go around. Grace is always going to get the first piece."

Liza gave him an encouraging smile. "That's one of the things I like best about you."

"It took me a while," he admitted, "but I'm perfectly capable of learning from my mistakes. I'm not a complete idiot, you know."

"Last night," she confessed, "I wasn't so sure. But you're winning me over."

"It's my irresistible charm."

Her laugh poured over his nerves with the electrifying effect of fine champagne—chasing away any lingering shadows. "I've always been quite impressed by the size of your ego."

"Actually, that's sort of what I wanted to talk to you about," he told her.

"Your ego?"

He gave her a dry look. "My mistakes. After last night—" He hesitated. "Are we all right?"

"You have to ask me that while I'm nursing the rug burns on my behind from this afternoon?"

He grinned at her. "I don't want to screw up again."

"I'll warn you first."

"Good." He leaned back in his chair. "You know, I haven't had a chance to really ask you how you think Grace is doing. She's very fond of you."

"The feeling is mutual."

"When I first met with Anna, she seemed quite certain that you and Grace would be a good match." He studied the dark liquid in his mug.

The sunlight streaming through his window had turned her hair to a glistening gold. If he kept looking at her, he'd want her again. "I think she's right."

"Grace is very talented."

He nodded. "She is. I've known that for quite a while." And Mara had known it too—she hadn't liked it, but she'd known. He, fool that he'd been, had let Mara's insecurities stand in the way of Grace's blossoming self-confidence. "Mara wasn't in favor of her lessons," he finally said.

"I gathered that from Doris's comments. Do you know why?"

"Frankly, I think Mara didn't like the idea of anyone, not even her own child, being more talented than she was." He shook his head. "Grace needed the assurance it would have given her to explore that talent. I didn't fight for it. I should have." He scowled. "Mara should have."

"Just because a person gives birth doesn't mean they're automatically suited to motherhood," Liza said. "It sounds like Mara had a lot of—issues."

"You could say that. Mara and I didn't agree on a lot of things. I think I failed Grace by not fighting harder about some of them."

Liza reached across the table to touch his hand. "Don't do that to yourself. You can only go forward, Eli. Concentrate on that."

He nodded in acknowledgment. "Still, she's not herself. She was never like this before. She's so excruciatingly polite. God, every time she calls me 'Father' in that stilted voice, I think I'm going to break something."

"She's afraid. Of a lot of things. You're working hard to allay those fears, and I know it's hard, but that's all you can do right now."

The words caused a cauldron of frustration to begin bubbling inside him. "I know it, but damned if I like it. She still barely talks to me. I paid every doctor in New York to do something, *anything*, for her, and she just looks at me with that vacant expression."

The shaft of sunlight spilled across their joined hands, heating his flesh. He studied the picture for long seconds, searching for a way to make her understand. "And the worst of it is," he finally said, "I have no idea how to help her. She seems terrified of me, too."

"No," Liza insisted. "I've seen the way Grace interacts with you. She is not afraid of you. Once Grace understands that you wouldn't willingly leave her alone, she'll begin to adjust. Children grieve too, Eli. They just do it differently than we do. She gave you a big part of the puzzle when she told you she didn't want to leave here. I think she meant she didn't want to leave you."

His thumb stroked a lazy rhythm on the back of her hand. "I hope so." With a low groan, his eyes drifted shut. "If I'd worked harder . . . But I had such trouble dealing with Mara."

"You couldn't have known what would happen."

But he should have, he thought cynically. It wasn't as if he didn't know Mara for who she was. "Mara and I had been divorced for five years, but we'd been estranged since the beginning."

"You started having regrets the morning after you said, 'I do,' " she guessed.

"How did you know?"

"Been there."

His eyebrows lifted. "You were married?"

"Sort of."

"How can a person be sort of married?"

Lord, why in the world had she brought this up? She *never* brought this up. He had a way of doing that to her. One piercing look from those amber eyes and she was spilling her guts. Liza reached for her nerve. "Legally, we were completely married. Emotionally—well, who knows what the hell we were doing."

"How old were you?"

"Eighteen."

"Eighteen," Eli mused. "You were young." His tone was thoughtful. "Had you known him long?"

"A week and a half."

"How did you meet him?"

"Is this an inquisition?"

He blinked, then gave her a slow smile. "Sorry. Scientist's innate curiosity. It's a reflex to probe."

"I'll consider myself forewarned. You were telling me about Mara."

"And you're changing the subject."

"You finish yours first."

"Hmm." He spread both his hands on his muscled thighs and leaned close. "Okay—Mara was a, 'hey, baby, what's your sign' type."

"Lovely image. I thought you said you were a brain man."

"I never claimed to have understood the woman."

"You understood her well enough to marry her."

"She married me, actually."

Liza's eyebrows rose. "There's a difference?"

"Like being sort of married," he acknowledged. "Mara pursued, and I chose not to run."

"How romantic."

His lips twitched. "I was twenty-seven. I was finishing my career as a student, and just beginning my career in biochemical research. I had won a few fellowships. Leonard owned a small pharmaceutical firm. He thought I'd go places and take him, his company, and Mara with me."

"Am I supposed to believe you fell into the woman's clutches?"

He laughed again. "You've met her mother, what do you think?"

"I think you should have thought about the fact that you might have turned sixty and found yourself married to another version of Doris."

He shuddered. "There's a lovely thought."

"It never occurred to you?" she asked in disbelief. "Come on, Eli. You observe things for a living."

"Actually, it's not as strange as you think. I was something of a science nerd in those days."

She choked. "Are you kidding?"

"No."

"Did you have plaid pants and a pocket protector?"

"It wasn't that bad," he acknowledged. "But I did wear horn-rimmed glasses." He slanted her a knowing look. "Mara insisted that I have my vision surgically corrected."

"I'm not sure," she said slowly, "that you would have looked so bad in horn-rimmed glasses."

"Thanks. I kind of liked them."

"But you listened to Mara?"

"I don't think I cared enough to argue. I'd been buried in a lab for years. I can at least thank Mara for teaching me how to function in the real world."

Liza leaned back in her chair. "What went wrong?"

He shrugged. "Everything, and nothing. When things began to fall apart, there weren't enough things about our relationship that were right to make it worth keeping."

"Except Grace."

He nodded. "Except Grace. I would have stayed in the marriage because of Grace, but Mara wanted out."

"That can be stressful on a child—to hear her parents constantly fighting."

"We didn't fight that much. We didn't actually *do* anything. Which was most of our problem. By the time we split, Mara and I had nothing in common but a good sex life."

Liza blinked. "Really."

He hesitated a minute. "Sorry. I shouldn't have said that."

"I understand."

"No, I don't think so." Eli drummed his fingers on the table. "Mara was—beautiful. She'd done some modeling before we were married, and wanted to keep on doing it. Which would have been fine, but having Grace changed her figure."

"She quit getting work," Liza guessed.

"Yes." He studied his hands. "Mara had an artificial side that I failed to notice in the light of her, er, other assets."

It was Liza's turn to smile. "You said you'd been spending a lot of time in the lab when you met her."

"A *lot* of time in the lab. Still—" he shrugged. "I was warned."

"That's what friends are for. Mine warned me, too."

"But you did it anyway."

"Some people have to learn things the hard way," she acknowledged.

"It's that lust for exploration I have."

"For *exploration*?" she quipped. "Really?"

He grinned at her. "Be nice or I'll quit spilling my guts."

"You can't stop now—not before the lurid details."

"Did I happen to mention that I was a nerd in those days?"

"Is that your way of telling me there aren't any lurid details?"

"Hmm." He nodded. "The only lurid detail in the whole story is that if Mara hadn't gotten pregnant with Grace, we might not have been married at all."

"Oh."

"I wasn't *that* much of a nerd."

"Evidently not."

"Grace was born six months after Mara and I were married." His voice softened at the thought. "If it weren't for Grace, I might have real regrets."

"That's a lovely thing to say," she said. "There aren't a lot of people in your position who would feel that way about their children."

"I mean it," he assured her. "Mara wasn't what I would have chosen for a wife. She couldn't understand the pressure of research. She resented the time I spent at the lab." He brushed his hand over the table. "To her credit, I could have done a better job at paying attention to her."

"Your career was new. I'm sure you were under a lot of stress."

"I was. But the more strained life became at home, the more time I committed to my work. Mara wasn't well suited to staying home alone with an infant. It wasn't what she'd planned."

"What had she planned?"

"A high-society life to match the high-society wedding." He couldn't suppress a twinge of bitterness. "Researchers with no track record and nothing but a fistful of unproved theories don't pull down enormous salaries. They work long hours for little or no recognition."

"I'm sure."

He shook his head. "I was as much to blame as she was though. I didn't want to work at my marriage. It took me a while to admit it, but I didn't even like Mara very much."

"Does Grace know you felt that way?"

"I hope not." Scrubbing a hand over his face, he released a long sigh. "Don't think I haven't thought about the possibility that my daughter is nervous about being with me because she senses I wasn't exactly her mother's biggest fan."

Liza shook her head. "I'm sure that's not true."

"It worries me, but I don't know what to do about it. Now that you've met the Paschells you can see why I'm not sure what she's heard from them."

"How much did they know about your relationship with Mara?"

His rough chuckle lacked humor. "They knew everything she told them—which I doubt was a very balanced perspective. I made sure, though, that they knew at least part of the truth. Before we were married Mara was extremely promiscuous. After Grace," he shook his head, "I paid closer attention." And he had. It had been the only rule he'd ever given Mara.

"She stopped?"

"As far as anyone knew—as far as I knew. I'm relatively certain that Mara didn't have an affair after Grace was born. If she did, she was extremely discreet. I wouldn't have tolerated that."

"That's certainly understandable."

"I'm not sure, however, that Mara appreciated the fact that I wouldn't allow it for Grace's sake. Had I ranted about being jealous, she might have taken it better. It even took me a while to realize it, but I didn't really care what Mara did. I just didn't want Grace to see that—to know that about her mother. It gave Mara one more thing to resent about me." He captured Liza's gaze again. "We began a slow descent into marital hell shortly after Grace was born."

"Grace is only ten. You hadn't been married long."

He shook his head. "Six months."

Liza frowned. "Are you sure Grace is—"

"She's mine," he said with unquestionable finality.

"But how—"

"She's mine," he said again. He'd never questioned it, and never allowed anyone else to question it either. "Grace is *my* daughter. I know she is. And that's all that matters."

He drew a calming breath. "If this doesn't work—" he shrugged. "If I can't get through to her while we're here, I don't know what else to do. The Paschells are convinced that I made an enormous mistake in bringing her here."

"You didn't," she assured him.

"They told me in that charming way of theirs that what Grace needs is to be around things that are familiar. Uprooting her, bringing her here—" he shrugged—"I took a big chance."

"Grace needs *you*, not New York."

"And I need her." He shook his head. "I never realized how much until she came to live with me again. Having Grace back—it's like walking out of a cell for the first time in years. I was in serious jeopardy of turning into a machine. She gives me a reason to feel things again. I can't lose her."

"You won't," she promised him. "This is my area of expertise, you know. I've seen hundreds of kids with problems every bit as complicated and difficult as your daughter's. You're doing the right thing, Eli. She just needs time to grieve."

He hesitated, then nodded. "You're right. I know you're right."

"Trust me. We teach kids a lot more than academics and performing arts here. We help them find their way."

Eli wrapped both hands around his mug. "Can I ask you another question?"

"Sure."

He pinned her with his amber gaze. "I've been here two weeks now. People like to talk."

"I'm pretty sure I warned you about that."

A tiny smile teased the corner of his mouth. "I've had a chance to hear others confirm what I thought the night I watched you dance."

She blushed, but didn't look away. "Oh?"

"I didn't ask. It's like I told you, people talk."

"There are a few members of the faculty that have been here as long as I have. They know I stopped dancing."

"Do they know why?"

"No."

"I'd like to know why."

"I'm not going to tell you."

He hesitated, wanting to press, but recognizing the need to back off. "All right."

He saw the same flash of irritation in her gaze he'd seen the night before when he'd rolled out of bed. "This isn't a game, you know? I'm not some oddity for you to play with while you're separated from your research."

Eli exhaled a long breath, then leaned forward. "Believe me, I'm not playing games. I want to know everything there is to know about you. I want you in my bed and in my life. I want to be your lover and your friend. It really isn't very complicated."

"It's extremely complicated."

"Because we don't have any privacy?" he asked.

"No. That's just part of the equation. You have a lot of baggage, and so do I. We aren't twenty-year-old kids with no past."

He reached for her hand. "I think I should probably explain something to you. Always in the past, I've pursued relationships the same way I pursue science. I've planned them, analyzed them, and approached them with methodical precision."

"You really know how to knock a girl off her feet, don't you?"

A grin slanted across his lips. "I think I've got knocking you off your feet down pat. It's the rest that worries me."

She groaned. "Have you always had this incredibly romantic streak?"

"I never claimed to be successful at this seduction thing."

"I can't imagine why."

"With you," he shrugged, "it's different."

She shook her head. "Maybe, but no matter what you think, I'm not one of your experiments. I'm not going to respond to the laws of science with the predictability of a chemical equation."

"Actually, I'm kind of counting on that. It's part of the appeal."

"Great."

He ignored that. "You're shivering right now. Do you realize that?"

"I've had a very long day. It's a delayed reaction."

He smoothed one hand down her shoulder. The soft faded denim of her shirt glided beneath his fingers. It made him think of how her hair had felt twisted around his hands. "I like it," he told her. "Shivering is a good thing."

"That depends," she said quietly, "on what's causing it."

He chuckled at that. "Chemistry. That's what's causing it."

9

She hadn't responded to that. She'd merely risen to leave, dumped the remains of her coffee in the sink, then told him she had to get ready for her meeting. He hadn't tried to stop her.

He'd walked with her to the door instead, where he could kiss her good-bye in a way guaranteed to leave her thinking about him for the rest of the day. He'd struck a nerve when he'd asked her about her dancing, and even he could tell she needed time to recover from that—so he'd given it to her.

After she left, he'd tried to concentrate on the stack of papers Martin had sent for his perusal, but found his concentration turning repeatedly to Liza and the events of the previous evening.

With several hours of his in-laws' accusations burned into his brain, he found it harder and harder not to wonder if they were right. The only time Grace seemed to open up to him was when she talked of her dance classes and of Liza. Eli had struggled with an irrational sense of jealousy when he'd realized Liza was reaching his daughter more successfully than he could.

Had he pushed her too hard by bringing her here?

Had he given her something to hide behind rather than dealing with the primary issue between them?

Had he expected too much and put her through too much by removing her from the environment she found familiar? She'd said she didn't want to leave Breeland, but he could never be sure whether she meant what she said, of if she were merely seeking to please him.

Only when he talked with Liza did he feel his equilibrium return. Somehow, coming from her, the assurance that he'd done the right thing rang true. When he thought of how close he'd come to blowing it last night, he flinched. He wasn't ready to lose the way she made him feel simply because of his own stupidity. It was the same feeling he got on the verge of an important discovery in the lab. There was something there, something no one else had seen.

He'd first recognized it when he watched her dance. Liza didn't merely exist, as he'd begun to fear he did, she lived. Even the way she dressed, he thought with a slight smile, betrayed a vim he envied. Like his daughter, she had a penchant for loud colors, bold patterns, and aggressive combinations. Today, she'd had on a red leotard, under a tropical-print denim shirt tucked into purple trousers. Somehow, she managed to tie it all together.

Liza, he could almost believe, had a way of making just about anything work. Even his pleasure in his work couldn't compare with the way he'd felt when he made love to her. That slight flush in her cheeks, that heightened sparkle in her eyes. It could become very, very easy, he suspected, to get addicted to that look.

He was still thinking about it the next morning when Grace entered the small study in the apartment. He was refiguring an equation for the third time—his concentration dimmed by memories of Liza—and didn't hear his daughter until she coughed. His head snapped up. "Good morning," he told her. "I didn't think you were up yet."

Grace's shoulders lifted in a slight shrug. "What are you doing?"

"Lesson plans," he explained. "I'm going over my notes before class today."

"Oh." She edged closer to the desk. "Are you busy?"

Deliberately, he put down his pencil. "No. What's on your mind?"

Grace shifted from one foot to the other. "There's a girl in my class—her name is Beth."

He pictured the talkative red-haired child who'd seemed attached to Grace's side for the past week. "You sit next to her in my class," he said.

"Yes. Do you like her?"

"I don't know her very well. Do you like her?"

Grace hesitated, then nodded. "Yes."

"I'm glad. You didn't have many friends your age at home. I'm glad you've met some here."

"So am I."

He waited while his daughter visibly gathered her courage. He had to clench his fingers on the edge of the desk to keep from demanding she tell him why she found such a simple conversation so burdensome. "Beth wanted to know," she finally continued, "if I could spend the night in her dorm room on Saturday."

He stared at her. Grace had not, as far as he knew, even considered a casual relationship like that with anyone since Mara's death. "She did?"

"Can I?"

"Of course. Yes, of course." He smiled at her. "I think you'd have a great time."

Grace tilted her head. "You aren't mad at me for wanting to stay there instead of here?"

"Of course not." He silently prayed that she'd give him at least a hint of what she was thinking.

It wasn't long in coming. "When Grandmother was here, she said that she wanted me to come home to visit her in New York this weekend, but that you said that you wouldn't let me."

He took a careful breath. He'd wondered how much Grace knew about the strain between him and his in-laws. More than he'd thought, obviously. "I thought we agreed you'd stay here with me for a while."

"We did. That's why I didn't know if you'd let me stay in the dorm."

"I'll miss you if you stay in the dorm, but that's not the same as a trip to New York." He gave her a slight smile. "New York is too far. If you're at the dorm, and I got really desperate, I could always kidnap you and bring you home with me."

"Mama used to say—" she paused, then shook her head. "Never mind. Beth says she's not sure she's allowed to have someone stay over in the dorm."

"We'll have to ask. I'm sure we can work something out. If you can't go there, maybe Beth can come here."

Grace frowned. "I'd rather stay in the dorm." She leaned a little closer to him. "Did you know that they stay up really late and paint each other's fingernails sometimes?"

"You don't say?"

"Yes. Beth says they're supposed to have their lights out, but they use flashlights to see with."

"I can see why that would be incredibly exciting."

She gave him a skeptical look. "No, you don't."

He fought a smile. "Okay, you're right. I don't."

"I still want to stay in the dorm."

"We'll work on it then."

"Will you ask Liza if it's okay? She's in charge. If she says yes, it'll be all right."

"Yes."

"Will you ask her today?"

"Yes."

She hesitated a second longer, then beamed at him—the first genuine smile he'd seen on her face since she'd come to live with him. "Thanks, Dad."

She ran out of the room then, and for the second time in two days, he found himself staring after a woman who'd left him feeling rattled. Lord, if he didn't soon get a grip on himself, Liza and Grace were going to turn him into a complete idiot.

That thought was quickly followed by another. With Grace gone on Saturday night, he'd have the apartment to himself. That thought had him tapping the eraser on his pencil on the desk in a rapid rhythm. According to Liza, they had a privacy problem. She was right about that. Her apartment was in the same building as most of Breeland's staff—and Liza wasn't the type to flaunt her private life in front of her colleagues. Since Grace lived with him, rather than in school housing, the situation was doubly complicated.

Until the miraculous and fortuitous arrival of Beth on the scene. His daughter's venture back into life, it seemed, could not have come at a better time.

With a chuckle, he picked up his pencil and refigured the equation with a few quick, decisive, calculations. Liza Kincaid was about to meet her match.

*   *   *

"How are things going, Anna?" Eli asked late that afternoon when he found the older woman in her office.

She smiled at him, the same warm smile that had charmed him from their first meeting. "Not bad at all. We haven't had any more crises that anyone's bothered to tell me about."

He winced as he lowered himself into the seat across from her desk. "No more lunatic grandparents showing up for a shoot-out at high noon?"

"It wasn't quite that bad, you know."

"Easy for you to say."

"Probably." She leaned back in her chair. "Have you heard from them since they returned to New York?"

"Not personally, thank God. I'm not sure I could have been civil. Doris sent a letter through Martin that she still wants to protest my moving Grace down here for the summer, but it's been quiet since then." He frowned. "Ominously quiet."

"I wouldn't worry about it," she assured him. "I'm certain that Martin has everything under control. Liza assured me that he's very efficient."

That softened his frown. "That's one way of putting it."

"And I'm glad you stopped by today. I've been meaning to ask you how you think Grace is faring after the run-in with her grandparents."

"That's why I'm here. She asked me this morning if she could spend Saturday night in the dorm with one of the girls."

"Really?"

"Yes. I think it's a positive sign. She appears to be taking this incident with the Paschells in stride."

Anna's white eyebrows disappeared behind a lacy fringe of bangs. "That sounds encouraging."

"I thought so. It's been a while since Grace has even expressed an interest in making friends—much less made any strides in that direction. I was very encouraged."

"Who's the lucky young lady?"

"Beth, er, Watson."

Anna's smile broadened. "Excellent. I'm really quite impressed with young Miss Watson. I had the chance to observe her in Caroline Kenner's debate class yesterday. She's very sure of herself—especially for a girl her age."

"Grace is attached to her, anyway. I've seen them together in my class. Beth seems to be good for her." His smile was rueful. "I can't remember the last time I saw my daughter giggle."

Anna's laugh warmed him. "Felt good, didn't it."

"Extremely. Even if I do suspect I was the subject of speculation."

"I don't doubt that for a minute. You seem to be the subject of everyone's speculation around here."

Exhaling a long breath, he settled back in his chair. "If I can safely assume that Grace has permission to stay in the dorm—"

"You'll have to ask Liza about that."

"I will. I wanted to clear it with you first. I know it's not the normal policy."

"We're here to help the girls," she said firmly, "not to enforce regulations."

He nodded. "Thank you for understanding that."

"That's what we're here for."

"So I'll speak with Liza this afternoon—which raises the other thing I wanted to discuss with you."

Her eyes twinkled. "I wondered when this would come up."

"Did anyone ever tell you that you're an extremely crafty woman?"

"That's not always the adjective they use."

Eli laughed. "Nevertheless, you don't let much get by you, do you?"

"I don't mind telling you that Liza has been a personal project of mine since she first came to Breeland twenty years ago."

"She cares for you very much."

"The feeling is mutual," Anna assured him. "In many ways, I think of Liza as a daughter. If I'd had children to raise, I would have wanted them to have Liza's spirit."

He steepled his fingers together as he carefully considered his next words. "She's very stubborn about some things."

"About relationships," Anna agreed. "She has cause."

"I'd like to know why."

"You'll have to get that from her."

He frowned at that. "She's not exactly open to discussing it."

"Keep trying. She likes you. Eventually, she'll trust you."

"I was hoping you'd give me some insight."

Her expression turned knowing. "You were hoping I'd give you a tactical advantage."

"That too," he quipped.

Anna shook her head. "One thing you'll have to learn about Liza. She plays straight from the deck. If you want to know her better, she'll expect you to work at it. Any information I gave you, she'd consider unfairly obtained. It would count against you. You'll have to trust me on that."

He hesitated, then nodded. "I will."

"Good."

Anna gave him a pointed look. "I think you can find Liza in the arts wing at this time of the afternoon. She likes to use the break between classes to go through some routines."

He glanced at his watch. "I have class in fifteen minutes."

"She'll know that—so she won't detain you. With a little strategy, you can arrange to meet her later to discuss the matter in more detail." She paused. "Privately."

He was still laughing when he found Liza in one of the rehearsal halls, executing a series of body-twisting stretches. The smile faded on his lips, however, as he watched her pull her body into a tight arch. Her hot pink leotard and green tights only served to highlight her lithe curves that virtually begged for his hands. Lord, she was going to be the absolute death of him. She must have sensed his presence. Her gaze met his in the wall-length mirror. "Hi."

Eli nodded and advanced into the room. "Hi."

She quit her routine and turned to face him with a warm smile. "Aren't you on your way to class?"

"Yep." He kissed her lightly. "I wanted to talk to you about something real quick.

Her gaze turned wary. "Have you heard from your in-laws again?"

"No," he assured her, "and I thank God for that every day."

"I'll bet."

"This is about Grace. She asked me this morning if she could have permission to stay in the dorm with Beth Watson on Saturday night. I felt I should talk to you about it."

"She wants to spend the night in the dorm. Really?" Liza's eyes lit. "That's very good news."

"I thought so." He traced a finger along the edge of her leotard where the hem was damp from her perspiration.

"I've noticed that they seemed to be bonding."

"So did I."

"What did you tell her?"

"I told her it was fine with me as long as it didn't break any rules."

Liza's shrug managed to be elegant. The slight roll of her shoulders fascinated him. "It does," she concurred, "but I'm not going to get hung up on that. I'll talk with the RD for Beth's dorm. I'm sure it won't be a problem."

"Thank you for being so accommodating."

Amusement flitted across her eyes. "It's what I live for."

"I'm counting on that."

Liza glanced over her shoulder at the empty hallway which would soon be filled with students. "Is that all you wanted. We need to clear out of here. There's a class starting in a few minutes."

He grinned at her. "It's not exactly *all* I wanted."

She gave him a chastising look. "Is it all you wanted that's reasonable given the present circumstances?"

He took a step forward. "Maybe."

She backed away from him. "Eli, we can't do this now."

"Can we do it later?"

"Is this why they call you The King of the Jungle—because you worry your prey to death?"

He closed the distance between them again. This time, she was backed up against the rehearsal bar with no place to go. Her scent, he noted, was that enticing combination of lemon and clean perspiration that made his head swim. It was the same smell that emanated from her when her flesh was heated from his touch. The thought had his fingers tingling again. "No. I got that name for my persistence. When I'm researching something, it's like a hunt. I have a hunger, and the only thing that's going to assuage it is finding the answer I want. Once I'm on the trail of a quarry, I don't lose it—once I've scented it, it's mine."

Liza started to laugh. "You're so subtle."

"Liza." He tugged her closer. "You're driving me crazy. I didn't sleep at all last night."

"Me either," she confessed.

With a slight groan, he tipped his head and brought his mouth close to hers. "We have got to do something about this," he said firmly, and he seized her lips in a searing kiss.

Pressing his hands to her spine, he molded her curves to his body so he could enjoy the exquisite taste of her lips. It was every bit as sensational as he remembered. Energy, high and tight, shimmered between them. Liza melted into him. Exultant, he deepened the kiss. Her lips were soft and sweet and he could easily, he knew, drown in the sheer sensation of kissing her. She made a tiny mewling sound in the back of her throat that drove him wild. Ravenous for her, he slanted his lips over hers again and again until he finally had to wrench his mouth away and suck in a desperately needed breath.

Liza didn't move. She kept her face pressed against his chest. Her breathing, he noted arrogantly, was as ragged as his. He moved one hand to cradle the back of her head. "Sorry," he whispered, his voice rough around the edges. "I shouldn't have started something I can't finish."

Liza merely nodded. So they stood that way for long seconds before he finally set her away from him. With a slight smile, he smoothed his thumb over the still-swollen curve of her upper lip. "If I promise I'll make it up to you later, will you forgive me?"

The slight widening of her eyes told him all he needed to know. Liza took a shuddering breath and stepped away from him. "I hate to break this to you, Liontakis, but it's considered tacky to suggest that a woman can't live without your, er, attentions."

Unrepentant, he grinned at her. "I know."

"You don't have to sound so pleased with yourself."

"Keeping you off guard seems to be the only way I have of getting under your skin."

"Where did you get an idea like that?" She leaned back against the exercise bar. "You've been under my skin since the day I met you."

"I'm glad to hear it."

"You would be."

She looked so disgruntled, he had to laugh. He thrust his hands into his pockets to keep from reaching for her again. "So, you want to come over tomorrow. My chaperone's going to stay out all night, and I have the house to myself."

"The board of visitors' faculty reception is tomorrow night. We're both expected to attend."

"I know. I was hoping you'd go with me and help me mingle."

Her lips twitched. "Are you kidding? You're the star attraction. You'll have women clawing for your attention. Now that your in-laws have been here, you're on the tip of every gossip tongue within a five-mile radius."

"Then maybe you can protect me from the masses."

"Maybe."

He studied the curve of her lips with peaking interest. He wanted to kiss her again. The energy thrumming through his blood told him he'd better curb his thoughts, quickly, or he'd have a hell of a time making it through his afternoon classes. He did not, however, resist the urge to trace the profile of her mouth with his index finger. To his infinite delight, her lips trembled.

Students had begun to file into the room, and they were watching Liza and Eli in open speculation. Liza kissed the tip of his finger, then pulled his hand away. "If I say yes, will you let us get out of here with some dignity still intact?"

"Absolutely."

She gave him a look that melted his socks. "Then prepare yourself, Liontakis. I'm going to wear you out."

10

"Crumb," Liza muttered, as she stared at her reflection in Eli's door knocker, "you're acting like a teenager."

Her palms were sweating. He did that to her. He had a way of turning her into a quivering mass of hormones. The way his lips tilted at the corner, the fierce light in his eyes when he spoke of Grace, the elegant way his hands moved to emphasize his point, they all combined to knock her equilibrium into a permanent tailspin.

And that was before he'd made love to her.

Now, her blood pumped faster every time she thought of him, of the way he touched her, of what it felt like to be that close to him. She was sinking faster and faster into an emotional quagmire with little hope of escape.

Of course, she thought, as she smoothed her

damp palms on her dress, it didn't help matters that Eli took every opportunity to shoot her looks so steamy she was surprised they didn't curl the wallpaper. At Thursday afternoon's faculty meeting, during her weekly briefing to the staff, he'd suddenly developed a fascination with tracing the curve of his upper lip with his index finger.

And Liza had seriously contemplated shooting him on the spot. *In for a penny*, she thought with a wry smile, and forcibly slammed the handle against the knocker on his front door.

Seconds later, Eli pulled open the door. He wasted no time getting right to the point. He tugged her inside, slammed the door shut, and wrapped her in his arms. "I'm glad you came," he whispered as his head descended to hers.

Liza surrendered to the sensual storm, which left them both breathless.

She blinked several times. "Nice to see you again." Her voice had turned husky.

Eli laughed as he scooped her purse off the floor. When had she dropped it? "The feeling is mutual." He hefted the purse from one hand to the next. "What do you carry in this thing? It weighs a ton."

She accepted it from him with a slight smile. "I keep a brick in there to fend off amorous males."

"I'll be careful." He dropped a kiss on her forehead as he eased past her. "I don't suppose you'd like to skip dinner?"

"You know what I have to say." She couldn't quite hide her smile.

"We have an hour," he pointed out.

"And I'd rather not arrive at the reception looking like I'd just taken a tumble in your bed."

He laughed. "Point well taken. Although, if they have a band, I feel I should warn you that we'll be doing a lot of dancing. I'm probably going to have a very hard time keeping my hands to myself."

"Restraint is the sign of a cultured gentleman."

He groaned. "Don't tell me. That was part of the Breeland code when you were a student here."

She grinned. "How'd you guess?"

"Intuition. I've really got to remember to ask my daughter what she's learning about boys." He shook his head. "And since I'm not going to talk you into something more—adventurous, we might as well eat." He headed for the kitchen.

"That's not the most gracious offer I've ever had," she called after him.

He shot her a look over his shoulder. "Chalk it up to days of sexual frustration. Why don't you make yourself comfortable?"

Liza ambled behind him. "Grace is already at the dorm?" she asked. A breakfast bar separated his kitchen from the living room. She wandered over to it and slid onto one of the high stools.

He pulled a pitcher from the refrigerator. "Yeah. I dropped her off earlier. We have the place to ourselves."

Liza pushed the remnants of fog from her brain and set her purse down on the counter. While he filled glasses, she swiveled on a bar stool to survey the room. She'd noticed the first time she came here that he'd added enough of his personal belongings to the decor to make it feel homey. Tasteful, masculine, but welcoming. She even liked the color of the walls. The controversial paint job now seemed the perfect foil for his unique style.

Eli set two glasses on the bar. "What are you thinking?"

"That I like what you've done with this place." She flashed him a smile. "I even like the paint. You were right about that."

"I wanted to give Grace a sense of home."

Another piece of her melted. "And here I thought you were just being egomaniacal."

"Score one for me."

"At least," she conceded. She reached for her glass. "Is this iced tea?"

"Yes. I made it myself."

Her eyebrows lifted. "Do they drink iced tea in New York?"

"Never. And if they do, they don't sweeten it."

Liza wrinkled her nose. "The barbarians."

He laughed. "I sweetened this, though. I spent an hour on the phone with Anna this afternoon mastering the recipe."

"Only a man could spend an hour trying to make iced tea. It's not that complicated." She accepted her glass.

"I'm a chemist. I like to be precise."

Liza took a tentative sip. "So there's a formula for this?"

His expression didn't flicker. "Five H_2O + two $C_{12}H_{22}O_{11}$ + one Orange Pekoe."

Liza choked on a laugh. "You made that up."

With a slight smile, Eli shook his head. "Nope. That's it. Scout's honor."

"Are you going to be demonstrating this to your class?"

"I don't know. How is it?"

"You haven't tasted it?"

"I was being polite by waiting for you."

"You were being a coward."

"Maybe. As you said, we don't drink iced tea where I'm from. It's alien."

She took another sip. "It's pretty good." Deliberately, she swirled her glass. "Robust, a little fruity, with a full-bodied aroma. Not bad for a first try."

"Thanks. I might actually get used to this southern living." He drank half his glass in one swallow.

She refused to entertain even a thought of what he could have meant by that. Instead, she kept her voice deliberately light. "Are we having stewed okra and fried chicken for dinner?"

"No way. Iced tea is one thing. Cholesterol poisoning isn't my idea of a good time."

"Wimp."

He kissed her again—a quick one on the lips that mingled with the sugar on her tongue. Liza sighed. Eli winked at her. "Let's go before you distract me," he said meaningfully.

When he pushed his plate aside a half-hour later and fixed her with a narrow stare, Liza felt a tremor run down her spine. His thumb caressed her knuckles. "Okay, time to talk," he said.

"I didn't know you were such a stickler for keeping a schedule."

The joke fell flat. Eli ignored it. "We don't get a lot of time alone. One of the things I'm learning is to take what I can with you. There are some things I want to talk about."

"Like when we can make more time for sex."

He frowned at her. "I know we're moving a little fast here, Liza, but it's not just about sex."

"I know that," she said quietly.

"Do you?"

She sighed. "It's harder for me than it is for you. It's been a long time since I've felt like this."

He tilted his head to one side. "Were you eighteen and thinking about getting married?"

Unnerved, as usual, by his perception, she met his gaze. "Yes, I was."

"Are you sure this is what you felt?" His fingers tightened.

"Close enough. I was out of control—dangerously out of control. I couldn't think clearly when I was with Drew, and I feel the same way with you."

"Liza, you aren't a kid anymore and neither am I. Just because you made some immature decisions—"

"You don't understand." Frustrated, she wiggled her fingers free. "Some people can afford to take enormous emotional risks. They have enough personal resources that if they lose part of themselves in the process, well, it hurts, but it's not devastating. Some people can't afford it." She gave him a close look. "I can't."

"Are you telling me," he said, his voice a hushed whisper, "that you're not emotionally involved with me? This is just a physical thing for you?"

She winced. It sounded so clinical when he said that. "No. I'm not saying that exactly."

"It sounds like it."

The condemnation she heard in his tone reminded her of the way he'd spoken of his former wife. "Sorry."

"I want more, Liza," he prompted. "I want everything." Eli slid his chair closer. "Sex with you—it's fantastic. I'll give you that. But it's not enough. I'm tired of waiting."

She pulled her gaze away and turned to stare out the window at the darkening sky. How much, she wondered, was she willing to reveal? "It's not a very interesting story."

"It's your story," he prompted. "I'm interested."

Drawing a deep breath, she searched for words. "My mother was very young when she got pregnant. She'd had an affair with a married man, and neither of them counted on facing any permanent consequences."

"Like children?"

Liza nodded. "He wanted her to have an abortion, and she refused. Frankly, I'm not sure why. She wasn't exactly the strong maternal-instinct type."

"Her parents were no help, I take it?"

"Thirty years ago, young southern girls did not have affairs with married men, and, if they did, they *never* got pregnant. I never met my grandparents—and, according to my mother anyway, that's how they wanted it."

She turned to look at him again. "Don't get me wrong. I'm not bearing some deep emotional scars because of this. My mother didn't mistreat me, she just didn't offer a lot of security. She was attractive enough to find men who'd put food on our table and clothes on our backs. We weren't destitute."

"Except maybe emotionally?"

"No." Liza shook her head. "No, it wasn't like that. I wasn't a victim and neither was she. She was only sixteen when I was born, so we sort of grew up together. We were more like sisters and less like mother and daughter. It wasn't ideal, certainly, but it wasn't horrible either."

He studied her for long seconds. "So how did you end up at Breeland?"

"My mother read an ad in the paper. She bought me some dance clothes and hitched a ride for us up here from Atlanta. I auditioned, and Anna let me in for the summer program. That led to a scholarship, which meant I could stay here year round. So my mother figured that was better for me than staying with her. She left me that summer and never came back."

His expression turned grim. "Lovely."

"It's all right," she assured him. "It sounds really shocking, but it wasn't. She was right about many things. Sure, I missed her, but I was happier here. I never had to worry about where my meals were coming from, or who was going to pay the rent. I didn't have to hide in the bathroom when she brought men home. I could dance, and I could go to school, and I could pretty much act like a normal kid. Anna took me in for the holidays, and I flourished here."

"Didn't you wonder what happened to her?"

"My mother? Of course."

"Did you ever find out?"

"No."

His gaze narrowed. "When did you stop asking?"

Liza fought the urge to squirm beneath his close scrutiny. "When I was eighteen."

"After your marriage?"

"Yes."

"I see."

"I doubt it."

He took her hand again, twining his fingers with hers this time. "Make me understand."

Liza resisted the urge to pry her hand free. "Drew was a dancer. I met him when his company came through Atlanta on tour. Breeland sponsored them for a couple of seminars. He paid a lot of attention to me. I was flattered."

"How old was he?"

"Nineteen. We were kids. He talked a lot about making it in New York. He made touring sound glamorous and exciting. I fell for it."

"When did reality set in?"

"The morning after we eloped. The company director called our motel to tell us the tour plans

had fallen through. We had no job and no pros-
pects."

"Couldn't you have returned to Breeland?"

She laughed. "If I'd been able to scrape
together the cash for a bus ticket and the courage
to admit I'd made a colossal mistake."

"What was Drew's reaction?"

Liza frowned slightly at the memory. "He was
used to it all. He didn't understand why I felt so
panicky. He laughed at me."

"You were scared." It wasn't a question.

"Petrified. I spent the first part of my life living
like that. I didn't want to go there again. Drew,"
she shrugged, "he had a certain capacity for it. I
just couldn't take it." She lapsed into silence as
the memories overcame her. She wasn't ready,
yet, to give him the full story, and she silently
prayed he wouldn't ask for it.

Eli stroked her fingers for long seconds. "What
did you do?" he asked finally.

"I got a job waiting tables. I begged Drew to
look for work, but he insisted it would interfere
with his auditions. We moved around a lot—living in rooms and closets we rented from other
dancers. My paycheck was the only steady
income we had. Drew auditioned a lot, but never
got work." She felt herself entering a verbal mine
field, and stopped to concentrate on what to say
next. Eli was an exceptionally intelligent man
with a naturally inquisitive mind. One clue too
many, and he'd hone in on her most vulnerable
spot.

And she couldn't give him that. She wasn't

ready to trust him that much—not when she was still fighting a sense of bitter resentment that he hadn't paid the same price for his mistakes that she had. Like him, her own plans had pivoted on the birth of a child once, but that dream had been stripped from her. Increasingly, she'd been forced to admit to herself that she was achingly jealous that he had his daughter to ease the sting of his failed relationship. While she, she had nothing but memories too sorrowful to discuss.

Eli broke the uneasy silence. "You were too busy working to worry about dancing?" he guessed.

"I was too busy surviving," she admitted. "I finally realized one morning that I couldn't take the terror anymore. It felt like I was six years old again, and wondering if my mother was going to come home that night." She met his gaze. "I was on the subway on my way to work when I found a hundred-dollar bill wedged between the seats. I didn't even hesitate. I went straight to the transit authority and bought a bus ticket to Atlanta."

"And you came home to Breeland."

"Yes. I also decided to stay here. I needed this." She freed her hand from his grip. "I need the security of living here and teaching here. I love what I do. I like the way we reach these kids. I like knowing that I'm going to have a job for the rest of my life, and that there aren't any risks involved."

"Including emotional risks," he prompted.

"Including emotional risks. I made up my mind when I came back to Breeland that I'm the kind of person who doesn't have a very high reserve of emotional energy. I can't afford to waste any of it."

He leaned back in his chair and regarded her with a shrewd look. "That's an interesting theory."

"It's also true. That's why I stopped dancing publicly. Each time I dance, I give something of myself away to the audience. I have always been afraid that I didn't have enough to spare."

Eli studied her face with unnerving scrutiny. Finally, he leaned forward and pierced her with a sharp gaze. "So if all that's true," he said softly, "why did you go to bed with me?" When she opened her mouth to respond, he held up a hand. "And don't bother telling me it didn't mean anything. That's crap and you know it."

Her breath drained from her lungs. He didn't move. She found a strange kind of courage in his stillness, as if he, at least, wasn't afraid of the storm she was about to unleash. "I've been thinking about this," she continued, "and I realized that you're right about some things. When you saw me dance—well, you took something from me. Something I can't have back. It made me vulnerable."

"I know."

"But now that you have it," she went on, "I feel sort of—connected." She met his gaze. "*Strongly* connected."

Eli surged from his chair. With a quick stride, he rounded the table and pinned her to her chair with his hands on her shoulders. "Thank you," he muttered a split second before his mouth descended to hers.

Liza gave up the struggle and let the sensation wash over her. She felt beautiful with him—as free and alive and graceful as she did when she danced alone on stage in a darkened auditorium.

11

"**G**race." Two days later, Liza interrupted the girl's progress as she headed for the door of the dance studio.

Grace gave her a wary look. "Yes, ma'am?"

"May I talk to you for a minute?" The other students were filing from the room. Lindsay glanced at Liza. "Do you need me?"

"No, go on to lunch. I just wanted to go over something with Grace."

"Okay," Lindsay reassured Grace with a slight smile. "I'll save you a seat."

Grace watched Liza carefully. "What's up, Liza?" she asked, when they were alone.

Liza sat on one of the low benches at the perimeter of the room and started unlacing her jazz shoes. "Why don't you sit down? I just wanted to talk to you for a minute. I've been noticing how well you're doing with the tap routines we've gone over in class. Every year in the closing recital, we have a few special numbers we do to allow time for the costume changes. I thought you might like to do a tap duet with Lindsay."

Grace's eyes widened. "A duet? On stage?"

"Yes." She waited. When Grace didn't respond, Liza prompted, "Would you?"

"I don't know." Grace had begun to look nervous. "I never thought about it before."

"The idea of performing without the rest of the group is a little nerve-wracking, I know."

"I think I'd be really nervous."

"That's not surprising." Liza suppressed a smile at the grown-up turn of phrase. "I get scared to death when I perform."

"Father said you don't dance on stage anymore."

"I don't." Liza wondered what else Eli had told Grace.

Just before they'd left for the reception on Saturday, Eli had received a cryptic phone call from Martin. As far as Liza could tell, his legal problems were escalating, but he'd been frustratingly withdrawn all night. Distracted and irritable, Eli had apologized to her, then left early. Liza had neither seen nor heard from him on Sunday until late that evening. He'd called to tell her he'd been tied up on the phone with his lawyers, his colleagues, and the other researchers and administrators at his lab for most of the day. He was sorry, he'd said. So sorry. She told herself she should feel relieved.

Now, she studied his daughter wondering what kind of effect her father's stress was having on the child's already fragile sense of security. She drew a deep breath and continued, "He's right."

"Why'd you quit?"

"I was afraid," Liza admitted.

"Seriously?"

"Sure. Haven't you ever been afraid of anything?"

"Yes." Barely a whisper. Liza waited. Grace studied her small, clenched hands. Several long seconds of silence ticked by. Finally, Grace raised solemn eyes to hers. "I'm afraid that I might have to live with my grandparents."

Liza drew a slight breath. So this fear hadn't been completely allayed. She'd expected as much. "You are?"

"Yes."

"Did you believe your father when he told you he wouldn't let that happen?"

Too many seconds passed before Grace responded. "I guess so."

"Grace—I know you want to stay with your father, but is there some other reason you feel like this about your grandparents?"

Grace hesitated. "Will you tell my father if I tell you?"

She studied the girl's tense features. "Probably not."

"But maybe?"

"Well, let me explain it to you like this. If you and I were out somewhere and I got hurt, what would you do?"

"I'd help you."

Liza nodded. "Uh huh. Would you go get someone to help?"

"Sure. If I needed to I would."

"Exactly. So if you tell me something, and I think maybe I need your father to help me, then yes, I would tell him. But if I think it's okay to keep it between you and me, then I won't. Make sense?"

Grace hesitated, then nodded. "I guess so."

"So do you still want to tell me?"

Liza watched the far-too-adult struggle on the child's face as she considered the dilemma. "Yes," she finally said.

"I'm glad." Liza waited.

Finally Grace relaxed against the bench and began to talk. "I like them okay. They're pretty nice to me. My grandmother likes to buy me stuff."

"Your father says your grandmother spends a lot of time with you."

"She does. She did before Mama died, but she does it more now. I think she misses Mama."

"Do you like being with your grandmother?"

Grace frowned. "Not really." She gave Liza a shrewd look. "She wants me to act more like my mother. Sometimes, I think she wants me to *be* my mother, if you know what I mean."

"What was your mother like, Grace?"

"Pretty." Her forehead creased in concentration. "She wore nice clothes. She always looked good."

"And your grandmother doesn't think you do?"

"Not really." Grace frowned. "She wants me to look—subdued."

The word made Liza groan. She could picture Doris saying that. Today, Grace wore a fuscia leotard, lime green tights and red and green striped leg warmers. Liza had a memory of the sneakers Grace had worn the day she'd met her. Based on Eli's description of his former in-laws, Liza could well imagine Grace's grandmother's reaction to purple hi-top sneakers. "Did she tell you that?"

"Sure. She says ladies look subdued."

"What does she mean by that?"

"She thinks I should wear more dresses and stuff."

"You don't want to?"

"I like dresses. Just not the ones she likes."

"I see."

The child nodded. "But my mother—she and my grandmother were just alike. She always dressed up. She always acted—right."

"You loved her very much, didn't you?" That, she knew, had been hard for Grace. She missed her mother even if Eli didn't.

Grace's eyes welled with tears. "Yes."

"I'm sure you miss her."

"I do." Grace drew a shaky breath. "Everyone liked her."

"They did?"

"Yes. She always had lots of friends. Especially men friends."

"Did you like her friends?"

Grace shrugged. "They were all right. I didn't like Paul very much."

"Who was Paul?"

"The man my mother was going to marry before she—before the accident."

Liza took a calming breath. A shiver slid down her spine as she silently prayed this conversation didn't take the nasty turn it so easily could. "Why didn't you like Paul?"

"He was an actor." Grace dropped her voice as if saying a distasteful word.

Liza prompted, "Is there something wrong with being an actor?"

"He pretended all the time. Even when he wasn't on stage—he still pretended. Mama didn't think so, but he did."

"What do you mean?"

"When Mama was there, he pretended to like me."

"But you don't think he really did?" She held her breath.

"He told me he didn't." Grace picked at a snag on her leotard. "He told me he thought I was a spoiled brat."

"When?"

"Lots of times. He used to say that when he and Mama got married, he was going to make me go away."

"What did you tell him?"

"That I could go live with my father."

"You could have."

"Paul said Father wouldn't let me."

Grace's lips had begun to tremble. Liza reached for her hand. "Did you believe him?"

She hesitated, then nodded. "Yes." Her fingers tightened on Liza's.

"Why?"

"Because Grandmother said so, too. And so did Mama. She used to tell me that Daddy never had time for me because nothing was more important to him than his work in the lab. He didn't come to see us very often. And that made me worry—" she sniffled—"Now I'm worried that if we leave here, he'll go back to the lab, and he won't want me in his way anymore."

Liza exhaled a frustrated sigh as she considered the possibility of tracking down Paul and giving him a liberal piece of her mind. "Did you ask your father about that?"

"No."

"Why not?"

"I was scared to at first. Then after—after the accident—I was more scared."

"Why?"

Grace's breathing had turned shallow. She pulled her hand from Liza's and slid off the bench. "I can't tell you."

"I'm your friend, Grace. You can trust me."

Grace shook her head. "I can't."

"Why can't you?"

"You'd tell my father, and he'd make me leave."

Liza carefully considered her next words. "Then is it all right if I ask you one more question?"

"I guess so."

"Was there any other reason you didn't like Paul?" Liza held her breath while she waited for Grace's response.

The child scooped up her gym bag and tossed it onto her shoulder. "He acted like a jerk," she said. "May I go to lunch now?"

Liza exhaled a sigh of relief. Grace's ready response told her more than enough to put her mind at ease about the circumstances surrounding Mara's relationship with her fiancé. "Sure. Just promise you'll consider the tap duet."

"I will."

"Why don't you talk it over with Lindsay, and the two of you can let me know tomorrow?"

"All right." Grace headed for the door, then turned back. "Are you going to tell my father what I said about my grandmother and Paul?"

"No." Liza gave her a shrewd look. "Are you?"

"I'm not sure yet."

"Fair enough. See you tomorrow."

As Grace hurried out the door, Liza, weak with relief, leaned back against the bench. Whatever was bothering that child, whatever scars she was carrying from her mother's death, they weren't as deep as Liza had once feared. The faceless Paul might have been a jerk, but at least he hadn't been a monster. She was fairly certain she wouldn't have had the courage to tell Eli if he had been.

* * *

"What the hell do you mean, you aren't going to tell me?" Eli demanded as he studied her in the dim light of the lab.

Liza glared at him. "Don't yell at me."

"I'm not yelling." Barely, he acknowledged, but he was managing to keep his voice under control. "But Liza, what do you expect? You come in here and tell me you had an extremely enlightening conversation with my child today, but you're aren't going to tell me the facts."

"I promised her I wouldn't."

It took a supreme effort of self-control, but he managed to wrestle his straining patience to the ground. "Well, excuse me, but I was under the impression that ten-year-old children aren't always in a position to know what's best for them."

"Oh, cut it out. Don't you think I'd tell you if it were something I felt you needed to know? For crying out loud, Eli, I'm on *your side*. Would you please remember that?"

He stared at her, breathing heavily. Finally, he uttered a soft curse as he raked a hand over his face. "Sorry."

She continued to glare at him. "You should be. I only told you because I thought you'd like to know that she's starting to open up a little—and that no matter what your worst fears are, they probably aren't grounded."

How could she have known, he wondered. "Are you sure?"

"Yes." Liza rounded the lab table to stand next

to him. "You were afraid that Mara's fiancé had
hurt Grace, weren't you?"

The words drove a wedge of ice through his
soul. He'd never voiced that fear aloud. His voice
sounded hoarse when he answered her. "How
did you know that?"

"I've seen a lot of the world," she told him gently. "Sometimes, I think I've seen too much of it—
even here in my little corner of Terrance, Georgia,
I've seen things I wish I hadn't. Any parent in
your position would have that kind of fear." Liza
touched his hand. Her fingers felt warm on his
suddenly cold skin. "I can't be absolutely sure, of
course, but based on what Grace told me today,
I'm almost positive. She didn't like Paul very
much, but she wasn't afraid of him."

Eli closed his eyes and let the feeling of relief
wash over him. "Is that all you're going to tell
me?"

"Yes. You'll have to get the rest directly from
Grace."

"Is there anything I can do to help her?"

"Continue to encourage her. Let her know how
much you love her. You saw how well she
responded to that when you talked to her in my
office. She needs to feel sure of you." *I need to feel
sure of you*, she added silently.

He nodded. "I'm trying."

"And you're doing really well." He must have
looked skeptical then, because Liza smoothed a
crease from his forehead with her forefinger.
"Really, you are."

"I've been told by a number of experts that my communication skills leave something to be desired."

"Then they're wrong. You communicate with me just fine."

He lifted his eyebrows. "I thought you said I was tacky."

"You have your moments."

"And I've been snapping at you all week?"

"You noticed."

Eyes full of laughter, he bent his head to kiss her. "Yes. Will it do me any good to apologize?"

"Maybe."

"What if I tell you that my only excuse is that Martin is nagging me like an old woman, my in-laws are being a royal pain in the ass, and you've got me tied into knots of sexual frustration? Hell, trying to be alone with you takes a field mar-shall's strategic expertise."

"Don't say I didn't warn you."

"Don't sound so damned happy about it."

"Sorry."

"Liar." He rubbed his hands up her spine. "When is this going to get better?"

"Beats me. If it's any consolation, though, your students love you. We're getting raves about your classes. Although I heard on the student grapevine that they're eagerly hoping for a repeat of the flower pot incident."

"I'm enjoying this. I wasn't sure that I would, but I'm finding that dragging tricks out of my bag to make the topic approachable is challenging."

"I've never heard such glowing reviews about acid/base experiments. What exactly *did* you do that day?"

"If you dissolve an Alka-Selzer in water, then dump the solution in diluted ammonia, it'll cause a titration and turn blue."

She gave him a slightly chastising look. "In English?"

Eli tweaked her nose. "If you multiply the ratio of an acid like Alka-Selzer to a base like ammonia, you can calculate the precise amount of time it takes for the mixture to react and change color. It's the same principle as litmus paper. I synchronized twenty vials to the 1812 Overture."

Liza laughed and the sound warmed him. "Very clever."

"The girls liked it."

"So I heard. The math teacher is complaining that the students like you best."

"The math teacher," he said with a slight smile, "is trying to teach them the Pythagorean theorem. Not much competition there."

"She's not as cute as you, either."

"She's sixty-three years old."

"See?"

He laughed again as he smoothed his hands down her back. "So now that we've established that I'm the most sought after male on campus—"

"You're the only male on campus."

"A guy's gotta love odds like that."

"You would."

He gave her an irreverent grin. "The operative

question here is, just what are you going to do with me now that you've caught me, Ms. Kincaid?"

She tucked a tendril of hair behind her ear. "I'm thinking of chaining you to the lab table and having my wicked way with your body."

Lord, Liza was the most genuine person he'd ever known. After his marriage, he'd invested the bulk of his passions and energies into his research. The few relationships he'd pursued had been with women sophisticated enough to know the rules of temporary liaisons. With Liza, everything was different. And that thought scared him to death—just not enough to walk away from it. "What if someone caught us."

"A little terror adds spice, I've heard."

He drew a shuddering breath as he smoothed her hair off her forehead. "Then except for the fact that I've got a ten-year-old daughter at home; you've got an apartment building full of faculty members; our class schedules; the three times a day I talk to my lawyers; and your endless round of meetings, this should be a piece of cake."

"I see you're beginning to get the hang of this," she told him with a wry smile.

"I am." He captured her gaze then. "That's why I think you should come to New York with me this weekend."

She stilled. "What?"

Eli nodded. "I've got to go. I didn't want to, but Martin has finally drilled it into my head that I've got to put the fear of God in the Paschells."

She studied his inscrutable expression. "Things are getting worse, aren't they?"

"The custody issue is adding fuel to the publicity fire. Martin thinks I can do some serious damage control if I just grant a few interviews with key people."

"I'm sure that's true."

He shrugged. "So I'm going to go up there on Friday evening so I can spend Saturday and Sunday talking to the press. I'm going to talk to my lawyer about the Paschells—and then I'm coming back on Sunday night." He paused. "I want you to come with me."

Liza eased out of his embrace. "You'll be busy. I'm sure I'll be in your way."

"No, you won't. I didn't say I was going to spend every waking moment with these people. Lord, they drive me up a wall after about an hour. I just want to reassure the lab that I'm taking this seriously and answer enough questions to make Dally look like an ass. The rest of the time, I'd be all yours."

He watched her closely. She began studying a row of test tubes as she ran her hands absently over the slate top of the lab table. "I don't know, Eli. It's difficult for me to leave campus, and I—"

"Anna told me it wouldn't be a problem."

"I'll bet she did."

He touched her shoulder, then eased her around to face him. "We'll have almost an entire weekend together. I'll make as much time for you as I can."

"That's not the point."

"You don't want to go," he said carefully. "Why not?"

"Good grief, Eli, experts agree that you're one of the greatest minds of the century. You figure it out."

His mouth twitched. "I'll let you in on a little secret. When they do those rankings, they don't ask questions on the test about how well a person handles his interpersonal relationships."

She gave him a pained look. "I'm not sure I can explain it. New York is—hard for me. And if I went with you, we'd sleep together. Every night. I'd know that was your expectation, and I'd have to plan for it." She scowled. "It would feel like *prom* night, for God's sake. And once was enough, thank you."

With the pad of his thumb, he rubbed the corner of her mouth. "I'd be lying if I said I didn't hope that would be the outcome, but actually, I just thought we'd have some time together. Some time when we didn't have the pressures of your responsibilities here." Or, he silently added as he fought a twinge of resentment, your worries about what people are going to say.

"When would that be? Coffee breaks during television interviews?"

"I'll make time," he assured her. "I'm capable of that."

"Like you were capable of it when you were married to Mara? Forgive my cynicism."

With a sharp breath, he pulled back, stung. "That was low, Liza. And it's not like you."

Her belligerent expression held a second longer, then crumbled into a look of contrition.

"No. You're right. I'm sorry." She shook her head. "This whole thing is hard on me, too."

His eyes drifted shut. He really was a selfish bastard. He hadn't even stopped to consider the toll that their stolen relationship, or the resultant gossip might be taking on her. He'd been so consumed with feeling sorry for himself, he hadn't given Liza's frustrations a second thought. "I'm a real bastard sometimes, you know that?"

"It's not that. Look. I'm sorry I can't be as blasé as you are about the whole thing."

Was she kidding? He searched her face for a clue. No, she was serious. Dead serious. How the hell, he wondered, had he managed to convince her that he wasn't unsettled by all this? His attraction to this woman—his *cravings* for this woman were beginning to consume him. And she thought he had nothing to be nervous about. "My God," he said quietly. "You're serious."

Her eyes turned cloudy. "You don't have to make fun of me."

"I'm not. Lord, whatever you think, don't think that. Believe me, honey, I'm just as much a wreck as you are."

He saw the look of surprise on her face. "You're kidding."

"No way."

"What have you got to be nervous about?"

He almost laughed out loud. "How about the fact," he said carefully, "that my last serious relationship—" she flinched when he said the word *serious*, but he plowed ahead—"turned into a spectacular failure? Or maybe we could talk about the fact that we've both agreed we aren't exactly well-suited temperamentally. I'm a serious mad scientist—"

"And I'm a neurotic, temperamental artist."

He gave her a lopsided grin. "If you say so."

"You could at least *try* to argue with me."

"Liza," Eli placed his hands on her shoulders. "I told you"—he waved a hand between them—"this is new to me. I'm not prone to impulsive acts, and especially not to impulsive relationships. You knocked the breath out of me, and I'm trying to deal with that. I just thought if we spent some time together out of this environment, we could better explore what's going on here."

"So it's sort of like changing the variables in a chemistry experiment?"

He winced. "I wasn't trying to make it sound clinical."

"You weren't." He wasn't sure if that was a question or not, so he kept silent while she studied his face. He wished he could read the enigmatic shifts in her expression. Finally, she wrapped her fingers around his wrists and eased his hands from her shoulders. "That's part of who you are, Eli. You like to carefully think things through before you make decisions. While I usually just jump off a cliff and worry about the consequences later."

He'd never thought of her that way. She seemed so—cautious. Except, an inner voice told him, when she danced, and, he'd learned, when she made love. Then, nothing held her back. "Come with me," he said quietly. "Please."

She studied him a moment longer, then laid her hand against his jaw. "I shouldn't let you do this to me."

"But you're going to?"

With a soft sigh, she nodded. "I'm afraid I am."

"What did she say?" Anna asked him the following afternoon.

"She said she'd go."

"Hmm." The older woman poured him a second glass of iced tea from the pitcher on her coffee table. "You'd better plan on kidnapping her. She'll probably change her mind."

Eli laughed. He had come to ask Anna if she'd be willing to watch Grace for the weekend. His daughter seemed to like Anna, and the feeling was obviously mutual. He'd seen them walking across campus together several times. "Do you think so?" he asked.

"Definitely. The more Liza thinks, the less likely she is to take a risk on something. She'll come up with a million reasons not to go."

"Do you think she should go?" he asked softly.

Anna gave him a sly grin. "Now, what kind of manager would I be if I suggested that my assistant go skipping off to New York while we're up to our ears in administrative details?"

"Someone who cares a lot about her."

Anna's eyes twinkled. "Well, that's true, at least." She took a sip of her tea. "What I think is that Liza could afford a little more impulse in her life."

"She just tried to convince me that she makes too many decisions without considering the consequences."

Anna scoffed. "That's because she still thinks she's paying for choices she made years ago."

"Drew," he said.

"That—" Anna shook her head. "And other things."

Eli frowned, but didn't press for more information. "She's very guarded," he admitted.

"And as you well know, she's missing out on things she should be experiencing."

"Like dancing?"

"Like life," Anna said firmly. "Liza loves to dance, it's true. And she's very good at it, but even if she chooses to spend the rest of her life teaching instead of performing, she'll still have her soul in the art. What I'm talking about is what happens to a person when they stop taking emotional risks. A part of them dies when that happens."

Eli studied her in the waning afternoon light. "We aren't talking about Liza anymore, are we?"

Wryly, she smiled at him. "I thought men were notoriously uninsightful."

"We are. I'm just better at probing than most. Comes with the territory of being a research scientist."

Anna nodded. "Yes, I suppose it does." He watched, fascinated, as her expression turned profoundly sad. "I think I found myself drawn to Liza," she explained carefully, "because I saw so much of myself in her."

Eli waited, sensing that Anna would need time to get the story out. When she continued, her voice had taken on a husky tone that told him she was rummaging through painful memories, seeking the ones she could most easily face. "Like Liza, I married young."

"You were still living in Austria," he softly prompted.

"Yes. And the Germans were taking over the world. It was a frightening time, a dangerous time. My husband, Rudolf, and I decided to leave Europe and come here."

"I didn't know you'd been married."

Her smile turned sad. "We had a child—a daughter, but she became ill the day we were supposed to sail. She couldn't make the trip. Rudolf was five years older than I, and I think he understood better what was happening. I wanted to stay there with him and Natalie, but he insisted I go ahead. He said he'd bring Natalie when she was better."

"I can't imagine what it was like for you to leave them." The lines on her face seemed to have grown deeper.

"I didn't want to. Rudolf and I argued, but he insisted that we could never afford to purchase two more fares if we sacrificed the tickets we'd already bought. He could stay and work to earn the money for a second fare while my mother cared for Natalie. I thought it would be a matter of a few months at most."

Eli studied her gentle face, usually ready with a quick smile and a laugh, now aged and worn almost beyond recognition. "He never came," he guessed.

Anna shook her head, her expression far away. "No. Natalie died of fever. Rudolf was arrested by the Germans, along with my mother and father. They'd been harboring Jews from the Nazis and it finally caught up with them. A friend of mine wrote and told me what had happened. I never saw or heard from my family again."

"Ah, Anna." Eli felt a twisting sensation squeeze at his gut. "I'm so sorry."

She gave him a sad smile. "It is in the past, Eli. I'm an old woman, and I have learned to love what I have. I regret what I lost, but I can't have it back."

He reached over to squeeze her hand. "You are a remarkable woman, Anna."

She met his gaze, then. "Not so remarkable. For years, I let the loss overwhelm me. I lived in fear of experiencing that kind of pain again." Her lips moved into a slight smile. "Fortunately, I had the lessons Rudolf had taught me. It took time, but soon, I learned to remember what he said. Rudolf was a wonderful musician. He wrote music that many considered dangerous and subversive." She laughed. "Now, it seems funny. If Rudolf's critics heard the music coming from the dorm rooms at night, no telling what they'd think."

Eli smiled at her. "I can see why you have so much passion for encouraging these young girls."

"Many of them have never had a chance to dream of anything beyond the day to day struggle of their lives, Eli. Everyone needs a dream. Rudolf believed that, and so do I."

"But you lost your dream."

"In a way." She set her glass down on the table. "When I lost Rudolf and Natalie, my dream changed. I wanted to teach music—it was part of Rudolf. So I studied, and learned, and got my certificate, and finally got a job here at Breeland. At first, being around the girls made me miss Natalie so much I thought I couldn't bear it. But Rudolf was fond of saying that, 'Every soul deserves at least one waltz in a lifetime.' The summer students, I realized, had never had that chance."

She glanced out the window, watched for several seconds as a sparrow fluttered against the pane. "I wanted to give them that chance. I knew Rudolf would want it. So I used some of his music that I'd brought with me, and began teaching my students how to play it, and how to write music of their own."

"You were criticized," he guessed.

"I was. Music teachers were supposed to teach theory and classics. Mozart belonged in the music class, not Rudolf Forian."

"But your students liked it."

"Yes. So I began teaching them the work of other composers as well. Scott Joplin, Cole Porter, Aaron Copeland. It doesn't seem so strange now, but you can imagine what happened when I introduced Elvis Presley into a classroom. Parents of the well-bred young ladies who were our regular students weren't entirely pleased, and the donors and administrators of the summer program weren't too certain they liked it either."

She laughed again. "I won't even discuss the backlash when the Rolling Stones became part of my curriculum."

Eli laughed, too. "I had no idea you were such a rebel."

"Oh, one of the worst. I loved those girls, though. That's why I did it. I didn't want them to see such a narrow view of the world that they missed their opportunity to waltz."

"When did Liza enter the picture?"

"Liza." Her face softened when she said the name. "Liza was an angry little thing when she came here. It's not surprising. She'd never had parents—not really. Her mother was as much of a child as she was."

"She told me that."

"So the rules took her by surprise. She didn't like them, and had no trouble telling me how she felt."

Easily, he could picture a ten-year-old Liza, hot-headed and temperamental, raging against a system that offered her so little. "She doesn't seem to have that problem with me, either."

Anna nodded. "Liza's a straight shooter. I told you that before."

"She loves you very much."

"We've been together a long time. We bonded. I needed Liza, I think. And Liza needed me. A part of me felt like I had a second chance to be a mother to Natalie."

"Liza's a remarkable woman."

"She is. And she has a remarkable will." The twinkle was back in Anna's eyes when she looked at him. "Before this is over, you'll be wishing you chose someone more amenable."

That made him laugh. "I didn't choose this. That's part of the problem.."

"Liza has a way of doing that. I'm glad you recognize it."

"Which brings us back to my question about New York. Do you think she'll go with me?"

"It surprised the daylights out of me that she said she would," Anna confessed. "As well as I know Liza, I've never been good at predicting her actions. I wouldn't have believed she'd even agree to, er, become involved with you, so I honestly can't say."

"But if you had to bet?"

"I'd bet that she'd find a way to squirm out of it at the last moment. Whatever excuse she gives you, it'll be an excellent one. You won't even be able to fault her for it."

He considered it a minute, then set his glass down on the table. "I'm hoping you're wrong."

"So am I," she told him. "And just in case I am, Grace is welcome to stay here for the weekend, or, if she wants, she can stay in the dorm with Beth, and I'll make sure the RD keeps an eye on them."

He rubbed his hands on his jean-clad thighs, then rose to go. "Thanks. And thanks for the visit. I've got to go, or I'll be late for class."

"One last thing, Eli," she said as he headed for the door.

He turned to face her. "Yes?"

"Liza tried waltzing once, and it hurt her badly. She's going to need some help learning the steps again."

He nodded. "I'll remember."

Anna smiled at him. "I believe you will."

12

"Okay, Liza, inquiring minds want to know. How good is The King of the Jungle in the, er, swing?" Liza's friend Rachel Ramsey dropped into the overstuffed chair in Liza's apartment. As always, Liza was delighted with the chance to visit with her close friend and fellow Breeland alumna. Rachel's bi-monthly business trips to the campus gave them ample time to linger in the pleasure of each other's company, catch up on gossip, and share girl-talk.

Liza pressed a cup of coffee into Rachel's hand, then settled onto the sofa. "That was smooth, Rachel, real smooth."

Rachel's eyes lit. "So, it's true."

"Eli and me? Yes. It's true."

Her friend looked positively exultant. "Oh, good. I want to hear every last delicious detail."

"Obviously, you already know most of them."

"Anna told me when I saw her today at the meeting."

"Great. I wasn't aware the details of my private life were the subject of board of visitor's meetings."

"We discussed you *before* the meeting, sweetie. The meeting was about Bill's grant proposal." She rolled her eyes. "Or lack thereof."

Liza leaned her head back against the sofa and let her eyes drift shut. As usual, the effervescent effect of Rachel's company was lifting her spirits. "Poor Bill."

"Poor Breeland," Rachel said. "The school had a great shot at that DeWhitley grant. Bill's proposal was wretched."

"He'll just end up giving the money himself."

"That's just my point." Rachel picked up her mug. "Liza, there's a reason you and Anna convinced the board to hire me as Breeland's fund-raising consultant."

"You don't have to convince me of that." She shook her head. Rachel, who had graduated from Breeland the year after Liza, had infused new life into the school's antiquated fund-raising efforts. "You've done wonders for the place."

"Then why can't I make the board understand that it's not prudent or farsighted to keep depending on Bill Maxin for the bulk of Breeland's funding?"

Liza laughed. "Be patient. You know how tradition-bound things are around here."

"Traditional enough for Breeland's star scientist to be attracting quite a bit of attention." Rachel tucked a strand of platinum blond hair behind her ear. "At least tell me if he's as hot in private as he is on television."

Hotter, Liza thought. "Can I plead the fifth?"

"No way, babe. I want to know exactly what's going on between you two, and I'm not letting up until you tell me."

"You know how I've always admired tenacity in a person."

Rachel's gaze turned probing. "You're stalling. You never stall with me."

"I'm not stalling. I already told you, the rumors are true. Eli and I have a mutual attraction—"

"That's not the way I heard it."

At the sarcastic comment, Liza gave her a dry look. "I don't care what Anna told you, Eli and I are hardly in the middle of a torrid affair. You know what it's like around here. When would I have the time or the privacy for a love life?"

"You'd find a way if you wanted to," Rachel assured her.

"I doubt it. My apartment building is filled with Breeland staff."

"And I understand Liontakis has his own apartment all the way across town."

"Where he lives with his ten-year-old daughter."

"Who likes to stay in the dorm on occasion." At Liza's scowl, Rachel laughed. "What can I say? I have my sources."

"Still, it's not as if I've got scads of free time on my hands. You know how demanding the summer session is. When, precisely, am I supposed to be conducting this fling?"

"You've made it work so far, haven't you? Where there's a will, there's a way."

"How original." Liza took a sip of her coffee.

Rachel leaned back in her chair with a soft sigh. Her pale blond hair framed her features in a modern cut that made her look simultaneously sophisticated and friendly. As teenagers, they'd bonded at Breeland and that relationship had blossomed into one of the greatest friendships of Liza's life. Which, she mused, was both a good thing and a bad thing. She could relax, completely, with Rachel, and know the other woman would still accept her, flaws and all. But she couldn't get away with much, either.

As if she read Liza's mind, Rachel probed, "This isn't about Drew, is it?"

Evidently, Liza thought, she couldn't get away with anything. "Of course it's about Drew. It's about Drew, and about my mother, and about—Josh."

"Oh, Liza." Rachel set her mug on the coffee table as she moved across the room to sit next to Liza on the sofa. "It never stops hurting, does it?"

Liza shook her head. When, she wondered, had the nerves at the base of her skull bunched into knots and her stomach begun to ache? About the time, she knew, that she'd decided she might be willing to risk everything for Eli. Things she hadn't felt since she'd lost her baby had begun to claw at her, and she was reeling from them. "I loved him so much," she whispered. A hot rush of tears threatened and surprised her. She met Rachel's gaze through a watery haze. "I loved him."

"I know."

"Having Josh was like—" she shook her head. "Sometimes I can't believe my baby died. I could never make myself believe that my baby died."

Rachel's arm circled her shoulders. "Oh, honey, I know. You can't imagine how much I wish I had been there for you."

"You were here." Liza wiped angrily at the tears now spilling from her eyes. "Where I should have been."

Rachel rubbed a hand on Liza's back while she let the wave of sorrow crest. "That's not true, Liza. You know that."

She shook her head. "If I hadn't—if Drew and I hadn't—well, it might not have happened."

"And if you hadn't married Drew and gone to New York, you wouldn't have had Josh at all. Liza," Rachel waited until Liza met her gaze, "you were nineteen years old. When are you going to forgive yourself for something you couldn't even control?"

"I don't know." She buried her face in her hands. "Do you know that a day doesn't pass when I don't think about Josh? He was so—perfect."

"I know."

"I didn't know it was possible to love someone as much as I loved my son."

"If you'd known that Josh would get ill and die so young, would you have made the choice not to have him?"

Liza hesitated, then shook her head. "I don't think so. I only had him for three months, but those were the happiest three months of my life." Shuddering, she allowed herself to relive the memories. "Since my mother—I wanted someone to love. I wanted someone I could take care of, and nurture and fight for." She glanced at Rachel. "My shrink says I was secretly getting revenge on my mother for turning me over to Breeland by investing my love in Josh."

"There was nothing secret about it," Rachel said softly.

Liza managed a slight smile. "That's what I told him. That's also when I told myself to get a grip, and I quit seeing him. I don't think I needed to pay five thousand dollars for someone to tell me that the reason I wanted to be a really great mother was because I never had one."

"What you went through—I can't even imagine." Rachel visibly shuddered. "But can you find a way to be thankful for the three months you had Josh in your life, without letting the tragedy overwhelm you?"

"Sometimes, I think so. Other times, I'm not so sure. I don't think it will ever stop hurting."

"It's probably not supposed to." Her expression turned thoughtful. "My guess would be that you'd be abnormally weird if you got completely over something like that."

Liza rubbed her eyes—hard, to rid them of the

lingering tears. "Did you learn that in Psych 101 at that fancy college you went to?"

"No way. I was too busy with business classes to give much attention to stuff like that." Her expression turned serious again. "But I know this: you can't keep locking away your emotions for fear of getting hurt."

"Why not?" Liza managed to quip. "It's worked 'til now."

Rachel glared at her. "Very funny. And it has not worked, either. Liza, you're an incredible person. You have so much to offer the world."

"And I've chosen to offer it here, at Breeland."

Rachel pursed her lips in a look Liza recognized as mutiny. "Just tell me this. How serious are you about Eli?"

"What did Anna tell you?"

"Only that there's a certain energy between the two of you. You know she'd never betray your confidence."

Liza nodded. "I know, but Anna has known me a long time, She hasn't seen me like this since Drew. I feel—out of control. Eli does that to me."

"Is that really such a bad thing?"

"It's a scary thing. Look what happened last time I let my heart talk me into something my brain kept saying was a really bad idea."

"I don't think you can honestly compare what was going on with Drew with what's going on with Eli. Liza, you were a kid. Kids do dumb things."

"I know, but that doesn't change the fact that I learned a really important lesson about who I am when Joshua died. I can't risk that much of myself, Rachel. I almost didn't survive."

Rachel sighed in exasperation. "But you *did*. I think you're the strongest person I know, and it kills me that you've isolated yourself here in Terrance because you're afraid of getting hurt again."

"Everyone's afraid of getting hurt, Rachel." The defensive note in her voice made her wince.

Rachel gave her a knowing look. "Don't you tell your students that they can never reach their potential if they don't take risks?"

Frustrated, Liza pulled away, physically and mentally. She leaned back against the arm of the sofa. "It's not the same."

"Maybe not, but how long are you going to keep yourself hidden away from the world?"

"First, I lost my mother, then I lost Joshua. I haven't got any more pieces to spare. I have to keep the rest intact." Anger was starting to wash away her grief. "Damn. I almost ended up in the loony bin after Josh died. I can't go through something like that again."

Visibly frustrated, Rachel glared at her. "I think you're selling yourself a little short. You're a survivor. You're not going to shrivel up and die if you suffer another blow to the heart."

"How do you know?"

"And how do you know that pursuing a relationship with Eli Liontakis is going to knock the wind out of you? How do you know you'll get hurt?"

Because, she thought silently, I could love him.

I could so easily fall completely and irrevocably in love with him. And if I do, an inner voice warned, he'll leave me—just like everyone else. "Eli is practically a national celebrity. He travels all over the world to give lectures about his research. He needs someone who can adequately share his life." She gave Rachel a pointed look. "Someone who can uproot themselves, move to New York, and be a part of his career. I can't do that. I won't do that."

"Liza—"

"I'm serious. Eli lives from project to project. Corporations hire him to find impossible answers to questions most people are afraid to ask. When he succeeds, he's an instant celebrity, until the next major breakthrough comes along. When he fails—and if he's doing his job right, he has to fail now and then—he doesn't have a friend in the world. Right now, he's based out of New York, but what's next? Chicago, LA, Paris maybe. He's like a gypsy—a brilliant, overeducated, incredibly talented gypsy. Nothing holds his attention for long. Once the problem is solved, it's time to move on. He even says that about himself in all those interviews he's been giving lately."

"And you think," Rachel said carefully, "that he'll move on from you, too."

Liza winced. She hadn't meant to reveal quite that much. "He's an incredibly sophisticated man, Rachel. Once he's solved the riddle, he'll be ready for a new challenge."

"You don't have a very high opinion of him, do you?"

Surprised, Liza insisted, "I have an extremely high opinion of him."

"Then *you're* the problem? You think you can't hold his interest."

"I know I can't hold his interest. I want to live here, in Terrance, Georgia, population six thousand, and teach kids to dance. What's he going to do? Teach chemistry lessons for the rest of his life? I don't think so."

Rachel shook her head. "Come on, Liza, tell yourself the truth at least. Liontakis can work anywhere he chooses. Hell, the Center for Disease Control is right down the road. Call me an optimist, but I'm pretty sure they'd hire a guy who's about to win a Nobel Prize for finding a better and more effective way to treat cancer."

"That's not the point. Even if he were to relocate here permanently, he couldn't stand the pace of my life. I like things nice and predictable. I like security and he doesn't."

"Don't quote me on this, but I'm pretty sure I've heard that opposites attract."

"Yeah, well, if you take a lesson from the world of chemistry, you can learn that opposites also destroy one another. When you mix polar properties, you end up with a big, giant mess."

"Or an entirely new compound." At Liza's killing look, Rachel held up her hands in mock surrender. "I won't press the point."

"Thank you."

"I will say, however, that according to Anna, faculty meetings are like watching the Fourth of

July fireworks. Whatever's going on between you, it's pretty incendiary."

"He's—" Liza searched for a way to describe Eli, "*here*," she said carefully. "He's extremely present. When he's in a room, all the eyes are on him. He commands the audience better than most performers I know. Has the subtlety of a class five hurricane."

"I've seen his interviews. He's incredibly charismatic."

"You could say that."

Rachel's lips pursed. "And because of what happened with Drew, you're resisting all that charisma?"

Suddenly deeply weary, Liza leaned back against the sofa. "Drew couldn't be there when I needed him. I'm not sure I can continue to hold that against him."

"I do," Rachel assured her.

"Thanks for that." Liza gave her a weak smile. "I don't know. He was as young as I was. It was hard. Probably the hardest thing a person can go through."

"But you still don't trust Liontakis."

"It's not that I don't trust him. It's just that I'm afraid of what he makes me feel."

"You know what they say—a life lived in fear is a life half-lived."

Liza frowned. "Who says that?"

"Anna."

That made her laugh. "The font of all wisdom."

"You got it. The woman's scraped me out of

my share of pinches. I've come to value every word she says."

"Me too."

"So why aren't you listening to her this time? She thinks you should go with him to New York."

"It's not New York he's asking for, you know. He wants a deeper commitment than we have right now."

"I always find that such a turnoff in a guy."

"Very funny."

"Liza—" Rachel folded her hands in her lap, "Don't let terror beat you. It sucks to live that way."

"Actually, you'll be happy to know that I'm strongly considering giving in to him."

"You're kidding?"

"Don't sound so shocked." She gave Rachel a wry smile. "I'm still in my prime, you know."

"So I've been telling you."

"You should be pleased, then. I'm thinking of doing exactly what you've been telling me to do. I'm going to have a meaningless affair with a man I find very attractive." Liza rolled her mug between her hands. "I'm going to enjoy the time we have together, I'm just not going to get emotionally attached."

"Liza—"

"But that doesn't mean I can't explore, uh, other aspects of our attraction."

"I don't think—"

"I've thought it over."

"That's what I'm afraid of," Rachel drawled.

"And I've decided that I'm old enough, and

sophisticated enough to find out just what will happen if I pursue a temporary relationship with Eli."

"A fling?"

"Yes. A fling. No commitments. No entanglements. No expectations."

Rachel's eyes narrowed. "Liza, you aren't the type to—"

"Maybe that's the problem. Maybe I shouldn't be so concerned about what type of person I am." She gave Rachel a harsh look. "I mean, is there anything wrong with admitting I have certain needs in my life?"

"That's not what I'm saying," Rachel said cautiously.

"Aren't you always telling me to take more risks—go out on a limb?"

"Are you trying to convince me, or yourself?"

The question hit a nerve. "I don't know," Liza admitted.

"At the risk of sounding too maternal, may I make one suggestion?"

"Sure."

"You aren't the type of person to give less than all of yourself to something, Liza. You're a total commitment type. When you give your heart away, it's going to be forever."

"I got over Drew all right. It was Joshua I couldn't get over."

"You weren't in love with Drew."

Liza's eyebrows rose. Rachel shook her head and continued, "You weren't. I shared a dorm room with you then, if you'll remember. I didn't know then. I wasn't old enough to tell the difference, but I am now. There are some people, like me, who can give their heart away a thousand times and always manage to grow a new one. You're not one of those people. If you really think you want to walk away from Liontakis, then you're right. You'll have to be very careful how much you dole out. It's going to be kind of tough to take all the pieces back once he's got them in his pocket."

A shudder tripped up Liza's spine. "There are times when I think I've lost my mind."

Rachel's look was pure sympathy. "It's not a pleasant feeling, is it?"

"No. Sanity is much more comfortable."

Nodding, Rachel leaned back against the sofa. "So here's the sixty-four-thousand-dollar question: How are you going to handle being in New York with him?" Rachel prompted.

"I haven't figured that out yet." Liza glanced around the confines of her apartment. The room that had seemed so secure in past years now left her feeling oddly trapped. "I always visit Josh's grave when I go there. It doesn't exactly put me in the mood for making merry."

"Or making love?"

"Or that," she said with a wry smile. "And I have a fairly strong indication that Eli would expect that."

"Maybe, and I'm going out on a limb here, you should consider just telling him about Josh." She paused. "I'm guessing you haven't."

"The man has enough grief in his life. His ex-wife is dead. His daughter is one of the saddest children I've ever seen."

"Sadder than you were at her age?"

"Maybe," she said. She was having trouble breathing.

Rachel seemed to sense her struggle and gave her a sympathetic smile. "If anyone can help her, it's you. I've seen you work miracles. And you'll tell Eli about Josh?"

"I'll think about it."

"Liza—"

Producing the remote from beneath a throw pillow, she tossed it to her friend. "I'll think about it really hard."

"I think you should."

"So noted."

Rachel frowned, then punched the button on the remote to activate the VCR. "Have you always been this stubborn?"

"For as long as you've known me."

"Or longer." Rachel's expression turned serious. "If the chemistry between you and Liontakis is half as magic as Anna claims, I don't want to see you throw it away. Okay?"

"Okay." Liza reached for her coffee cup. "Do you want more coffee?" She sensed the concern in Rachel's hesitation, but deliberately didn't meet her friend's gaze.

"Liza—"

"It's okay, Rachel. Really."

Rachel's sigh of frustration was audible in the still room. "All right, but look. I'll be back in New York all next week. I've got a couple of clients coming in from Canada, but I'll find time for you if you need me."

"Thanks."

"Promise me you'll call, and then I'll shut up."

"Fine. If I decide to go, I'll call you while I'm there."

Rachel searched her expression, then finally relented. "All right. You're off the hook for the rest of the night."

"Thank God."

Rachel laughed. "Go get the coffee. I'll start the movie. And when you get back, you can tell me how Amelia Pankhurst's pursuit of Liontakis is faring."

Eli looked at his daughter's profile in the dim light of his bedroom. He was tossing clothes into his suitcase, and she was sitting on his bed, idly picking at a loose thread on the linen comforter. "You're sure you're okay with this?"

"Sure." She didn't meet his gaze.

"I'm only going to be gone for two days. I'm leaving tomorrow night, and coming back Sunday night."

"I know." No change.

He reached for his patience. "Honey, is something bothering you?"

"No, sir."

"I thought you'd enjoy staying in the dorm with Beth. Would you rather stay with Mrs. Forian instead?"

"No, sir." She was about to unravel a two-inch section of the bedspread.

Eli frowned. "Anna could come here. You and Beth could stay here with her for the weekend."

"The dorm is fine."

Frustrated, he dropped to the bed with enough force to nearly bounce her off. She looked at him in surprise. Her eyes had that fathomless look he was growing to dread. "Grace, if you don't want me to go, I won't."

She didn't say anything. He waited. The silence dragged between them. Eli searched his brain for something, anything, that might break her carefully maintained facade. Hell, even a tantrum would be preferable to this cold, extended silence. He dragged breath into his lungs and stared at her bent head. Patience, Liza had told him, patience and consistency. At the moment, neither Liza nor Grace seemed to be responding to his best efforts. It had taken something extreme—first the kiss in her rehearsal room, then the one in his apartment—to get Liza to admit she felt the attraction between them. What, he wondered, would it take to get Grace to admit why she couldn't look him in the eye tonight?

He frowned as he pondered the problem, reaching into the crevices of his memory for something he might have missed. What was it Grace had told him the day she'd asked permission to stay in the dorm with Beth? Eli replayed the conversation in his head. Slowly, a picture

formed. She'd never finished that sentence. She
had started to explain something to him, something Mara had told her, he realized, that suggested that he didn't particularly enjoy his
daughter's company. Tamping down his anger at
his former wife, he concentrated on his daughter's face. "Grace," he said gently, "do you want
to come with me?"

Her head shot up. "What?"

"Do you want to come to New York with me?"

"Could I?"

Eli nodded. "Of course. Absolutely. The only
reason I didn't ask you if you wanted to come is
because I thought you might be bored there. I
have to go to a lot of meetings. Martin and I will
be gone a lot. I knew you were making some
friends here, and thought you might prefer to
spend the weekend with them, but if you want to
come, I'd love having you with me."

"You would?"

He wanted to strangle Mara, he realized. "Definitely. You're very good company." He leaned a
little closer. "You're much more interesting than
my bosses from the lab, that's for sure."

A slight smile touched her lips. "Martin likes
them."

"He likes you better."

That won a tiny laugh. "Do you have to meet
with Mr. Everson?"

She knew the name of his attorney, he realized
with a frown. Chances were, she'd picked that up
from his in-laws. He made a mental note to rattle

Doris Paschell's cage until he found out just what the hell she'd been telling Grace. "Yes."

"He's a mean-looking man."

Eli laughed. "Lawyers are supposed to look mean. It's part of their job."

Her expression turned thoughtful. "Is Liza going with you to New York?"

Sucking in a sharp breath, he resisted the urge to ask her just how she knew *that*. Evidently, Grace was paying keen interest to the details of his life. "I don't know," he admitted. "She hasn't given me a firm answer yet."

"If she goes, can I still go too?"

"Yes." He tucked a strand of hair behind her ear. "Actually, if you want, I can call and tell her that you and I decided to go together, and that maybe it would be better if she stayed here this weekend."

Grace's face registered a series of emotions. "I don't know, Daddy. She might get mad if you did that."

"No, she wouldn't," he assured her. "Liza would understand. I promise."

Grace's fingers, he noted, had fisted into the comforter. "Would you—" The question trailed off.

"Would I what?"

She drew a fortifying breath. "Would you get mad if I went instead of Liza?"

"No." Eli kept his voice deliberately calm. Damn, Mara, he thought. He'd suspected that Mara's relationship with Paul whatever-his-name had left Grace feeling terribly insecure. "No, I wouldn't," he finally said. "If you wanted to go with me, I'd be very glad to have you— whether Liza went with us or not."

Grace seemed to think that over. When she looked at him, her eyes had lost their hollow look. "I think," she said slowly, "that I would like to stay here with Mrs. Forian and Beth this weekend."

He absorbed the comment, feeling his way through what he sensed was a mine field of a conversation. "You would?"

"Yes. Did you know that the Ballet Magnificat is going to perform here on Saturday night?"

"I'd heard that."

"I want to see them. Lindsay says they're really, really good."

Eli nodded. "If I didn't have to go out of town, I'd like to see them, too."

"If I stay here, Beth and I can go."

"Yes. Mrs. Forian said she'd take you."

"I want to do that, then."

"Okay," he assured her. "I'll miss you."

"I'll miss you, too."

He levered off the bed and started filling his suitcase again. "Daddy," she said. "Are you going to take that tie?" She pointed to the one in the suitcase.

"Yes," he confirmed.

"I wouldn't," Grace said, her expression slightly pained.

He raised his eyebrows. "Why not?"

She paused for several seconds, then said, "It makes you look like a dork."

Eli stared at her. It was such a *normal* comment, it had him reeling. "Do you think so?" he asked her.

"Yes," she said, her voice more firm. "I do."

He snatched the tie from the suitcase and tossed it to her. "I'll take your word for it, then."

Grace slung the tie around her neck with a slight smile. "Good." She waited while he added a pair of folded jeans to the suitcase. "And, Daddy?"

"What, sweetie?"

"If Liza goes with you to New York, you should take her to Tapeka."

"The restaurant?"

"Yes."

"Why?"

"Because it's a fancy place. Girls like it when men take them to fancy places. It says you think they have class."

He felt a smile tugging at his lips. Never in his wildest dreams had he pictured himself receiving dating advice from his daughter. "Really?"

"Yes," she assured him. "You should dress up." She slipped from the bed and walked to the closet. Her carriage, he noted, looked just like Liza's. She had a dancer's elegance. "You should wear something really nice." Grace disappeared into his closet. "Something that makes you look handsome and elegant." Her voice sounded hollow in the confines of the large walk-in space. She emerged seconds later with his black suit. "You should wear this."

Eli accepted the suit from her. "Why this one?"

"Because it makes you look very exotic."

He almost choked. "Oh?"

She studied the suit for a minute, then went back into the closet. She returned with an ivory collarless shirt. "Wear it with this. No tie." She handed him the shirt. "It's very fashionable."

"So I've heard." He started to remove the shirt from the hanger so he could add it to his suitcase. "Anything else I should know?"

She studied him for a few seconds while he put the suit and the shirt in his bag. "Yes," she finally said. "When you go to dinner, open the door for her."

"The door?"

"Good manners are important. She should feel like you enjoy paying attention to her."

"I see."

"Oh, and tell her the color of her dress makes her look really good."

"How do I know what color it will be?"

Grace gave him a pained look. "Daddy," she said, her voice slightly strained, "it doesn't matter what color it is, you're just supposed to tell her she looks good in it. Girls like that."

"Oh," was all he could say.

Grace smiled at him. "I have to go now. I have to finish my homework for tomorrow," she told him.

"Do you need help?"

"No. I just have to finish writing a story for Mrs. Petrie."

He had a fleeting memory of Liza referring to sex as the transcendental plane of existential bliss. "Do you want me to check it?"

"Are you too busy?"

"No," he assured her. "If you want me to read it, I'll be glad to."

"Okay. I'll bring it in when I'm done."

"Deal."

She turned toward the door. "Grace—" Eli arrested her attention.

"What?"

"I love you."

She hesitated, then smiled at him again. "I love you, too, Daddy."

She left the room and Eli sank down on the side of the bed, reeling from the shock.

13

How in the world, he wondered the next evening as the plane cut through the ocean-black sky, had he gotten so fortunate? He tilted his head slightly so he could study Liza's profile. "Did I happen to mention how glad I am that you decided to come?"

Liza pulled her gaze from the window where she'd been staring at the inky sea of clouds. "Twice."

"How many times did you think about changing your mind?"

"Too many to count," she confessed. "I had a hundred reasons to stay home."

"Then why didn't you?"

"If I told you, you'd think I was nuts."

Eli wished the lighting in the plane weren't so dim. He'd give a year of his life if he could decipher her expression. What he needed were a few halogen lightbulbs and a stainless steel work surface. Liza was showing him that, despite his theories to the contrary, courting a woman was nothing at all like conducting research. At least in chemistry, some things were delightfully predictable. "Try me," he prompted.

"I heard the music," she said without blinking. "I decided to dance to it."

Eli froze. Liza continued to watch him through narrowed eyes. "I can't really explain it, Eli," she told him quietly. "I'm smart enough to know that after this weekend, we'll no longer have what might be called a casual fling. This is a planned sort of thing. The stakes change when you plan things."

"Yes."

"So, I'm basically insane for doing this, but do I need to understand why?"

He shook his head. "No."

Her gaze dropped to her lap. "Can I ask you something?"

"Anything."

That won him a slight smile. "You're a brave guy. What if I ask you to talk about your feelings?"

He braced his hands on the arm rests of his seat to keep himself from reaching for her. "I assure you, I've not only survived the tender mercies of the paparazzi, but I've lived through psychotherapy. You can't shock me."

She swallowed. He liked the way a heated recognition flared in her gaze. "I'll, uh, try to remember that."

"So what is it you wanted?" he prompted. He knew *exactly* what he wanted, and the closer he leaned to her, the more he wanted it. Her scent, citrusy and delicate, had haunted him for days.

"I want to know what your plans are for tomorrow morning."

A rush of energy shot through him when he considered just how to answer her. The dim cabin light made her eyes look black and exotic. Clad in a purple tee-shirt and slim-fitting green jeans she looked simultaneously innocent and seductive. His plans, he mused, were to wake up with Liza wrapped around him—preferably in the king-sized bed in his apartment, but he was willing to compromise on the venue. "I was hoping," he said carefully, "that since we'd be taking some of the pressure off by getting away from Breeland for a couple of days, we'd be able to spend some quality time together on the 'transcendental plane of existential bliss.'"

"Did they teach you this subtle conversation technique in PR class?" she quipped.

She was adorable—not to mention sexy as hell. He was fighting the urge to kiss her, knew she'd be embarrassed if he did. "Yes. I didn't think you'd respond well if I told you I planned to wake up with you draped all over me. Naked."

Her mouth twitched. "You're honest at least."

"I try." He lifted his eyebrows. "But I think I've become the master of understatement and subtlety since I've been at Breeland. Your colleagues are, uh, interested in what's going on between us, and they aren't shy about asking questions."

Liza gave him a chastising look. "You don't think it has anything to do with the way you flirt with me at faculty meetings, do you?"

He shook his head. Her lips were trembling just enough to taunt him. "Who said I was flirting?"

Liza tried to frown at him, but the expression didn't quite reach her eyes. "I think you were in top form when you asked me if I'd be personally modeling the new uniforms we're considering for the students."

"I'm a scientist." He deliberately kept his voice bland. "I need to do significant research before I can make a decision."

Liza drummed her fingers on the arm rest. "Is that why you told Anna you considered this trip to New York to be a fact finding mission?"

He winced. What was he supposed to have said when Anna had pinned him for an answer—that he was hoping if he spent three days making love to Liza it might take some of the edge off his desire for her and help him think straight again? He shook his head. "I told her that because I didn't know what else to say."

"It seemed repugnant, maybe, to say you were hoping for a little uninterrupted quality time in the sack?"

That made him frown. "Don't make this sound ugly. It's not."

She momentarily closed her eyes. When she opened them again, he saw a hint of storminess there. "Sorry," she said quietly. "I'm edgy, and I'm taking it out on you."

"It's okay. I just don't want you to think I'm not taking this very seriously."

"Me too."

"Good." He paused. "So what are *your* plans for tomorrow morning?"

She took a deep breath. "I want you to promise," she said softly, "that you'll go somewhere with me. We can do it early if you have a meeting, but I have something I have to do."

Curious at the thready note in her voice, he narrowed his eyes. "My meetings don't start until after noon. I wanted the morning to spend with you."

"So you said. This doesn't fit into your plans," she warned him. "I wouldn't exactly refer to where we're going as a transcendental plane."

He reached for her hand. "Is there something you want to tell me?"

"Not until tomorrow morning," she said. Her fingers fluttered in his. "I was sort of hoping you'd help me forget about it until then."

His eyebrows lifted. "Liza—"

"I meant that the way it sounded," she assured him. "I've heard that existential bliss is an excellent remedy for anxiety and stress."

"Ah, Liza," he muttered, and gave in to the urge to kiss her. Made necessary by the presence of the other passengers, he kept it brief, but when he raised his head, his pulse had shot as high as their present altitude.

A lingering sadness still touched her gaze; she seemed to fight a mental battle with it, and finally won. "Since this obviously isn't going anywhere until we're on the ground, why don't we talk about something else?"

He glanced quickly at the cabin, gauged the proximity of the other passengers. "This is worse than faculty meetings," he admitted.

A laugh escaped her. "Uh huh. If it makes you feel any better, I think I read somewhere that the anticipation is almost as satisfying as the, er, culmination."

"I'll bet you a thousand bucks you read that in a woman's magazine."

"How did you know?"

"Because any self-respecting male would tell you that's a crock. Culmination beats the hell out of anticipation every time. Hands down."

Liza laughed. It tickled his nerve endings into razor sharp awareness. The throaty sound of it had him straining for patience. And, he thought wryly as he shifted in his seat, other things, as well. In a deliberate effort to end his own torture, he seized on her invitation to change the subject. "By the way," he said, "I didn't have a chance to tell you about my conversation with Grace yesterday."

Liza's eyes lit. "Something good happened, didn't it?"

"I think so."

"She seemed—different—in class today. Lighter. Does that make sense?"

"Yes." He told her about his conversation with his daughter, careful to leave out Grace's advice about his relationship with Liza. "Sometimes," he said as he finished the story, "I wish Mara were still alive. I'd like to give her a piece of my mind."

Liza squeezed his hand. "I'm so glad, Eli."

"You knew how anxious she was. You tried to tell me."

"I suspected at first, but after the conversation you two had in my office, and then that day she talked to me about it after class, I knew. She didn't actually say it, but I sensed it. Evidently, Paul told her she'd have to go to boarding school after he and Mara were married. When she said she'd live with you, he told her that wouldn't be an option."

Eli swore. "The bastard."

"My sentiments exactly."

"Who the hell did he think he was?"

"Who knows." She rubbed her thumb over his hand. "The important thing is, though, that Grace trusted you enough to let you see how insecure she felt. It means a lot, Eli."

"I know. After she left the room, I practically sobbed."

Her smile was incredibly tender. "I would have stayed, you know. If she'd wanted to go, I would have stayed."

He pressed a kiss to the back of her hand. "I know. I never doubted it."

"I hope Grace didn't either. I hope she knows it would have been all right if she'd decided to come with you."

"I think she does. Actually, I don't think she really wanted to come. It was almost a test, really." He remembered her parting advice about how he should go about wooing Liza and suppressed a slight smile. Actually, he admitted, Grace had seemed downright ecstatic.

"I'm sure you're right," Liza said. "Just knowing you would have brought her was all she needed."

He smiled at her then. "Oh, and before I forget, that shirt is a great color on you."

Liza tamped down a shiver as she slid into the back seat of the town car with Eli. Tomorrow, she would face the demons. Tonight, she needed oblivion.

Charlie shut the door behind them, then rounded the car to slide into the driver's seat. He met Eli's gaze in the rearview mirror. "Where to, Doc?"

"Home," Eli said, and crushed Liza's hand in his.

Charlie nodded, then silently closed the privacy window between the seats. It slid shut on a soft whir and Eli wasted no more time. He pulled Liza into his arms with a slight groan of triumph. His lips slanted over hers. His hands molded her to him, and her last cognizant thought was the grateful realization that she wouldn't have to beg for oblivion after all.

He couldn't remember the ride from the airport. Nor did he recall the trip up the elevator or the act of finding his key. As he broke their kiss, Eli realized that he and Liza were in his apartment, standing just inside the door. The dim light from the back hallway told him that Martin had stopped by to make sure the place was ready for his arrival—Martin always left a light on.

His lungs ached from the effort he was making to breathe. Liza's lips were pressed to his throat, while her hands held him impossibly tight. The tingling sensation in his fingertips drew his attention, and, finally, he realized that he'd worked his fingers under a portion of her tee-shirt. He slid them over her flesh, delighted with the way it quivered and flexed beneath his hands. Lord, the woman was going to kill him.

As if she'd read his mind, Liza nipped his earlobe. "Eli—" Her voice sounded husky. "Are you still with me?"

He managed a slight smile. "I'm not going anywhere."

She tugged at his head. "Kiss me again."

"Liza." He rubbed his hands up her spine. "Honey, we have all night. Let's slow down a little."

"Why?" Her fingers worked their way to the buttons of his shirt. "Don't want to," she mumbled against the hollow of his throat. "Can't."

Eli mentally paused, aware that something seemed wrong. He couldn't pin the thought down—couldn't pin anything down as Liza's mouth worked its way up the column of his neck. But why slow down, indeed, he thought?

Eli took charge again, covering her mouth with his, making love to her lips with deep, marauding kisses. He couldn't remember the last time he'd felt this gnawing, aching hunger—perhaps never. Liza was pulling on his hand, so he followed her, oblivious now to everything but the scent and taste of the extraordinary woman in his arms.

A faint popping sound alerted him that she'd lost patience with his buttons. He felt several of them bounce off his bare feet. When had he lost his shoes? Liza had his shirt open now, and was moving her fingers over his chest, skimming the waistband of his jeans.

Eli gave her tee-shirt a sharp tug and wrenched it free of her jeans. "Lift your arms," he muttered. She did, and he sent the shirt sailing across the room. Her bra followed—a filmy wisp of a thing that he dimly noted on its way to the floor— when he thought that maybe he wouldn't lose his mind if he didn't have her soon.

"Eli," she said against his skin as she pushed his shirt off his shoulders. The cuffs caught at his wrists.

She yanked until those buttons popped off as well. He dragged breath into his lungs. "Honey, wait a minute—"

She shook her head as she reached for his mouth. He turned away so her lips skimmed his jaw. "I've got to get something from my room," he said softly.

"Later," she mumbled.

"Honey," he captured her hands, brought them to his chest. Liza's eye drifted open. At that moment, he thought, she looked heart-stoppingly beautiful. Her lips were swollen, a flush stained her cheeks, and her eyes glowed with a fierce passion. He was fairly certain that no woman had ever looked at him with that 'take me, I'm yours' look in her eyes. He swallowed, hard, and held her hands still. "I can't protect you," he said. "I've got to go . . ."

Liza shook her head. "You don't. I took care of it."

The admission sent heat rocketing through him. Could she have known how much he craved the undiminished feel of her? "I'm healthy," he said, years of medical training exerting their influence. "You don't have to worry."

A smile teased the corner of her mouth. "I never do when I'm with you. You wouldn't let anything happen to me." She skated a hand across his collar bone. "Can we stop talking now?"

He groaned, a deep, guttural kind of sound that simultaneously shocked and amazed him. He'd experienced passion—he'd even had what he'd thought of as really great sex, but nothing in his experience had prepared him for the unraveling sensation he felt whenever Liza touched him. How was she doing this to him? *What* was she doing to him?

Seconds later, he admitted that he didn't care as they sank to the carpet—he didn't care that a perfectly decent bed was a few steps away, or that he should be taking his time with her, or that maybe she wouldn't want it this way. All he cared about at the moment was joining himself to her. He needed it, he realized. He ached for it.

"Liza," his voice was gravelly. It hurt to talk. "Baby, tell me—"

"Yes," she hissed. "Oh, yes."

Eli didn't need further encouragement. With a

swift flex of his hips, he put himself where he most wanted to be. An instant later, she was following him to the moon. Liza clung to him when they toppled over the edge. She held him so tightly, his ribs ached.

It felt good. So damned good. He closed his eyes and reveled in the sense of freedom that followed the realization that they belonged to each other now. Threading his hands through her hair, he smoothed it over the carpet. He brought his mouth to hers, nipped gently at her lower lip. "You're amazing," he whispered. "Amazing."

Her breath fanned across his cheek. Her eyes were still tightly shut. He could feel the little aftershocks rippling through her body, and he fully absorbed each one. A soft smile touched her lips before she opened her eyes to meet his gaze. "Thanks. I'm kind of fond of you, too."

Something close to exultation shot through him. With a slight groan of triumph, Eli slanted his mouth over hers again, and kissed her until he felt her begin to shiver. Heat followed the shivering. He wasn't sure anymore where he ended and she began.

"Eli—?" She met his gaze in the dim light.

He inhaled a great breath of her citrusy, musky scent. "Wanna go again?" he said with a slight smile.

Liza flexed a strategically placed hand. "And again, and again . . ."

* * *

She awoke to a wealth of strange sensations. Her hand was asleep. The front of her body was freezing, while the back was impossibly warm. Her legs ached as if she'd spent too long on a new routine. And the bed felt—grainy. Like carpet.

Liza's eyes popped open. It *was* carpet. She and Eli had fallen asleep on the floor of his living room after he'd taken her places she'd never even dreamed of. He lay stretched against her back, with his arm wrapped tightly around her waist. The carpet, she realized, was rubbing her skin raw, and her hand was asleep because she'd been using her arm as a pillow. Gently, she eased away from him and sat up.

Muscles creaked and groaned from the effort. Liza rubbed at a particularly stiff spot on her neck. A large, warm hand covered hers. "Sore?" he questioned.

That slight purr of his accent was back. It made her shiver. He lay in the shadows, and his skin looked dark against the pale gray carpet. With his black hair spilling over his forehead and shoulders, and his amber eyes glittering at her, he reminded her of a black panther—sleek and hard and beautiful. "It's just stiff," she answered him, then moaned when his thumb found a particularly tender spot.

His lips curved into a smile. His fingers kneaded the flesh, working at the knotted muscle. "Hold on," he told her. "You've got quite a knot here."

She could feel the muscle rolling beneath the steady pressure of his fingers. "How do you do that?" she asked, tipping her head to the side.

"Physiology training. I took classes in med school."

Something about that seemed impossibly funny. Liza couldn't quite stifle a giggle.

"Are you laughing at me?"

She shook her head. "Just wondering what else you learned in, er, physiology."

His grin turned wicked. "Enough to keep you awake for the rest of the night."

"I was sort of counting on it." She groaned again when his hand worked its way up the knotted muscles in her neck.

"Good grief. You're as tight as a bowstring up here." He eased her around so she sat between his legs, her back pressed to his chest. "Lean forward a little."

She didn't want to. It felt too good where she was. He must have sensed her hesitation because his hand applied an easy pressure to her neck until she tipped forward. Gently he pushed her hair over her shoulder, then began massaging her back in slow, smooth strokes. "That's it," he crooned. "I'll have you feeling better in no time."

She closed her eyes and let the sensation have her. The rhythm of his hands began to lull her into a deep lassitude. She was so relaxed, she hardly noticed that one of his hands had worked its way around her rib cage and to the front of her body. When it swept a slow, sensuous path from her hip, across her abdomen and lower, the lassitude gave way to an entirely different sensation. "Eli, what are you—"

His laugh was a low purr in her ear. "What do you think?"

Liza dropped her head back against his shoulder. "Is my massage over?"

"Just starting." He kissed her nape.

Liza smiled. "You want to try the bed this time?"

He nipped her earlobe. "Actually, I was thinking of the shower . . ."

"You're assuming that I can walk."

"I'll carry you."

That made her laugh. "How chivalrous."

"If it offends your feminine sensibilities, you can carry me next time, how's that?"

It had never been like this for her, she realized. She'd never had a lover who could play and tease and laugh with her—never at her. After Drew, she'd had few relationships, and those had been short and unmemorable. An unexpected rush of tears pricked her eyes. Liza turned in his arms so she could press her mouth to his. She poured everything she had into that kiss, and when she finally released his lips, he looked at her with gentle bemusement. "What was that for?" he asked.

"Chemistry lessons," she told him.

Eli managed a slight laugh, then levered himself to his feet. "Come on." He extended his hand toward her. "I want that shower. I've got carpet burns on my butt."

Liza accepted his hand and let him pull her to her feet. She swayed once she got there. With a low chuckle, Eli wrapped an arm around her waist. "Maybe I will have to carry you."

"Maybe," she said absently. Something white on the carpet caught her eye. It was a button, she realized, and then spotted another. A vague memory had her reaching for his shirt. When she shook it out, she was surprised to see the shredded placket where the buttons had put up such a fight. The cuffs, too, were torn. Liza studied the shirt for an instant, then looked at Eli in amazement. "I tore your clothes off," she announced.

His eyes glittered. "I noticed."

Liza blushed. She felt it race over her skin and was suddenly aware that they were naked. Why hadn't she realized it before, she wondered? She pressed the shirt to her chest. "I—I'm sorry. I'll fix it."

Eli gently pried the mangled shirt from her fingers. "Don't bother," he told her. With a flick of his wrist, he slung it over his shoulder. "I think I'll keep it as a souvenir."

Six hours later, Eli stood with his feet braced apart, staring out the window at the weakening darkness. Orange wedges of sunlight intruded into the night sky, pushing away the inky black cover that softened the edges of the city and knocked the glare from reality. He cast a glance over his shoulder where Liza lay sleeping in his bed. This morning, he suspected, would change things forever.

She'd been incredibly open with him—he'd seen a side of Liza Kincaid that she'd always kept closely guarded, even when they'd made love.

Last night, however, she'd shown him that part—the same part he'd seen while watching her dance. He turned toward the window again. He'd been so close to her, but not, it seemed close enough.

With a slight sigh, he padded toward the shower. Soon, the sun would be up. With the advantage of daylight, he could look more closely for answers.

"Hi." Liza, wrapped in his robe, walked into the kitchen.

Eli leaned back against his kitchen counter with a cereal bowl balanced in his hand. "Good morning." He studied her over the rim of the bowl. She looked relaxed. He was glad. He was fairly certain he would have hated it if she'd been nervous.

Liza wiped a hand through her hair as she crossed to the refrigerator. "Do you have anything in here besides Grace's cereal?"

He indicated his bowl with a nod of his head. "Sorry. I forgot to tell Martin to stock the place. I cleaned it out before Grace and I left for Terrance."

"*You* have milk," she said, her eyebrows lifting as she looked at his bowl.

"Powdered."

"Ugh."

He laughed. "I don't suppose it would do me any good to point out that chemically speaking, there's no difference between this and the real thing."

"I still can't believe you're eating that."

"I'm hungry." He set the bowl on the counter. "I'm also curious."

Liza pulled open the refrigerator and stuck her head inside. "About what?"

Eli took a deep breath. "Liza—"

Her head appeared from behind the door. "Geez, Eli, you don't even have preserves in here. I thought for sure I could find crackers and jam."

"I want to ask you something," he said quietly.

She emerged from the refrigerator with a bottle of applesauce. "What?"

He studied her face for a second, the same face that had looked at him with unbridled passion when she'd called his name. The same eyes that had met his gaze with uninhibited honesty. The same lips, he hoped, that would finally tell him the secrets that had put those shadows on her heart. "Who," he said quietly, "is Joshua?"

14

Liza froze. "What?"

"Joshua," Eli repeated. "Who is he?"

The color drained from her face. "Why do you ask?"

"You said his name last night in your sleep." Eli took a step closer. "I want to know why."

She blinked rapidly. "Oh."

"Is that all you have to say?"

"No." She shook her head. "No, I have a lot to say. I just—" Her expression had turned vulnerable—"I want you to go with me somewhere before I tell you."

His eyebrows lifted. "You mentioned this on the plane last night."

"Yes."

Her eyes, he noted, had misted. She was visibly struggling to maintain her composure. Baffled, Eli frowned. "Where are we going?"

"I'd like to get there first. Then I'll explain."

Wariness crept through him. He had visions of meeting one of Liza's former lovers for a bagel and coffee. He was fairly certain he'd have trouble controlling himself if she introduced him to some self-centered bastard who'd done a number on her self-esteem. "I don't think—"

She disarmed him when two tears spilled down her cheeks. "Don't ask me," she whispered.

Frustrated, Eli wiped a hand over his face. "I've never—"

She didn't let him finish the thought. She interrupted him by racing across the kitchen to wrap her arms around his waist. "You've given me so much, Eli. Give me one more hour. Please."

His hesitation eroded. Enfolding her in his arms, he kissed the top of her head. "I'm not going to let you run away from me. Not after what happened last night."

Her arms tightened. "I know."

Tangling a hand in her hair, he tipped her head back to meet her gaze. "Do you?" he probed.

A long second passed, then she averted her eyes as she stepped away from his embrace. "I'm going to take a shower. I can be ready in ten minutes."

"I'll call downstairs and ask for the car."

"No." She thrust her hands into the pockets of the robe. It made her look impossibly vulnerable to him. "If you don't mind I'd rather take a cab."

Impersonal, he thought, with uncharacteristic

insight. She was taking every opportunity to distance herself, from him, and from the world in general. With little or no imagination, he could picture her like this, as an eighteen-year-old kid scraping together enough money and energy to run home to Terrance, Georgia. He released a long breath. "All right," he told her. "Whatever you want."

Liza fled the kitchen. Eli stood for long seconds watching the spot where she'd stood. He had the same feeling he experienced when a new theory began to form in his mind. Elements, as yet unexplained and disconnected whirled about in apparent chaos. Instinct told him that this morning's venture would serve as the catalyst to bring him new insight into her world.

Liza leaned back against the emerald tiled wall of Eli's shower and took deep, calming breaths. The icy spray pricked her skin and stung her eyes. She tried, hard, not to succumb to the numbing fear that was clawing at her insides. She had shared this trip to Joshua's gravesite with no one. Drew had never been willing to go. For a long time, she'd hated him for that. It had taken her years to realize that although Joshua's death had thrust her mercilessly into adulthood, Drew had escaped the same fate. The bitterness she'd felt had slowly given way to pity as she'd grown to see Drew for what he was: an immature and irresponsible young man who'd run away at the first sign of adversity.

Still, she'd never had the courage to take
another person into her personal hell. Drew's
refusal to experience even a portion of her pain
had given her an iron-resolve to harbor the agony
as her own. No one, she'd persuaded herself, had
the right to see the depth or the horror of what
that time in her life had been like.

But from the moment she'd met him, she'd
sensed a connection with Eli. Maybe it was
the palpable fear that sometimes edged through
his normal reserve. His fierce love for his child,
and his terror that she was slipping irrevocably
away from him, had found a place deep in
Liza's heart she'd thought she'd buried with
her baby.

Drawing a deep breath, she shut off the water.
The time had come to face those demons.

She found Eli in the living room, clad in a pair
of jeans and a denim shirt, sitting on the single
chair he'd left behind when he'd had his furniture
moved to Georgia. "Ready?" he asked quietly.

Liza shuddered. "Not really."

Eli surged from the chair to cross the thick carpet in three strides. Reaching for her hand, he
raised it to his lips. "You look petrified."

She managed a weak smile. "What tipped you
off?"

"You don't have any color in your face." He
scrutinized her closely. "You're scaring me."

Giving his hand a quick squeeze, she shook her
head. "It'll be all right. Just don't let go."

Eli tucked her hand close to his side. "No
chance."

* * *

They made the trip to the cemetery in silence. Eli gave her a curious look when the cab delivered them to the main gate at the cemetery, but said nothing as Liza paid the driver to wait for them. She stopped at a vendor car near the entrance and purchased a small bouquet of flowers.

The walk along the brick-paved paths took minutes, but Liza felt each step draining the energy from her. Eli's grip on her fingers remained tight and reassuring. They rounded the final turn, and Liza led him through the grass to the small white stone that marked the place where she'd buried a large portion of her heart.

She stooped to place the flowers on the impossibly small plot of land the charity-run cemetery had allotted for her son's grave. Her hand felt cold where it rested in Eli's. "This," she said, her voice thready with tears, "is where my son, Joshua, is buried." Unexpected tears pricked at her eyes. She hadn't cried here in years.

Eli sucked in an audible breath as he pulled her into his arms. "Oh, Liza. Oh, God." She could hear the tremor in his voice, knew he was thinking how easily this could have been his tragedy. Not so long ago, he'd faced the reality that he could have been burying his child as well as his former wife. "I'm so sorry. I didn't know. I had no idea. God, I'm so sorry."

She clung to him—she, who had never clung to anyone in her life—drawing strength from his solid, dependable presence. "He lived three months after he was born," she told him. "He died from pneumonia. I couldn't afford to take him to the doctor. He needed antibiotics, and I couldn't get them for him."

Eli's arms tightened. Liza pushed her face against his denim shirt. "If I'd taken him to the hospital, they would have treated him—even without insurance. I could have—"

"Don't do that," he said harshly. "You can't second guess yourself like that. You'll go crazy."

"I did," she told him sadly. "For a while, after he died, I became unbalanced."

"You were so young."

"Joshua was born less than a year after Drew and I were married."

His hand slowly stroked her hair, long, soothing strokes that helped ease some of the chill in her blood. "You were just a kid, Liza." His arm tightened around her shoulders. "You couldn't possibly have been ready for this much responsibility."

"Then I shouldn't have taken it on, should I?" she asked bitterly.

"When are you going to forgive yourself for this?"

"Probably never," she admitted. Tipping her head back, she met his gaze. "If it were Grace, could you have forgiven yourself?"

He hesitated. "No," he told her. "I don't think so."

With a nod, she turned to look at Joshua's grave marker. "That's what I thought."

They stood in silence for long minutes, she lost

in her pain, while he sought for a way to reach her. When he finally spoke, his voice had the same husky quality she'd come to associate with him whenever he talked about Grace. "I wish I'd known him. I wish I'd known you."

"I had no one but Drew. We hadn't been here long, and we didn't know many people. Drew couldn't handle it." Her hands tightened convulsively on his shirt. "He wouldn't talk about it." She swallowed. "He never came here."

The steady rhythm of his heart beat against her ear. "Have you ever brought another person?" he asked quietly.

"No."

"Does Anna know?"

"She knows. But I've never asked her to come with me."

"This is where you were that morning you came to New York with me to meet Grace." It wasn't a question.

"Yes."

"Liza—"

She met his gaze again. "It's okay, Eli. You don't have to make this better. I've had five thousand dollars worth of therapy to help me cope."

Eli simply held her for several more minutes. She couldn't remember, later, what he said to her in the somber stillness of that place—that place that had always seemed so desolate and barren. When they finally turned, by silent consent, to make their way back through the shaded paths, something had changed. For the first time, the burden she carried away from this place where her childhood had died a miserable death, seemed easier to bear. Eli unconsciously now shouldered part of it for her. She tipped her head against his shoulder as tears rolled uninhibited down her face.

Finally, they had come. She'd waited for them for years. Each time she'd come here, she'd wondered when she'd finally be able to shed them. Now, they poured freely, dripping onto her shirt, soaking the fabric of his sleeve. He offered his handkerchief. When she accepted it, she admitted to herself that she'd given him her heart in return.

By unspoken mutual consent, they didn't speak of Joshua, or the cemetery, for the rest of the day. Eli took her home, where he spent several necessary hours with his colleagues from the lab. Liza polished a couple of routines for her class, then spent the bulk of the time visiting with Rachel Ramsey. Rachel listened sympathetically to Liza's report of the morning—then nailed her with a shrewd look. "You're in love with him, aren't you?"

Liza cringed. "I don't know."

"Yes, you do. You're in love with him."

"Rachel—"

"It's not the end of the world, you know."

"Easy for you to say. You've been in love, what? Seven hundred times?"

A smile played at the corners of Rachel's mouth. "I lost count after five hundred thirty-two."

"I'll bet."

"But as it happens, my, er, extremely active love life is not the point here."

"I know. My non-existent one is the point." Liza swirled her coffee in the mug as she glanced out the window of the small cafe where she'd met Rachel for lunch. "I like it that way. It's safer."

"Then why did you take him to see Joshua's grave this morning?" When Liza didn't answer, Rachel prodded. "You've never taken anyone else, Liza. Not me, or even Anna. It meant something for you to show him that."

Liza finally met her gaze. "Eli and I—we have a connection. I can't explain it."

Rachel nodded. "I know."

"How?"

"You had that look. You sort of—glow."

"I'm exhausted."

Rachel's laugh was warm. "Maybe that's what causes that look. I don't know. I just recognize it and know what it means. And you've got it."

"I think what you're seeing is lunacy."

"Trust me, babe. I'm the expert on this. The King of the Jungle has you under his spell."

Which, Liza thought, was exactly what she feared. "You're probably right."

"So why do you look so miserable?"

"I don't know." Liza suppressed an inner voice that told her she knew exactly why. Rachel was right, as usual. Fool that she was, she'd given away the last piece of her heart. And terror was threatening to overwhelm her. "I suppose Amelia

Pankhurst would be thrilled to be standing in my shoes."

Rachel laughed again. "From what I hear, about half the women in the free world would trade their eye teeth to have that man even glance their way."

"It's, um, potent," Liza admitted. "Having all that single-minded attention, I mean."

"I'll bet." Rachel leaned closer and lowered her voice. "Are you feeling up to telling me the baser facts, or are you going to leave me dangling?"

"I see you were snoozing through Miss Martin's etiquette-for-young-ladies class while you were at Breeland."

"I skipped it as often as possible. Besides, I'm pretty sure that Old Maid Martin never covered the proper way to ask a girlfriend just how well her guy comes through in the sack."

Liza gave up the fight and laughed, genuinely, for the first time that day. "I assure you, I lived in fear of getting caught skipping class. I went to every session and we never went over this. I would have remembered."

Eli was staring out the window of his apartment when he heard Liza let herself in later that night.

"Eli?" she said into the semi-darkened room. "Are you here?"

"I'm over here," he said from his place by the curtains.

"Are you all right?"

He faced her, and felt his heart lift at the sight of her standing just inside his door. "Yes. I'm tired. And frustrated, but I'm all right."

She dropped her key on the hall table and walked toward him. "Things didn't go well today?"

He shrugged and held out his arms. Liza came into them without hesitation. "They went okay."

"You talked to the Paschells?"

"Lord, this is such an unnecessary psychodrama. I'm seeing Doris and Leonard around noon, and then we can get the hell out of here."

Liza rubbed her cheek against his shirt. "I thought you liked it here."

"Not without Grace." His hands caressed her back. "Not without you. I missed you today."

She laughed. "Liar. You were concentrating on your interview notes and you didn't give me a second thought."

"You're selling yourself short. Every time I noticed the lack of furniture in my living room and that expanse of carpet, my concentration was shot."

Her smile dazzled him. "Oh. What a nice thing to say."

He narrowed his gaze, trying to determine whether or not she was teasing him. "I have it on fairly decent authority that my conversational skills leave something to be desired."

"Really?" She was nibbling the side of his neck.

His concentration was beginning to unravel. "Really," he said. When she flicked open the top button of his shirt with her tongue, he flailed about for several seconds to find the thread of the conversation. "Mara used to say that I was the only man she knew who could make a compliment sound like a clinical dissertation."

"I thought we established," Liza whispered against his ear, "that Mara was a moron."

He choked out a laugh. "Did we?"

"Uh huh." She gently bit his ear. "And I don't really want to talk about her. Especially not now."

He tipped his head back when Liza traced the whorl of his ear with the tip of her tongue. "Why now, especially?" he gritted out.

"Because," there was unmistakable laughter in her voice, "I'm going to ravish you, and I don't really give a rip what your ex-wife thought of you." Her hand slid inside his shirt. "I've got a few opinions of my own," she assured him. "And they're getting stronger by the minute.

His lingering frustration melted away. "Are you going to let me take you to dinner tonight?" he asked.

"Hmm. Maybe later."

His hand settled on her shoulders. "You have to," he assured her.

With visible reluctance, Liza met his gaze. "Why?"

"Because Grace gave me specific advice on how to impress you. I want to try out her lines and see if they work any better than mine."

A smile twitched at the corner of her mouth. He couldn't resist the urge to kiss it. Liza's hand

threaded into his hair. "If they work any better, I
might not survive until tomorrow morning."

"Oh, hi, Dad." Grace looked up from the kitchen
table when Eli walked into the apartment they
shared in Terrance. And his world righted itself
again.

"Hi, sweetie. I'm home."

She smiled at him. "I'm glad."

"I'm glad, too," he assured her. The smell of
baking brownies filled the apartment, and he
wasn't surprised when Anna walked out of the
kitchen to greet him.

"You're home. How did things go?"

He gave her a telling look. "The interviews
were tedious, and the meetings were boring," he
said, deliberately leaving out the details for
Grace's sake. "Liza and I had a lot of time to talk,
though. She'll probably want to talk to you about
it."

Anna's expression told him that she understood. She smiled at him. "I'll look forward to it."
She looked at Grace. "Can I trust you to take
those brownies out of the oven when the timer
rings?"

"Yes, ma'am." Grace nodded vigorously.
"They smell good."

Anna pulled the dishtowel from her shoulder
and wiped her hands on it. "I thought you two
would rather eat here than at the dining hall
tonight."

"Aren't you going to join us?" Eli asked.

She shook her head, then glanced meaningfully at Grace. "I think dinner *a deux* is a good idea."

Eli thanked her with a silent smile. She handed him the dishtowel. "There's a lasagna in the oven. It's ready when you are."

He walked with her to the door. "Thanks, Anna."

She laid a hand alongside his cheek. "She did well," she assured him. "Let her talk tonight. You'll probably learn some things."

"I will." He looked back at Grace. Her head was bent over her notebook where she was intently working a math problem with a pencil. "Honey, thank Mrs. Forian for staying with you."

Grace gave Anna a genuine smile. "Thank you. And thanks for taking us to the ballet. I had a really good time."

"So did I. I'll see you tomorrow." She gave Eli a knowing look as he pulled open the door for her. "And I'll call Liza tonight."

"Tell her I said, HELLO."

"Anything else?"

He laughed as he shook his head. "Nothing else I'm going to tell you."

"I'll wheedle it out of Liza."

"I'm sure you will."

She winked at him. "Have a good evening with your daughter. And if you would, er, like to let her stay in the dorm again one night soon, I'm sure that could be arranged."

Eli ushered her out the door with a firm hand at her elbow. "I'll remember that. Thanks again."

When she stood just past the threshold, she reached for his hand. "Eli, one thing. Did she—do you know now?"

He didn't pretend to misunderstand her meaning. "About Joshua?"

Anna looked relieved. "She told you."

"Yes."

"I'm glad."

"So am I."

For her part, Liza welcomed the solitude of her second-floor apartment in the small building on the western side of Breeland's spacious campus. After the intensity of the weekend, normalcy felt good, and comforting. She kicked off her shoes, adjusted the thermostat, checked her messages, then settled herself on the sofa with a cup of coffee and her class notes.

The wonderful feelings from the weekend, she knew, would yield all too soon to the relentless pressure of the students, the classroom schedule, and the demands of Breeland's multifaceted programs, but she couldn't keep her mind on her work. Her skin felt unnaturally sensitized, as if Eli's hands and mouth had left permanent imprints. She could feel the layer of clothes against her flesh—abrading the particularly sensitive spots that still thrummed with energy. She allowed her eyes to drift shut as the feeling of remembered bliss washed over her.

She'd felt closer to him than she'd felt to anyone in her life. And her body ached from the effects of their too-soon separation. She drifted into a light sleep, where her dreams focused on the passion she'd seen in a pair of leonine amber eyes.

When the phone rang two hours later, she frowned at it. Her machine picked it up, and she heard Eli's voice. She reached for the receiver. "Hi, I'm here."

He sighed. "What are you doing?"

"Paper work."

"Really?"

"No, not really. I'm supposed to be going over the enrollment applications for the next session, but I keep finding myself distracted by certain, er, memories."

"I know the feeling."

She laughed. "Are you any more ready for tomorrow than I am?"

"Are you kidding? I was a little—preoccupied—this weekend. I didn't have much time to review my lecture notes."

"I noticed."

"You don't sound very contrite," he said.

"I'm not."

"Good," he said. "I'd hate that."

Liza sank deeper into the couch. Something about his blunt, decisive way of expressing himself gave her an incredible feeling of intimacy. "I'm sure you would."

"Did Anna call you?" he asked.

"Yes. She said Grace did well this weekend."

"We had a good evening," he assured her. "She seemed to have a great time with Anna."

"It's easy to have a great time with Anna," Liza assured him. "I always did at Grace's age."

She heard him shift the phone to his other ear. "I think I'm really close to getting through to her, Liza. It feels good."

"I think you're close, too. Just be patient."

"I'm trying. It's not my strong suit."

That made her laugh. "I kind of noticed that."

"Are you complaining?" he growled.

"Not in the least. It, uh, suits me."

"Yeah, *I* noticed that."

"Cretin," she muttered.

"Hey, I've got the scratches on my shoulders to prove it."

Liza felt her blush bury itself in the roots of her hair. "So, uh, did you want something, or was this just going to be an exercise in seeing how frustrated we can make each other?"

"Actually"—she could almost hear his teeth grinding—"I called to make sure you knew how much I appreciated having you with me this weekend. It meant a lot to me, Liza."

"Oh. It meant a lot to me, too."

"I was concerned that maybe you thought I was pulling away from you when we didn't talk about Joshua again after Saturday morning."

She had, of course, and she'd spent most of her remaining moments cursing her own neuroses. "I needed the space," she told him. "It was okay."

"It wasn't," he insisted. "If I hadn't been so busy—"

"Eli, it's okay."

"I'm serious."

She sobered. "So am I. I'm sorry." She shifted the phone against her ear. "I really appreciated what you did for me this weekend. I want you to know that."

"I want you here with me."

"I want that, too, you know," she reminded him.

"When am I going to see you again?"

"You mean without the supervisory eyes of the entire faculty and student body?"

"That's exactly what I mean."

"We'll figure something out."

"Anna mentioned that Grace might like to spend another night in the dorm soon."

"Do you think so?" Did he hear the eagerness in her voice?

"Grace asked me tonight if I could get her a room there for the entire next session."

That made Liza laugh. "I see the advantages of living with a hundred girls her age are beginning to dawn on her."

"I think it would be good for her—and before you say something smart about ulterior motives, I mean that sincerely."

"I think it would be good for her, too," Liza assured him. "You know I supported that from the beginning."

"Yes."

"We can talk about it tomorrow."

"I think it might kill me to sit across from you in the dining hall," he confessed. "There's significant scientific research to suggest that sustained periods of sexual frustration can have a permanent disabling effect on a man's brain."

Liza laughed. "Will it make you feel better if I tell you that I have arranged to take tomorrow afternoon off? I'm free from three to five."

"My free period starts at three-thirty."

"The fact had not escaped my notice."

He chuckled. "Just how long were you going to wait to tell me this?"

"I was thinking of surprising you at the lab."

"Oh, really?" His voice was almost a purr.

"Hmm. Would you rather go for something more mundane—say, my place at four?"

"Hell, no," he assured her. "You're not going to set me up like that and then leave me dangling."

"It won't be a surprise, now. You know about it."

"I'm sure you'll think of something," he assured her. "Good night, Liza."

She smiled into the receiver. "Have nice dreams, Liontakis."

15

"It was supposed to be . . ." Liza's voice trailed off.

Eli interjected. "I know. A surprise." He kissed her bare shoulder. Her head dropped back against the shelf of the supply closet.

"I was the one doing the surprising. Ah—what are you doing?"

"Surprising you all over again."

Twenty minutes later, Eli summoned the energy to stand upright in the cramped space. "Are you all right?" he asked her.

She gave him a sleepy look. "You have to ask me that?"

He laughed. "Okay, how's this? Are you feeling as worn out as I am?"

"Fishing for compliments?" She reached for

her shirt. It was tangled with the leg of his trousers on the bottom shelf.

"You bet." He retrieved one of her shoes from a half-empty box of paper.

"Okay." She pulled his tie from a carton of paperclips. "I'm completely exhausted. I'm pretty sure I won't be able to stand up straight for at least a week. And I think I have Liquid Paper in my hair. Satisfied?"

He grinned at her. "Absolutely." He'd cornered her outside her office and lured her into the supply closet immediately after his last class. Then he'd spent the next forty-five minutes working off the sexual tension that had been steadily building since he'd dropped her at her apartment the day before. With studied diligence, he buttoned her blouse for her, then paused to kiss her long and lingeringly.

Finally, Liza broke the kiss. Her fingers threaded into his hair, and she tugged until he lifted his mouth from hers. "We can't stay in here all day, you know?"

"Why not?" He would have kissed her again, but she evaded him. "Because, it's Monday. And on Monday afternoons at five o'clock, we have faculty meetings."

"I know." He smoothed his hands down her back to cup her bottom. "They're the highlight of my week. It turns me on to watch you run them."

"So I take it you aren't planning to restrain yourself this afternoon."

"Hell no."

She laughed. "I should have known."

"You should have." They'd finished righting their clothes, and done what they could about mussed hair and flushed skin. Eli swung the door open. And they came face to face with Amelia Pankhurst. At the poor woman's startled gasp, Eli gave her a beatific smile. "Amelia. Where in the world have you been lately? I've been meaning to tell you how much Grace enjoyed staying in your dorm the other night."

Amelia looked from Eli to Liza, and back again. "Excuse me?"

Liza cleared her throat, painfully aware that her lips were still swollen from Eli's kisses. "Grace Liontakis stayed in the dorm with Beth Watson last week. I know Anna talked to you about it, but we both wanted to thank you for making the exception."

Amelia looked positively dazed. Eli decided to take advantage of her disorientation. "Liza, since we couldn't find those supplies I need here, what do you say we check the closet near the lab? Maybe they're in there." Liza blushed, and he adored her for it. Amelia, on the other hand, looked dangerously intrigued. Eli looped his fingers under Liza's elbow and led her quickly away.

They were barely out of earshot of Amelia when Liza started to laugh. "Did you see her face?"

"It's not nice to laugh," he chastised her.

"It's your fault. You're the one who—"

She never had the chance to finish the sentence. Anna, her expression grim, interrupted their progress. "There you are. Liza, I've been trying to page you for the past hour." She looked closely at Eli. "You weren't answering."

"No," Liza admitted with admirable sang-froid. "I wasn't. What's up?"

Anna, Eli noted, looked weary. "I need to see both of you in my office. We have a—situation."

Eli scowled. "Does this have something to do with the Paschells?"

"Not precisely. Come with me."

The three of them made the short trip down the hall to Anna's office in silence. Liza gave Eli a concerned look, but said nothing, while Anna's countenance remained inscrutable. She pushed open her door, and Bill Maxin, along with a handful of men and women Eli recognized as members of the Breeland's board of visitors, waited inside. At their entrance, everyone stood. And Bill looked guilty.

Liza's eyebrows lifted as she entered the room. Anna waited for Eli to follow, then shut the door softly behind her. "Thank you for coming," she said. "I thought this would best be settled in person." She gave Bill a sharp look. "Bill, do you want to do the honors."

He flushed. "Now, Anna—"

She held up her hand. "We've been through this. I think you all need to hear what Dr. Liontakis has to say on the matter before we go any further."

Eli looked at Bill. "What's going on?"

Bill cleared his throat. "Well, it's like this. We've had a couple of disturbing reports lately. I understand your in-laws are suing for custody of your daughter."

"They are."

"And that they're citing your, er, personal life as part of the reason."

"They are," he said again, his voice sounding ominous.

"There are some concerns on the board that this could reflect poorly on the school. If that happens, we might have—problems."

Eli muttered a soft curse. "What, exactly, have you been told?"

A woman dressed in a blue silk suit—he remembered her name as Rose something or other—answered his question. "Is it true that you are being investigated for allegedly stealing another researcher's work?"

"No," he said. "There is no investigation. There is a researcher named Jonathan Dally who made some claims to the press. I responded to those claims. The matter is closed."

"Word has it," a blue-haired woman whose name he couldn't recall chimed in, "that your Nobel prize nomination could be in jeopardy."

He took a calming breath. "If the allegations were true, then that would definitely be the case. But they aren't true, and it's not an issue."

Bill, who was rocking back and forth on the balls of his feet, extended a manila folder to Eli. "I think you'd better take a look at this."

Eli accepted the folder, flipped idly through the contents. Most were the assorted newspaper and journal clippings Martin had sent him. "I've seen these. Where did you get them?"

"A friend of the school sent them," Rose answered.

Eli frowned. "Would that be a friend named Doris Paschell?"

Rose sucked in a sharp breath "I don't think it's appropriate—"

"Damn it," he said, his voice harsh. "That woman is a—" he trailed off on a string of curses that had Anna giving him a satisfied look while her fellow board members paled.

Liza laid a hand on his sleeve. "Eli, it's okay." She looked at the board. "Dr. Liontakis is currently having a legal battle with his former in-laws regarding the custody of his daughter. Because of complications regarding his relationship with his late wife, her parents believe the courts shouldn't have awarded custody to him. He believes, as do I after having worked with Grace Liontakis and met her grandparents, that his daughter's interests will be better served if she stays with him."

Anna nodded. "I agree." She gave Bill a knowing look. "And so did you—until this morning, evidently."

"Now, Anna—"

Anna shook her head. "I'd like to know what changed your mind, Bill."

He had the grace to wince. "I'm concerned about Breeland's reputation, that's all."

"You needn't be," Liza assured them. "Dr. Liontakis has the respect of his colleagues and other professionals in the field. This type of thing isn't terribly uncommon in pharmaceutical and medical research. They know a sham when they see one, and it's merely a matter of time before Jonathan Dally is silenced."

Rose scoffed. "How do you know what's going to happen, Liza. We're all over our heads here."

"I've met some of Eli's contacts. I've spoken with them on this very matter, and I'm assured that the situation is well under control."

"But then," Bill said quietly, "you're not exactly objective on the subject, are you?"

Liza's quick intake of breath reverberated along Eli's nerve endings. He turned a frigid glare on Bill. "That's out of line."

"Someone has to say it," Bill said. "I realize that in the broader world, Liontakis, this kind of thing is commonplace. But not at Breeland. Our faculty are expected to act as role models for the students. In every way."

"Oh, shut up, Bill," Anna snapped. "You sound like a dinosaur."

He looked stung. "I don't see how—"

"Because," Anna interjected, "were it not for that handy little packet of clippings, and the blistering lecture you received from Leonard Paschell today, you wouldn't even be bringing that up. Eli and Liza are entitled to keep their personal lives private."

"Not," said the blue-haired woman, "at the expense of Breeland."

"And the only expense involved here," Anna

said coldly, "is the proposed donation from
Leonard Paschell." She surveyed the members of
the board with a condemning gaze. "Since when
do we allow ourselves to be held hostage by a
potential donor? If we give him what he wants
now, what will he demand in the future?"

"It's a lot of money, Anna," Rose said firmly.

"Yes, it is. Money we didn't even think we'd
have before today, and money we don't need if
the price tag is Leonard Paschell's control of
school business."

Rose frowned at her. "I hardly think his request
is unreasonable. You know I had concerns about
bringing in a male faculty member from the
beginning. Dr. Liontakis is only here on a trial
basis. We agreed we'd see how he fit into the
Breeland environment for this first six week session, and if all went well, then we'd extend an
offer for the rest of the summer."

From the corner of his eye, Eli saw Liza shoot
Anna a surprised look. Anna had informed him
early in the process about the board's reservations, so the revelation came as no surprise to
him. Liza, evidently, didn't know.

Rose continued, "All Mr. Paschell is asking is
that we don't extend an invitation for Dr. Liontakis to continue on here if we feel it's not in the
best interest of the school. The information he
provided was merely—"

"A load of crap," Liza said angrily. "Damn it,
Rose. Can't you see what's going on here. The
Paschells are trying to harass Eli into giving them
what they want. Once they get him and Grace

back in New York, they have every intention of launching a media campaign designed to completely discredit his work and his reputation."

"I'd rather that didn't happen," Bill said, "while he was here at Breeland."

"It's not going to," Eli said. "I can assure you of that. The Paschells intend to exert an enormous amount of pressure, but Leonard's career is dependent on his contacts in the field of medical research. He won't support Jonathan Dally's claims at the risk of ruining his own reputation."

"You can't guarantee that," the blue-haired woman told him. "Custody battles can turn messy."

"They can," Liza agreed, "and we've been in the middle of our share of them." One by one, she looked at the members of the board. "And for as long as I've been affiliated with this school, we've had two objectives: to help our students, and to create a family atmosphere among our faculty. I hope that's not going to change."

No one answered. Liza looked at Anna. "If you're through with us—"

"We are," Bill said. "I think we need to discuss—"

"We're through with the discussion, Bill," Anna told him.

"But—"

"We're through with it."

Rose interjected, "I think we need a vote."

Anna glanced around the room. "Don't be ridiculous, Rose. We don't begin to have enough facts to make a decision like that. If it weren't for the fact that you're still angry you lost on the issue of bringing Dr. Liontakis here in the first place, you wouldn't even be considering this."

Rose's gasp echoed in the tense room. "How dare you—"

"And I'm not in the mood for your histrionics," Anna bit out. "There's no evidence here to suggest anything other than an informational discussion. Which we've had and I've closed."

"Well, I move that we vote," Rose insisted.

Anna looked around the room, studying each board member in turn. "I sincerely hope there's no second to that motion."

Long seconds of silence ticked by. When no one spoke, Anna looked at Eli. "On behalf of the board, Eli, I want to apologize for this little scene."

"I understand," he told her. He glanced at the other occupants of the room. "You have my personal guarantee that I will do whatever I can to protect Breeland's reputation. This place has come to mean a lot to me, and to my daughter. She's a different person than she was when she came here, and I'll always be grateful to you for that."

Liza slid her hand into his—a show of unity, he knew—that cost her something. He squeezed it, then continued, "I give you my word that I'll do whatever I can to prevent the publicity to spread to Breeland. I have a team of incredibly qualified professionals working on resolving the matter. I trust them implicitly."

"So do I," Liza added. "And I trust Dr. Lion-takis."

Bill looked at Eli through narrowed eyes. "Paschell's serious," he warned.

"Not as serious as I am," Eli assured him, then he led Liza from the room.

She found him, late that evening, in the school's lab, studying a pile of research notes and calculating a string of complex-looking equations. A sole lamp shone at his desk, casting long shadows across his face. There was a vacancy in his expression she hadn't seen since she'd let herself into his apartment the Saturday night they'd stayed in New York. The other time he'd worn it had been the day after the Paschells had descended on Breeland. She was coming to recognize that expression as the armor behind which he protected his deepest wounds.

With a slight frown, she softly whispered his name, "Eli—"

His head shot up. He stared at her several seconds, then blinked. "Hi. What are you doing here?"

"Looking for you."

"I thought you had a meeting."

"I skipped it." She walked slowly toward him. "I talked to Anna. She said Grace is spending the evening with her."

"Yes. Something about a costume for her recital. I think Anna's making it."

"Probably." When she reached the work table, she laid a hand on his sleeve. "Are you all right?"

"Of course. Why?"

Because you've barely spoken to me since this afternoon. They'd gone straight from Anna's office to the faculty meeting. Their conversation had consisted of her asking questions to which he gave terse, uncommunicative answers. At the meeting, he'd sat near the back of the room, his face the same expressionless mask he wore now. The moment she'd adjourned the meeting, he'd left without a word. She hadn't heard from him for the rest of the day. He didn't answer the phone at his apartment. "I tried to call you this evening. You didn't answer."

"I was here," he told her, turning his gaze back to the papers.

"Are you working on something?"

"Yes."

She reached for her patience. "Look, I know that confrontation in Anna's office today was disturbing—"

He continued to scratch equations on the paper. "Frustrating as hell is more like it. How do you stand these people?"

She recognized the ploy to pick an argument with her, and refused to take the bait. "I'm sorry I couldn't have predicted it would happen."

"You did," he assured her without taking his eyes from the paper. "You told me that if you and I got involved, this is exactly what would happen."

"I don't recall telling you that you'd get flayed alive by Rose and her cronies."

His expression didn't flicker. Liza drew a deep breath as she rubbed her hand on his shirt sleeve. "Eli, please tell me what's bothering you."

He didn't respond. So she waited. The clock on the wall ticked an audible rhythm. Without warning, he grabbed an empty beaker from the work table, turned and slammed it against the wall. The glass shattered and fell to the floor in a shimmering cascade.

Liza, startled, jumped back. "You heard from your in-laws," she guessed.

He turned and wrapped his arms around her. "The bastards."

"Tell me what happened, Eli."

His hands moved restlessly over her back. "Evidently, while Leonard was placing his phone calls to the Breeland board of visitors, Doris was busy making calls of her own. She got one of the doctors who treated Grace to say that there's a strong possibility that Grace's anxiety over the accident is linked to the disassociation she feels from me. Doris is using that as psychological justification to demand a hearing."

Liza swore. Eli's expression turned ravaged. "And she wants to challenge my paternity as well as my right to custody."

"Oh no."

He met her gaze, and she saw the pain deep in his amber eyes. "I've never questioned it, Liza. You know that."

"Yes."

"I don't know if I can prove it," he said, his voice just above a whisper.

She hugged him close. "Maybe you won't have to. If you don't question it, why should the court?"

"What judge is going to believe I can adequately provide for the emotional needs of my child when I can't get her to talk to me about anything more personal than the weather?"

"Don't do this to yourself, Eli. It's not true."

"Hell, she won't tell me what happened the night of the accident. I had to hear from you that that bastard Paul LeMan didn't touch her—because I couldn't figure out how to ask her that myself. You had to tell me she's afraid of living with her grandparents. You had to tell me she's uncertain around me. You had to tell me what her dreams were—what her hopes are." His voice sounded raw. "I'm supposedly smart enough to help find a cure for the plague of the millennium, but I can't have a meaningful conversation with my own daughter. What does that say about me?"

She threaded her fingers into his hair. "Listen to me. I know it's easy to get impatient, but you are getting through to her. You said today that you've seen how much she's changed just in the short time you've been here. She trusts you. It's just a matter of time before she trusts you with everything."

"There are times when I think I hate Mara for what she did to her. She turned her against me."

"I know."

"It's not fair to do that to a child."

"I know," she said again.

Eli lifted his head and met her gaze. "But you also know," he said quietly, "that part of what she said was true. I can't give Grace what she needs from me for the same reason I couldn't give it to you."

Her eyes widened. "That's not—"

"It is true," he insisted. That day you took me to see Joshua's grave—I turned my back on you."

"You were busy."

The self-derision in his gaze nearly undid her. "I was a bastard, and you know it."

She couldn't answer him, so she stared. He slid his hands down her back and molded her more closely to him. "I don't think I realized it before, but I do that when I don't want to feel things. I bury myself in something safe—" With a nod of his head, he indicated the notes on his desk. "Something predictable, and I shut everything else out."

"Everyone has a different way of dealing with grief. It's not—"

"Please, don't make excuses for me. I don't think I could stand that."

"You didn't let me down, Eli," she told him.

"But I didn't support you either." She couldn't deny that. He nodded. "That's what I thought."

"So you learn. And you grow. That's how life works."

"But this time, with Grace, I learned too late. She couldn't count on me when her mother was alive, and she can't count on me now. And she knows it."

"No." Liza shook her head. "It's not true."

"Then how do you explain it? How do you explain the fact that my daughter has been living with me for almost a year, and until we came here, where she has you and Anna and her friends, she was living in a emotional closet?"

"Whatever happened the night of the accident, it was incredibly traumatic to her. There are lots of reasons why she can't talk about it. And of course it's going to be a barrier between the two of you. You're the last real link she has to her mother. Her grandparents want her to replace Mara, and Grace knows she can't do that."

He swore, low and violently. "That's just what I mean, Liza. You shouldn't have to tell me things like that about my own daughter."

"You aren't being fair," she insisted. "If I had a medical problem, I couldn't possibly diagnose it without help. I'd need someone with the experience and knowledge to tell me what to do, what to look for. No one expects you to solve all the problems of the world."

He flinched. "Some people do."

"Then they're idiots." Frustrated, she drummed her fingers on his chest. "When you decided to bring Grace here, you trusted your instincts. You have those instincts because you love her, because you're her father. And it was the right choice. You knew her well enough to make that decision, trust yourself to know her well enough to be there when the time comes."

"I'll fail her," he said.

"No, you won't."

He shook his head and she sensed the war raging in his soul. "Liza, you don't know. You don't—"

She kissed him softly to end the argument. "I know that I have seen thousands of children come through these doors. They've had every kind of problem and family crisis you can imagine. And I've never seen one who had the kind of devotion from her parents that Grace has from you."

"I've got to go to New York again," he told her. "I can't trust this to anyone. The stakes are too high."

"I know." Liza recognized the slightly desperate look in his eyes as the same one she'd had when she'd contemplated taking him to see Joshua's grave. "When are you leaving?"

"As soon as possible."

"Are you taking Grace with you?"

"Lord, no. I don't want her anywhere near this."

"Would you like me to stay with her?"

He nodded. "I'd feel better about that than anything else. Do you mind?"

"No."

"Is this going to cause problems? With my classes I mean."

She shrugged. "We'll take care of it. Breeland has a long history of taking care of our people."

His expression turned bitter. "Until today?"

She knew he referred to the confrontation in Anna's office. She scoffed. "Oh, that. Don't even worry about it. Rose is prone to, er, fits of temper."

"What about Bill?"

"He'll come around."

"You're sure?"

She wasn't, but didn't say so. He needed a clear head, not one filled with worry about the situation he was leaving behind. "I'm sure."

His eyes drifted shut. "What am I going to do, Liza?"

She smoothed her hands over his face, remembering how lacerated her emotions had seemed that night in New York. Then, she'd needed the respite he could give her—the simple, life-affirming act of being with a person who cared for her. Just as he needed it now. She could give him this, and she would, gladly.

She raised up on her tiptoes to kiss him fully on the mouth. His response was longer than usual in coming, but he finally groaned deep in his chest and crushed her to him. "Liza—"

"I know," she told him again. "It's all right."

He devoured her. His hands moved over her, seeking, demanding, asking for things she'd never given before. Seconds later, she found herself seated on the cold slate work desk and threw her head back to surrender to the sensual storm, guiding him with her to a place of sweet abandon.

When he called her name at the end, and held

her so closely that they shared one heartbeat, she admitted to herself what she'd been denying for days: he had stolen her heart—and she could never have it back.

16

Eli left two days later. Liza had chosen to move some of her things to his apartment so she and Grace could stay there. Grace seemed tense, but not overly concerned. As the week wore on, Eli called to speak to them at least once a day, and though he always asked, she deliberately didn't tell him how things were developing on campus. The petty in-fighting on the board, and the increasing speculation among the faculty seemed ridiculously unimportant next to his own mounting problems.

Thus far, he assured Liza, he'd managed to prevent Doris from getting a court order for paternity testing, but he sounded wearier each time she talked to him. By week's end, she noted, he changed his pattern. He'd speak to Grace first, ask about her classes, assure her everything was fine, then talk to Liza—as if he couldn't make himself maintain the positive tone he used with his daughter for more than a few minutes.

By the following Monday, Liza was a mass of nerves. She looked at Anna in the early morning light as they shared their morning routine. "Did you speak to him last night?" Anna asked.

"Yes. He sounds terrible."

"He must be exhausted."

Liza gave her a worried look. "'Good Morning America' is carrying a piece on Paschell's case this morning."

"Eli's talking to them?"

She shook her head. "They're interviewing Doris and Leonard."

"Oh, dear."

"I know. Eli's furious. He sounds really weary when he calls."

"It's got to be taking a toll," Anna said.

Liza studied the gray circles under her friend's eyes. Anna looked older, slightly strained. "Speaking of that"— she lifted her eyebrows— "how is the board taking this."

Anna's expression altered. Liza saw the determination in her faded blue eyes. "I can handle the board."

"Which means they're not taking it well?"

The older woman shrugged. "You know Rose. She's like a dog with a bone." She managed a slight smile. "One of those annoying little yipping dogs with a bone."

That made Liza laugh. "I've never envied you

the task of dealing with that woman. She makes me crazy."

"You, and just about everyone else."

They sipped their coffee in silence for long seconds. Liza finally broached the subject she'd been avoiding. "How is Bill?"

Disappointment, and something else, flickered in Anna's gaze. "He's fine. Why?"

"He seemed, uh, agitated, that day in your office."

"He's under a lot of pressure. Leonard Paschell is offering us three million dollars."

"It's not like Bill to—"

"I know," Anna said coldly.

Liza worried her lower lip with her teeth. She'd suspected, for years, that Anna and Bill had a deep affection that went beyond the bounds of friendship and professional respect. Anna had never brought it up, so she'd respected her friend's privacy and never asked. Still, she sensed that Bill's apparent betrayal was hurting her deeply. "Anna," she said carefully, "if I can—"

Anna shook her head. "Don't worry about it, Liza. I've got everything under control."

Like always, Liza mused. "May I come to the next meeting, at least?"

"I don't know if that's a good idea."

"I'd like to be there. You should have someone who's on your side."

Anna thought it over. "It's not going to be pleasant. I've protected you as much as I can."

"Anna," Liza leaned forward in her chair,

"you've been protecting me for most of my life. I'm all grown up now. I can look after myself."

"I don't think you understand—"

"Sure, I do. Rose is casting aspersions on my character because I'm sleeping with Eli Liontakis. Someone needs to tell her that if she concentrated more on Breeland's students and less on other people's business, she'd be a lot easier to get along with."

"We have a very traditional environment here. You know that."

Liza frowned. "What are you trying to tell me?"

"All I'm saying is that with the scrutiny the summer program gets because of our work with government sponsored institutions, we're not as autonomous as we'd like to be."

"Anna—"

"Don't get me wrong. I'm not telling you that I don't think you and Eli had every right to get— involved."

"But—"

"But there are several members of the board who feel that the two of you could have exercised more discretion."

"More discretion?" She fought a bubble of outrage. "Are you serious? We've hardly been together since we got back from New York. We've *never* even indicated that we were having a relationship in front of the students, or the faculty, to my knowledge."

"Faculty meetings—" Anna began.

"Oh, these people need to grow up."

"I'd agree with you there."

Liza took a calming breath. "I thought that the issue here was the publicity surrounding the Paschells' custody case and the possible reflection it might have on Breeland."

"It is—" She sounded unsure.

"But it's really about the fact that he's having sex with me?"

Anna gave her a shrewd look. "Is that all it is?"

"What's that supposed to mean?"

"It's not like you to be crass. I realize I'm a generation or two ahead of you, but I've never heard you refer to your personal relationships like this."

Liza drew a shaky breath. "I'm sorry. I'm seriously irritated this morning."

Anna pursed her lips and studied her across the desk. "Are you serious about him?"

"Define 'serious,' " Liza hedged.

"I mean, would you consider marrying him?"

"Who said anything about marriage?" She fought the urge to squirm. Anna knew her too well, and had never allowed her to hide behind a facade—no matter how carefully planned.

"It's been a while—unless I miss my guess, a *long* while, since you were intimately involved with someone. I just wondered what you were expecting from this relationship."

"I'm not expecting anything."

"So, what are you putting into it?"

"Anna, I don't think—"

She held up a hand. "Listen to me. You're in a twist because you think the board is judging you, and him, unfairly. But ask yourself this: if you're not serious about him, and he's not serious about you, then aren't the two of you involved in a casual fling with no meaning and no strings attached?"

Liza winced. "I wouldn't say *that* exactly." How could she explain that she felt her survival was contingent on thinking of Eli in the here and now? If she thought of a future with him, the stakes would go too high.

"But you wouldn't say that the two of you have a commitment, either?"

"We haven't discussed it."

"What do you think Eli expects?"

"I don't know."

"Really?" Sarcasm laced her tone.

"Don't look at me like that," Liza protested. "I'm serious. We've never discussed the future. As far as I know, he's content to enjoy what we have, then move on." At Anna's frown, she continued. "What else can there be? At the end of the summer, he's going back to his life, and I'm going back to mine."

"And you intend to tell him that all this meant nothing more than a pleasurable interlude in your life?"

"That's not fair. It isn't that simple."

"But you're not willing to sacrifice to keep it?"

Liza swallowed. "Hell, I don't know. I'm not sure he is either. Why should I be the one to make all the changes?" She met Anna's gaze with cool determination. "I did that once before, if you'll recall, and it didn't work out so well."

Anna shook her head. "You don't have to pay for that for the rest of your life, you know?"

"You sound like Rachel."

Anna didn't respond. Instead, she spread her hands on the desk and leaned forward so Liza felt pinned by the searching look in her eyes. "Tell me this, then, if you're not taking your relationship with him seriously, why should the board?"

"Excuse me?"

"If it's nothing more than a summer fling with him, why do you expect the board of visitors to view it as anything else?"

"It's none of their business what it is."

"Isn't it? You're smart enough to know that the publicity surrounding Dally's claims could damage Eli's reputation. If that happens, it could reflect on Breeland."

"He didn't *do* anything wrong," Liza said through gritted teeth.

"So he says."

"And I believe him. You should believe him."

"I do. That's not the point. The thing is, there are several members of the board who feel that, maybe, you've got clouded judgment."

"Because I don't think we should just fire him without substantive justification? If we fired every faculty member who'd ever had a scandal in their life, we'd never keep anyone."

"Liza, try to understand. Most of the members of the board have known you since you were a student here. They have trouble thinking of you as an independently-minded adult. To them, you're still that kid who came here with no direction and no hope."

"Despite the fact," she said bitterly, "that I've been married, had a baby, and buried that baby?"

"Which some of them don't even know."

"I can't believe this," Liza muttered.

"It's sticky," Anna said gravely, "and Rose and a couple of board members are making it stickier. I just want you to be aware of that."

"I am."

"You know how much resistance there was to bringing Eli here. The people who lost that battle are now feeling vindicated."

Liza muttered a curse. "One of the things I like about this place is the way we take care of each other. Eli needs all the friends he can get right now. What right do we have to turn our backs on him?"

"They don't feel the same loyalty you do," Anna pointed out. "And like I told you, your situation is a little different. You might find it difficult to be objective."

Feeling outraged and uncomfortable, Liza gripped the arms of her chair. "I thought you were on his side."

"I am." Anna held out her hands. "I am. But I'm also trying to understand why Rose is so determined."

"Because she's a meddlesome old hag."

A smile tickled Anna's lips. "Who happens to love this school just as much as you and I do. All

I'm saying is that it wouldn't hurt you to be a little sensitive to the delicacy of the situation. If you want to come to the meeting, then do. They're open to the faculty. I couldn't stop you even if I wanted to."

"Do you want me to come?"

"I want you to think very carefully about how you might respond if someone verbally attacks you or Eli."

"May I throw Rose out the window."

Anna smiled. "You may not."

"Damn."

Anna's tinkling laugh filled the room. "He's rubbing off on you, you know. Before he got here, I had you trained down to 'crumb' as an expletive." Her expression sobered. "Just promise me that you'll consider what I said."

"Which part?"

"You know which part."

She did, of course—the part about what she expected from her relationship with Eli. The part that had kept her up nights wondering if she'd lost her mind. The part that told her it was way too late to protect herself, because he already owned her heart. The part that said soon, too soon, she was going to have to make tough choices, and she was too much of a coward to make them.

When Liza didn't respond, Anna folded her hands on the desk top. "It's going to be all right," she said softly.

Liza met her gaze. "Are you sure?"

"Yes. No matter what happens, as long as Eli stays focused on maintaining custody ˙of Grace, the rest will take care of itself."

"I know."

"Does he know?"

"Yes," Liza said softly, "he does."

"Then that's all that matters."

"I'm still coming to the meeting."

Anna gave her an amused look. "I'll look forward to it."

"I'm sure you will."

Picking up the stack of reports on her desk, the older woman determinedly set her coffee aside. "Now, let's get to this. We've wasted enough time for one morning."

Liza walked into Eli's apartment late that afternoon to find Grace, huddled on the sofa clutching a stuffed elephant. Tears ran down the child's face as she sobbed uncontrollably into the blue fur.

Alarmed, Liza dropped her bag and rushed forward. "Honey. Grace, what's wrong?" Grace was supposed to be rehearsing her tap routine with Lindsay this afternoon, not home alone in obvious misery.

Grace didn't respond. Liza stroked her shoulders. "Did something happen. Where's Lindsay."

Sniffling, Grace wriggled until she produced a crumpled piece of paper from beneath her and thrust it at Liza. "I didn't go to rehearsal. I got that in my mailbox."

Frowning, Liza smoothed the paper open. Every student at Breeland had a personal mailbox for inter campus mail and personal mail from family and friends. Grace had evidently been assigned a box despite her unusual living arrangements. Liza's frown deepened when she saw Doris Paschell's spidery signature at the bottom.

Quickly, Liza scanned the letter, fighting a surge of anger. Doris took great pains to assure Grace that although Eli's legal troubles were mounting, and that things didn't look good for him, that she'd always have a place to go where someone loved her. Doris and Leonard, her grandmother wrote, would welcome her no matter what horrors might befall her father. Smothering a dark curse, Liza thrust the paper aside and pulled Grace into her arms. "It's all right, sweetie."

"Is she right? Is that Dally guy really going to get Daddy in trouble?" Grace asked.

Liza tried to decide how to answer her. Children, she knew, were exceptionally perceptive. If she lied, Grace would know. "Things don't look good."

Grace clung to Liza "Why is Dr. Dally doing this?"

"He's jealous, I guess. He wants the recognition your father is getting."

"But he's lying," Grace insisted. "Why can't people see that he's lying?"

"I don't know." Liza stroked her hair. "But

your father's going to make people understand that. When they believe him instead of Dr. Dally, then everything will be all right."

"What if they don't?"

"He knows lots of people who will tell the truth, Grace. He can get them to persuade anyone who's interested, that Dr. Dally is lying."

Grace's lips quivered as she fought a fresh surge of tears. "It's not fair, Liza. Daddy didn't do anything wrong. Why is Dr. Dally lying about him?"

"Sometimes," Liza said carefully, "people lie for all kinds of reasons."

"If Dr. Dally wins, will I have to go live with my grandparents?"

"I don't know," Liza confessed

Grace's shoulders jerked. "I don't want to."

"I know. Your father doesn't want you to either."

Wiping her nose on her sleeve, Grace tried, valiantly, to stop crying. "She's mean," she said softly.

"Your grandmother?"

"Yes."

Liza squelched the urge to offer a hearty agreement. "I think she wants what she believes is best for you."

"Then why doesn't she want me to stay with my father? I don't want to live with them. I've always wanted to live with my father. Even when . . ." Her voice trailed off.

Liza thought about the barrage of angry words she'd witnessed that afternoon at the board meeting. Adults could be brutal. "I'm not sure it's that she doesn't want you to stay with him, it's more that she wants you to live with her."

Grace shook her head. "That's not it. She hates him. She doesn't even think he's really my father."

Liza's eyes widened. How in the world— "How do you know that?"

"My mother told her that he wasn't."

Lord, Liza thought, was there no end to Mara's selfishness. She forced down her anger. "You heard her say that?"

"Yes. I was in the next room, and she didn't know it."

"When did you hear her say that?"

"A while ago. Maybe a year before she died."

A sudden thought occurred to her. Liza gently tucked Grace's hair off her tear-streaked face. "Honey, I know you told me that Paul said your father didn't want you to live with him. Did your mother tell you that, too?"

Grace hesitated. "Not really."

"You're sure?"

"Yes. Mama said that she and Daddy got divorced because he was really busy all the time, and that we got in his way. He didn't want either of us living with him anymore because he couldn't work."

"Do you think that's true?"

The child shrugged. "Maybe. I used to. But if he did feel that way, he doesn't anymore."

Very wise, Liza thought as she searched her gaze. "No, not anymore."

They sat in silence for long seconds. Liza kept her arms wrapped around Grace, who would occasionally hiccup on a latent sob. Grace spoke first. "Liza?"

"Hmm?"

"I'm really scared of what's going to happen."

Me too, Liza thought. "I know, but you don't have to be. Your father isn't going to let anyone take you away from him."

"What if—" Grace flinched. "What if he has to take that test and he can't prove he's my father?"

Liza didn't bother to ask how she knew about that. "You have to trust him, Grace. I know it's hard, but he's fighting for you—that's much more important to him than anything Dr. Dally is doing."

Grace nodded. Liza continued to stroke her hair in slow, soothing strokes. "Liza?"

"Hmm?"

"Do you think he's scared too?"

Liza stilled. "Your father?"

"Yes."

She thought about that. Probably, she admitted. He was facing the battle of his life, and he was probably terrified. "I don't know, Grace."

"Everyone is lying to him and about him," Grace said. "Even my grandmother. She's telling everyone he's not my father."

"Do you believe he is?" Liza probed gently.

Grace gave her a startled look. "Of course he is," she said. "He loves me."

How could anyone doubt, Liza wondered as

she studied the piquant face and wide dark eyes, that this was his child? She had his heart.

Something started to break loose in Liza's heart. She stared into the small face and wondered what her life would have been like if Joshua had lived. Would she have had that kind of faith directed at her? It made her ache inside.

Grace eased out of her arms. "I wish I could talk to him. I feel better when he talks to me."

"I'm sure he'll call tonight."

"I know. It's not the same." She sounded forlorn.

"It'll be over, soon, Grace. I'm sure it will."

"I know," she said again. This time, she slipped off the couch. "Thanks for talking to me. I'm sorry I skipped rehearsal."

"It's okay."

Grace hesitated. "I'm really glad you're here, Liza. I'd be scared the whole time if I were all by myself." Grace left the room, and Liza sank back against the sofa cushions while she struggled with her anger at Doris Paschell—and the larger question of whether or not to tell Eli what had happened.

He'd want to know, but he had enough to deal with without her adding to his load. Besides, she thought with grim certainty, he might strangle his mother-in-law if he found out. For that matter, she'd like to help him.

The thought made her wonder how he was faring with no one to confide in. Each time he called, she'd noted, he sounded a little more isolated, distracted. He'd shared his frustrations with her, and she'd heard the weariness in his voice, but she sensed that he had withdrawn. He was, once again, the man who attacked a problem with ruthless determination—and to hell with the consequences.

Like Grace, she found, she didn't like to think of him facing all those demons alone. Everyone, Grace had said, was lying about him. There had to be times when he felt like he didn't have a friend in the world. It couldn't help that as he'd left Breeland, he'd known the board of visitors was divided over his position. Not even here, on the small campus where he'd come to fight for his relationship with his child, did he have unqualified support.

That realization made her heart ache until she almost doubled over from the physical pain. Once, she'd been alone in her own grief—with no one to help her face the fears or the burdens. It had been the most devastating time of her life—and she'd had no one to turn to. No one told her things would work out. No one promised that she'd survive. No one offered succor or comfort when the fear threatened to overwhelm her.

And she couldn't bear to think of him like that.

She pondered for several minutes the thoughts tumbling through her head—wondered what Anna would say when she told her what she'd decided. Probably, she thought, reaching for the phone, she'd assure her it was about time.

* * *

Eli stood, his back to the door, studying the city under the cloak of night. The last time he'd really looked at this view, Liza had been in his bed, sleeping off a long night of lovemaking. Then, he'd felt energized. He remembered thinking that the rush of adrenaline that had driven him from the bed compared to the same feeling he got on the threshold of a new discovery. Then, everything had seemed new, and possible, and promising.

All he felt now, was a bone-deep fatigue and the surge of anger and fear in his blood. He'd believed, foolishly, that if he let Liza bring him back to life, if she taught him how to feel again—how to live again—he'd be better for it.

His lips twisted bitterly. What a fool he'd been. Living, he'd found in the last few days, robbed a man of any vestige of peace.

"Eli?"

He tensed and wondered when he'd started to hallucinate. That couldn't be Liza's voice.

"Eli, what are you doing?" The voice was closer.

He turned, to find Liza and Grace standing in his bedroom. He was without words.

Grace slipped her hand from Liza's and started across the wide expanse of gray carpet. "Hi, Daddy. We came to help."

She catapulted into his arms. "Hi," he managed, his gaze seeking Liza's in the dimly lit room. He pressed a kiss into Grace's hair. "I'm so glad to see you."

Her slender arms were wrapped tightly around his neck. "Liza said you would be. I missed you."

"I missed you too." His voice sounded husky. He held out one arm to Liza. Without hesitation, she stepped into his embrace, and wrapped her arms around his waist.

"I thought you might need us," she said softly.

"Daddy," Grace leaned back so she could study his face. "I got a letter from Grandmother. That's why we decided to come."

He lifted his eyebrows, looked quickly at Liza, then back at his daughter. "Oh?"

"Yes," Grace said. "Liza read it."

"Did she?"

Liza eased out of his arms. "Why don't I go fix us all something to drink while you two talk about it?"

He studied her, seeking answers. She pressed a light kiss to the corner of his mouth. "Grace will tell you all about it."

"Liza—"

Liza shook her head. "When was the last time you ate?"

He frowned at that. "I don't know. I think I had something for lunch."

"We can order out," Grace chimed in. "There's a pizza place right down the street. Their sauce is great."

There had been a time when he'd thought eating one more ordered pizza would probably kill him. Tonight, the blessed normalcy of it all made it seem like the rarest of delicacies. "I would love a pizza," he assured her.

Liza smiled at him, and his world began to right itself. "I'll take care of it," she promised, and quietly left the room.

17

Later that night, Liza laid curled up against Eli on the sofa while Grace slept in her room. His fingers traced a lazy pattern on her shoulder as they listened to the stillness.

"Thank you for coming," he said softly. "I'm not naive enough to believe it didn't require some major planning on your part."

Liza smiled against his chest. "Well—there were some rumblings about my taking Grace off campus without your permission."

He snorted. "I can imagine."

"And Rose wasn't exactly thrilled that I'd miss a week or so in the office."

"I hope—"

"Don't worry about it," she assured him. "Everything is covered. There are other dance teachers who can go over the routines for the recital. Crumb, Lindsay's as good with the younger kids as I am. And by this time into the term, the office practically runs itself. They won't even miss me."

He squeezed her shoulder. "Liar."

"All right, maybe they'll miss me a little. Still, you needed Grace here, and I wasn't about to put her on a plane by herself."

"I needed both of you," he assured her. "There have been times over the past few days when I felt like I didn't have a friend in the world."

"What about Martin?"

That made him laugh. "Martin's not exactly the overtly demonstrative type. I'm pretty sure he'd never agree to lie on this couch with me and tell me everything's going to be fine."

"It is, isn't it?" she asked.

"Yes," he said firmly. "As soon as I get my hands on Doris I'm going to wring her neck, but other than that, I think we're going to be okay."

"No paternity test?"

His grip tightened almost painfully. "No," he said. "I told her, and her friend the judge, exactly what I thought of that idea. The judge knew if I wasn't contesting it, there was no way he could justify ordering the test."

"I'm glad."

"It wouldn't have mattered," he said. "I know what it would have said. Still, I wouldn't have wanted Grace to find out I'd even agreed to that."

"It's bad enough for her to know her mother doubted it."

Eli swore viciously. "Sometimes, I can't

believe—" He took a shuddering breath as he reached for control. "It's hard to imagine what that woman was thinking. Or Doris, either, for that matter. I can't believe she sent Grace that letter."

Liza twirled her finger on one of his shirt buttons. "She's hurting, Eli. I'm not excusing her, but it's not going to do you any good to stay angry at her. She's lost her only child, and anger is the only thing she has to hold onto right now."

"If she hurts my daughter—"

"I know." Liza tipped her head to meet his gaze. "She won't. You won't let her."

"No."

She linked her hands so she could rest her chin on her fingers. "What are you going to do?"

He sighed harshly. "I phoned Martin earlier. He's going to talk to Doris and Leonard tomorrow and set up a meeting. I'm going to try to reason with them."

"And if you can't?"

"Then I'm going to threaten them."

She laughed. "I'll take Doris if you'll take Leonard."

For the first time in days, he managed a slight grin. "Deal."

They lay in companionable silence for long minutes more, enjoying each other's presence. Eli felt fatigue winning the battle for his concentration. He tipped her chin up so he could see her face. "I want to take you to bed," he whispered.

A smile crept across her lips. "I know, but your ten-year-old daughter is in the next room."

"It does sort of dampen the mood."

"Probably not the best idea. Besides," she smoothed a frown from between his eyebrows with her index finger, "you look exhausted."

"I'm not *that* tired."

Her finger trailed over his mouth. "Well, I am. I've barely slept since you left."

He kissed her finger. "Sorry."

"It's okay. I've been worried. I feel better now."

"Me too," he told her. "So if we aren't going to share a bed, why don't you sleep in my room, and I'll take the couch."

"Don't be silly." She flexed her legs. "You'd be really uncomfortable here. It's too short. Just give me a pillow and a blanket, and I'll be fine."

"I'd feel better if—"

"Eli." She sat up. "Didn't you tell me that in addition to your dealing with the Paschells tomorrow, you also have some work to do at the lab?"

"Yeah."

"Then that about settles it, doesn't it? You're exhausted. I can see it just looking at you. I think what you really need right now is a good night's rest—and you aren't going to get it if you stay on this couch twisted up like a pretzel."

He hesitated for a long second, then agreed. On impulse, he wrapped a hand around Liza's head and brought her mouth to his. "What in the world," he muttered, seconds before he kissed her, "would I do without you?"

* * *

The next two days passed in a whirl of activity. If possible, Eli was even busier than he had been on their last trip to New York. Liza spent most of her time with Grace, and the rest of it she split between trying to facilitate his life and keeping a growing feeling of panic at bay. It felt frighteningly normal, this routine they'd fallen into. She spoke with Anna daily, and knew from their brief conversations that the board seemed, at least temporarily, to have tabled their criticism of Eli.

However, their criticism of Liza, and her decision to join him in New York, was another matter. For her part, Liza categorically refused to entertain the notion that her position was forever altered. Eli asked dozens of questions about her conversations with Anna, but Liza deliberately glossed over what she feared was the reality—for both their sakes.

At least, she thought one afternoon, the enormous legal and public relations pressures Eli's team was bringing to bear on Dally seemed to be having an effect. She was watching a report on CNN, and it seemed that Dally's story was beginning to show signs of inconsistencies. A few more days, she told herself, and this would all be over.

An unrelenting knocking on the door drew her attention. She checked her watch. At her insistence, Eli and Grace had taken a couple of hours that afternoon to shop for the costume Grace would need for her recital duet with Lindsay. Grace needed the time with him, and God knew, Eli needed the diversion. When she'd learned that he, somehow, had managed an afternoon free, she'd offered him the excuse to spend some much needed time with his daughter. He'd tried to persuade her to accompany them, but Liza was growing increasingly wary of the picture he was painting that included the three of them together in terms longer than a few more weeks.

The knock sounded again, and she contemplated whether or not to ignore it. Eli's doorman hadn't announced anyone. To her knowledge, no one was expected. It must be, she concluded, a neighbor. No one could have entered the building from the street level without buzzing in.

She headed for the door praying the interested party wanted nothing more than a cup of sugar. She felt fairly certain that Eli wasn't prepared to handle a group of curious neighbors. At the renewed insistence of the knocking, Liza frowned. This had better be one incredibly important cup of sugar, she thought irritably as she jerked open the door.

An angry Doris Paschell, flanked by Leonard, and a man Liza knew must be the elusive Martin Wilkins, stood glaring at her. "It's about time," Doris snapped. She shoved her way into the apartment. "Where's Eli? Where's Grace?"

Liza ground her teeth. Damn, she should have trusted her instincts. Deliberately ignoring Doris, she held out a hand to Martin. "You must be Martin Wilkins. It's nice to meet you finally."

Amusement gleamed in his silver-gray eyes. He looked nothing like she'd suspected. He was short and unassuming. From her conversations with him, she'd expected a giant. He enfolded her hand in both of his. "I am. And you're Liza Kincaid. Welcome to our world."

She couldn't quite suppress a smile. "Thanks. Come in."

Doris stood in the middle of the living room, fuming. "Stop that fawning, Martin. You said Eli would be here."

Liza gathered her composure. "He's out," she said. "So's Grace."

"Out?" Leonard snapped. "Out where?"

"Out," Liza said again. "Is there something I can help you with?"

Doris's face flushed. "I think you've done quite enough. My God," she looked at Martin, "is she *sleeping* here?"

"Apparently," Martin said. He sounded pleased.

Liza found herself liking him better by the minute. Deliberately, she kept her gaze on Doris and Leonard, instinct telling her not to even turn her back. "Was there something you wanted?" she asked.

Doris frowned. "You bet there is." She reached into her handbag and produced a folded piece of paper. "I just received this from Eli's lawyers, and I want to know what the hell it is."

Leonard snatched the paper from her, his eyes glittering as he faced Liza. "It's a court order. He had his attorneys draft an order to keep us away from Grace."

"Did he?" she said blandly.

Martin rocked gently back and forth on the

balls of his loafer-clad feet. "It seems," he explained, "that Everson and the rest of Eli's legal team feel that perhaps the Paschells are putting an unnecessary amount of stress on Grace. The judge, apparently, agreed."

"Really?" Liza asked. She'd been present when his lawyers had informed him that they intended to call the Paschells. She leveled a cold look at Doris. "I'd say that about sums it up, then."

Doris launched into a stream of obscenities that made Liza wince. She made a mental note to thank Anna for every opinion she'd every offered on the unbecoming nature of swearing women. Leonard's face turned a dark red. "I want to know where that son-of-a-bitch is," he demanded. "And if you know, you'd better tell me."

"Or what?" Liza snapped. "You'll send me a nasty letter telling me that maybe the man who claims to be my father really isn't—but don't worry because I can come live with you?" She glared at the malevolent pair. "Is that really the best you can do? Picking on a ten-year-old child you claim to love?"

"How dare you," Doris sputtered.

Liza managed a slight laugh. "You're one to talk."

"This is none of your business," Leonard barked. "We're here to talk to Eli—and to ensure Grace gets what's best for her."

"And that would be living with you?" she asked. She looked at Martin. "I can't believe you brought these people over here."

Martin's expression didn't flicker. "Sometimes a head-on collision is the only way to stop a runaway train."

"I've had enough of this," Doris spat out. "Where's Eli?"

"I'm right here," came his voice from the doorway. "What are you doing here?"

Leonard swung around to face him. "You're back, I see."

Grace, Liza noted, was not only clinging to her father's hand, but had stepped behind the shelter of his leg. "We are," Eli said softly.

"Grace!" Doris moved forward. "Thank God. I've been so worried about you. Are you all right?"

"I'm fine," Grace said. Her voice had the same emptiness Liza remembered from the first day she'd met her.

"For God's sake, Doris," Eli snapped. "She's been out shopping with me, not in the clutches of a serial killer. Will you rein in the melodrama?"

Doris gave him a look that could have frozen the Gulf of Mexico. "If I choose to express concern for my granddaughter's well-being, I hardly see how you can find that offensive."

Eli snorted. He gave Grace's hand a quick squeeze. "Honey, why don't you and Liza go back to my room so you can show her what we bought?"

Liza held out her hand. "Good idea."

"Okay." Grace eased forward, giving Doris a wide berth. Martin brushed her shoulder as she passed, and she flashed him a slight smile. She took Liza's hand, then virtually tugged her through the hallway toward the back bedrooms.

When they entered Eli's room, Grace slammed the door. "Why are they here?" she asked Liza, wide-eyed.

Liza decided to tell her the truth. "Your father's lawyers got a judge to agree to keep them away from you until the custody case has been decided. And they're angry about it."

Grace hesitated. "I'll bet they are."

Liza sat on the edge of the bed. "Grace, is there something you want to tell me?"

Grace dropped the plastic bag she carried and twisted her hands together. "They really hate him, Liza."

Liza's eyebrows lifted. "Your father?"

She nodded. "Yes."

"I don't think they hate him, exactly—"

"No, they do. I've heard them. Grandfather thinks that Daddy kept him from making a lot of money. He says that Daddy knew when he released the results of that last study that it would bankrupt him and grandmother." Her eyes filled with tears. "That's why Mama was going to marry Paul. He had a lot of money, and we didn't anymore."

Startled, Liza leaned forward. "Grace, I don't think—"

"It's true. I heard them," the child wailed. "Grandfather said that if Daddy's research was published it would mean that some drug his company was developing wouldn't reach the market. I heard them, Liza. You have to believe me."

"I do," Liza assured her. "I believe you."

Grace ran across the room to climb onto the bed next to her. "Grandfather told my mother she had to marry Paul because his company was big enough to buy grandfather's company."

"Grace," Liza stroked the child's shoulders, "does your Daddy know about this?"

"No," Grace shook her head. "I didn't tell him."

"Why not?"

"I thought after Mama died that Paul would go away, and I didn't . . ." Her voice trailed off.

"You didn't what?"

"I didn't want to tell him everything," she said quietly. "I was scared."

Liza frowned. "Do your grandparents know that you know this?"

Grace hesitated, then nodded. "Yes."

Which explained, Liza thought bitterly, their ruthless insistence that Eli send Grace to live with them. At no cost did they want her to tell him what had occurred. It probably also explained why Paul, and Mara, evidently, had taken great pains to ensure that Grace wouldn't easily trust her father. The maliciousness of it all made her shudder. She tamped down her anger and deliberately kept her voice gentle. "Honey, if we go out there right now, are you willing to tell your Daddy what you just told me?"

Grace's lips quivered. "Will it make my grandparents quit trying to take me away from Daddy?"

"I think so," Liza assured her. "I'm almost certain."

She could see the indecision on the child's face, and hated the loss of her innocence. "Will you come with me?" Grace finally asked.

"Absolutely," Liza assured her. She took the child's hand, and they walked toward the door. "All you have to do," she told her, "is tell your father what you just told me. Just trust him, Grace. He'll take care of everything."

As they walked down the hall, the angry voices coming from the living room grew louder. Leonard was shouting, accusing Eli of everything from unscrupulous research methods to criminal activities. Grace and Liza stood unnoticed in the doorway for long seconds while Doris stalked toward Eli. "You'll never know," she spat out, "what this has cost us. You dirty bastard. Not only did you set out to ruin Leonard's reputation, but you took our daughter and our granddaughter from us." She threw the subpoena at him. "If you think you aren't going to pay for that, then you're crazy. You drove Mara to her death, and you know it. If it hadn't been for you, she never would have gotten mixed up with Paul LeMan. If some judge asks me exactly what I think of you, I have every intention of telling him that not only are you a lying, thieving cur, but that you're a murderer as well."

"Doris—" Leonard held out a hand.

"It's true," she snapped, giving her husband a

cold look. "He made sure we'd have nothing left, and then he drove Mara with his demands until she couldn't take it anymore." She turned on Eli once more. "You might as well have put a gun to my daughter's head and shot her, you bastard. You killed her."

"No!" Grace screamed. "No, that's not true."

Every head in the room turned their way. Liza looked at Grace startled. "Grace—"

"It's not true," the child yelled again. "It's not Daddy's fault. He didn't even know why Mama was with Paul. He had nothing to do with it."

Eli took a step forward. "Honey—"

"You didn't, Daddy. I know you didn't." She gave Eli an anguished look. "It isn't your fault that she died, it's mine," she said, her voice a broken sob. "I'm the one that killed her."

Grace ran back down the hall before Liza could stop her. She had the barest second to recognize the ravaged look on Eli's face as he pushed past her and hurried after his daughter. Liza drew a deep breath and turned to face Doris and Leonard. "It's time for you to leave," she said firmly.

"I've got to go to her," Doris said.

Liza moved to block the doorway. "No. You need to leave."

Leonard glared at her. "We're not leaving her like this. She has to understand—"

"She understands perfectly," Liza bit out. "And you need to leave." She glanced at Martin. "Martin?"

He nodded. "I'll see them out."

348 Neesa Hart

Doris sputtered. "You can't throw me out of here, you little bitch. I have a right to see—"

Martin walked forward and clamped his fingers on Doris's elbow. "The lady wants you to leave," he said, his voice lethal. "And I suggest you do before I'm forced to call the police and inform them that you're in violation of the restraining order Eli has against you."

Leonard exploded. "You bastard."

Martin looked to Liza. She nodded and said, "If you don't leave now, I can call security and have you arrested."

Doris started swearing again. Liza decided to leave the details to Martin. She turned and walked back down the hallway, but not before closing the pocket door and throwing the lock.

Eli found Grace flung across his bed, sobbing. "Honey," he said, easing carefully into the room. "Baby, it's okay."

"I should have told you before," she wailed. "I'm so sorry. I'm so sorry this happened."

His chest ached. He took a badly needed breath as he sat next to her on the bed. "Shhh." He gathered her into his arms so she could sob against his chest. Easing back against the headboard, he pillowed her against him as he gently stroked her hair. "It's all right, honey. Daddy's here."

Grace's sobs were breaking his heart into millions of shattered pieces. She shook her head. "It's"—she hiccuped—"it's true. Everything I said. If it hadn't been for me, Mama wouldn't have died in that crash."

His eyes drifted shut. "Oh, honey, that's not true. Your Mama died in an accident, and no matter how it seemed, it wasn't your fault."

"It *was* my fault," she insisted. "You don't understand."

His hands were shaking, he realized as he made a concerted effort to control his voice. "Why don't you tell me what happened?" He continued smoothing her whisper soft hair with his large hand.

She sucked in several tear-laden breaths. "We had a huge fight that night. I was really mad at Paul and I kept yelling at her that she shouldn't marry him."

"Why?" he asked softly.

"He was lying about you." Grace rubbed her face on his shirtfront. "I heard him on the phone with Grandfather. Paul said that after Mama married him, he could make sure that you wouldn't keep Grandfather's company from selling Arid—Arril—"

"Arillium," he supplied the name of a drug he knew Leonard's company had been developing—a drug that had lost significant value since the results of Eli's most recent study had been released.

"That's it. Paul said he could make it worth money again after he married Mama."

Eli raised a brow. "Are you sure?"

"Yes. He said that if you didn't do what they wanted, that he'd never let you see me again and

that you'd give in. Mama and Paul, and sometimes Grandfather and Grandmother would have
long meetings with him. At first, I didn't know
why."

He did. His temper spiked several degrees
higher. "Why did you argue with your mother
that day?"

"Because Paul came over before she got home.
I heard him tell Grandfather on the phone that if
he didn't get someone to corro—corro—"

"Corroborate?" Eli prompted.

"Uh huh. What does that mean?"

"It means that they needed someone to back up
their claim that the study I'd released wasn't
true."

"Oh." She sniffled. "Paul was yelling at him.
He said if Grandfather couldn't get someone to
do that, then he wasn't going marry Mama. He
said that Grandfather better find a way to make
you look like you were lying or they'd both lose
everything." Grace tipped her head back to look
at him through tear-laden eyes. "He was lying,
Daddy."

"Yes," Eli agreed.

"I didn't know what was going on, so I asked
Mama, and she got really mad at me for listening
to Paul's conversation. She told me I shouldn't
have done that, and that I'd better not tell Paul. I
told her I hated him anyway, and I didn't want
her to marry him. And she started yelling at me. I
didn't know what to do. I told her I was going to
call you and tell you everything. That's when she

called Paul and told him we were coming to see him."

Eli swallowed. "The night of the accident?"

"Yes. She told Paul that he'd better think of a way to explain things to me because I was going to ruin everything by telling you. She said that he never should have told me you wouldn't let me live with you."

"He shouldn't have," Eli agreed. He swept her hair behind her ear. "He lied about that."

Grace dropped her head back to his chest. "We were fighting the whole time we were in the car. I didn't want to see Paul. I wanted to call you, but she wouldn't let me. She called Grandmother and Grandfather, and they were supposed to meet us there."

"But you and your mother didn't make it to Paul's house because of the accident?"

She had begun to sob again. Eli held her closer. "Shh, baby, it's all right. Everything's going to be all right."

Grace clung to him. "We were in the car, and I kept trying to reach the cellular phone. I was going to call you and tell you to come get me. Mama was trying to take it away from me when she hit the truck." Her shoulders were jerking spasmodically. Eli felt a burning sensation in his throat. "And then," Grace continued, "she swerved off the road. When I saw the truck, I screamed, but Mama couldn't stop. She hit it, and she—the windshield shattered and the bumper of the truck hit her in the head. She was bleeding, and I kept screaming. There was no one there. The phone wouldn't work, either. I couldn't call anyone. I was really scared. I didn't know what to do."

"Oh, my God." He felt the sting of tears in his own eyes. "I'm sorry I wasn't there for you."

"I was scared to tell you," she said through a fresh burst of tears. "I was afraid that if I told you you'd be really mad at me for causing the accident, and then you wouldn't want me anymore. I didn't mean to do it, Daddy. I swear I didn't."

Eli's cradled her head in both his hands. Gently tipping her head back, he met her tearful gaze. "Grace, it was an accident," he said carefully. "Your mother died because she wasn't driving as cautiously as she should have, and she crashed her car. It was *not* your fault." He stroked his thumbs over her wet cheeks. "And I will *always* want you. Always. I love you."

Grace searched his eyes. "I'm so sorry. I'm so sorry."

"Shhhh, Baby, I know. It's going to be okay." She sobbed against him for what seemed like an hour. Eli held her and stroked her hair while the aftershocks rolled through him.

Finally, Grace tipped her head back from his shoulder. Her lips trembled. "What if—what if Grandmother proves that I'm not even your daughter?"

"You are," he told her. "I've never doubted it. You're my daughter. No one is going to take you away from me."

She stared at him gravely. "Are you sure?"

"I'm very sure."
"Daddy?"
"What?"
"I love you."

18

A week and a half later, Liza wearily rubbed her eyes with her thumb and forefinger as she listened to Bill Maxin making a pseudo-conciliatory speech at a special meeting of the board of visitors. The stifling afternoon heat was classic Terrance, Georgia, summer weather. There was a time, she knew, when she would have found it comforting. Today, it grated on her nerves.

As had everything else, it seemed, since she'd returned from New York. With Grace's story in the open, the Paschells had been forced to back down on their custody demands. As predicted, the publicity was dying a long, dreary death. Eli had remained in New York to finish tying up loose ends, and Grace had returned with Liza to Breeland.

At her own request, Grace was staying in the dorm until her father returned. While Liza was staying, very much alone, in the apartment that had been her safe-haven for the last twelve years. It felt more like a prison every day, she admitted.

"So," Bill was saying, "I hope we can finally put this behind us and move on to some of the pressing issues about Breeland's future."

He sat down. Rose gave him a sour look, but kept her mouth shut. Anna looked carefully around the table, studying each board member in turn. Liza watched her, worried. She hadn't been herself since Liza's return from New York. Despite the fact that Anna's support of Eli had finally been backed by the board—the crucial vote hadn't occurred until *after* Jonathan Dally's claims had been publicly refuted. It had taken a toll, Liza knew, on her friend.

"I have one more thing to say," Anna said carefully. "For the past few weeks, I've tried to listen to all of your opinions. I've made every effort to give equal time to anyone who demanded a voice. And I hope when we look back on this, you'll all remember that I was fair and equitable in the way I handled it."

"Of course," Bill insisted. "That was never an issue."

"We wanted," Rose added, "what was best for Breeland. Your leadership of this board and of the school were never questioned."

Anna pursed her lips. "Be that as it may, I know we haven't always agreed, but I like to believe that we disagreed agreeably. Which is why," she drew a deep breath, "I have one final statement to make on the matter. When I came to this school, what drew me here was the fact that Breeland put the needs of its students and the growth of its faculty ahead of programs and numbers. We've had our share of detractors, and we've suffered our share of criticisms. Not everyone agreed on our approach to education. We've been accused of being too traditional, too radical, too serious, and too frivolous all at the same time. But through all of that, I have always believed that this board, this *school* shared one common purpose: to give the girls who attend our programs during the regular school year and in the summer an unparalleled educational experience that would help them be better women, not just better students."

Liza frowned. She suspected this was going somewhere, and she wasn't going to like it. Bill sent her an anxious look. Anna leaned forward in her chair and folded her hands on the polished conference table. "That," she continued, "has always been what mattered most to me. As a teacher, here, I found that I loved the chance to teach these girls how to fly. I believe that if we didn't save lives, we at least saved spirits—and that made every frustration worthwhile."

Anna looked around the room again, her gaze noticeably saddened. "But all good things finally come to an end, and I've found in the last few weeks that I just don't have the energy to do this job the way it should be done. What you need on this board is someone who can fight for the students, someone who won't back down when the pressures mount, someone who can give you the passion and leadership that makes Breeland what it is. I can't be that person anymore. So after today's board meeting, I'll be stepping down as head of the summer program and chairperson of this board."

A collective gasp sounded in the small room. Bill held out a hand. "Anna, please. That's not necessary."

"No, Bill," Anna said. "It's time. And it's not a sad thing. I don't want any of us to walk away from here thinking this is anything other than a great opportunity for us to move forward. It's my recommendation," she told the rest of the board, "that you elect Bill Maxin as your new chairman." She looked over her shoulder at Liza, "And that you appoint Liza Kincaid head of the summer program."

Liza's eyes widened. She couldn't imagine doing the job, even being a part of the summer program without Anna's firm, yet compassionate leadership. "Anna—"

"It's the right thing, Liza," she said quietly.

Three hours later, Liza leaned back in the chair in her office and stared out the small window. Her insides were still quaking with the magnitude of Anna's announcement at the board meeting, and the way things had changed. Everything, she thought grimly, had changed.

Before she'd left New York, Eli had tried to pin

her into telling him when she'd return. Like a coward, she'd managed to avoid him. She'd paid a visit to Joshua's grave on her way out of town, and found that even there things felt different. In the past few weeks, everything she'd come to count on, everything she believed in, had shifted. She wasn't sure she could face another major transition in her life. It made her feel panicky.

The phone on her desk rang. She picked it up with a frown. "Liza Kincaid."

"Hi, it's Rachel. I just got your message. My God, is it true?"

"About Anna? Yes, it's true."

"Lord, Liza, it's just too weird to think of Breeland without her. What's she going to do?"

That question, at least, Liza had settled with Anna over lunch. "She's stepping down as chairman of the board, and as head of the program, but she'll still be a part of what goes on here. I'm not sure I could even contemplate the summer program without her influence."

"I'm glad." Liza heard Rachel shift the phone against her ear. "So you said in your message that you had an idea for a send-off. What's on your mind?"

Liza leaned back in her chair. "Can you raise several thousand dollars for me in a week?"

"Sure. You got a current alumni list?"

"Yes."

"Email it to me. I can have the office make the phone calls. What are you planning?"

Liza gazed out the window again. "Anna has spent most of her life making dreams come true for people like you and me, Rachel. I think it's time we paid back the debt."

Eli turned into the parking space outside Breeland's largest auditorium, and switched off the ignition. The first time he'd seen Liza Kincaid dance, it had been in this very building. Then, she'd bewitched him.

"Are we going in, Daddy?"

He looked at Grace. She wore her dance recital costume tonight. It made her look impossibly grown-up. It had been two weeks since he'd last seen her. After that tumultuous day at his apartment, they'd spent three days together talking to each other, talking to a child psychiatrist friend of Eli's, and generally healing from the past few months.

Finally, by mutual consent, he and Grace had agreed that she should return with Liza to Breeland to finish her classes while he stayed behind in New York to tie up his legal battles—and to make sure the Paschells knew he wouldn't tolerate any more interference. He called every night, and to his increasing delight, Grace opened up to him more every day. Now that the truth was out in the open, and now that she no longer feared any backlash from her mother's death, she was free to express her own grief in her own way. With Liza's help, and the help of the counseling staff at Breeland, she seemed to be doing fine.

He was the one who'd turned into a basket case.

Liza, he knew, had been incredibly busy. The first of the three summer sessions was drawing to a close, and Liza had the dance recital, as well as the closing ceremonies to plan. Still, their few conversations had grown increasingly impersonal. She'd sent him a written invitation to the recital. Until he'd opened the envelope, he wasn't even sure he'd be welcome. Rachel Ramsey had relayed a number of requests to him—including Liza's instructions for the gift he'd brought Anna—but as far as he could tell, Liza wouldn't care whether he showed or not. That thought, along with an instinct that told him she was steadily pulling away from him, had his gut tied in knots.

"Daddy," Grace prompted.

He realized he still hadn't answered her question. "Yes," he said, simultaneously determined and trepidant. "We're going in. Do you have Anna's present?"

Grace shook the silver-wrapped box. "Right here."

He gave her a lopsided grin. "Do you have Liza's present?"

"It's in my pocket," she assured him. Rachel Ramsey and Lindsay had brought Grace to the Atlanta airport to meet his plane. He and his daughter had had plenty of time to talk in the hour-long trip back to Terrance as they'd followed Rachel and Lindsay in a rental car. Grace, at least, seemed confident about the evening.

Eli nodded. "Then let's go."

The auditorium hummed with energy and life.

Appropriate, Eli thought, for an event Liza had planned. Across the crowded foyer, where a mob of parents and students milled about snapping pictures and chattering above the din, Eli spotted Martin. He led Grace toward him. "Hello, Martin. You made it, I see."

"Wouldn't miss it." Martin stooped to hug Grace. "You look fabulous, darling."

Grace laughed. "Daddy said you were on vacation in the Caribbean and might not make it tonight."

Martin gave Eli a sidelong glance. "I was personally invited to this event by you, Grace, *and* Liza. What made you think I wouldn't be here?"

"A personal invitation," Eli said dryly. "Really?"

Martin nodded. "Yes. Liza and I have become quite good friends."

"She likes you," Grace told him. "She didn't think she would at first, but she does."

"The feeling is mutual," Martin assured her with a smile.

Grace beamed at him, then handed him Anna's wrapped gift. "I have to go get ready backstage. You and Daddy better get a seat or you won't be able to see me dance."

Eli watched, feeling a bittersweet longing as she disappeared backstage. Martin prodded him in the ribs. "The lovely Miss Ramsey is saving us seats near the front."

Eli looked at him with raised eyebrows. "The lovely Ms. Ramsey? I wasn't aware you two were so close."

Martin's long-suffering look was almost laughable. "You would probably be surprised at how much you haven't been aware of for the past several months." He poked him again. "Let's go. I don't want to miss anything."

An hour and a half later, Eli leaned back in his chair and watched with a mixture of pride and delight as his daughter charmed the audience in a tap duet with Lindsay. Liza had been right once again—not only did Grace have a natural talent, but she loved dancing. She had the audience, him included, in the palm of her hand as she and Lindsay finished the duet. The number concluded the annual dance recital, and brought the loudest cheers. Which, he noted with paternal pride, it fully deserved. He made a mental note to talk to Liza about Grace's continued lessons as soon as he could get her to have a personal discussion with him.

As if he'd conjured her up, Liza walked on stage, ushered in by the wildly appreciative applause of her audience. She gave them a broad smile as she accepted a wireless microphone from a stagehand. "Thank you," she said, waiting for some of the noise to die down. She was having trouble, Eli noted, gaining the audience's full attention. Ironic, he thought, as she had managed to rivet him the moment he'd seen her.

To catch his attention, Martin thrust Anna's package into his stomach so hard, it forced Eli to suck in a startled breath.

"Keep breathing," Martin warned him. "You'll pass out and embarrass me."

Scowling at him, Eli clutched the box and looked at Rachel. "Now?" he asked.

She shook her head. "Soon. Liza's going to make the announcement, then she'll ask for the gifts on stage. Yours is the last one."

"Great." He was rapidly calculating the chances of rushing the stage, abducting Liza, and kissing her senseless until they were both breathless. If Liza looked at him with that same cool, impersonal stare he'd seen as she boarded the plane to leave New York, he was fairly certain he'd do something rash.

His gaze shifted to Liza. She was talking about Anna's contributions to Breeland. Maybe if he moved quickly enough, he could get to the stage before someone stopped him. Once he had her in his arms, he wouldn't give her time to think. He'd make damned sure she was panting before he asked her what the hell was wrong with her. Then maybe, if he was lucky, she wouldn't tell him that she'd decided he couldn't be the man she needed.

He'd failed Mara like that. And if he hadn't, Grace never would have suffered through his ex-wife's bitterness. When Liza had told him about Joshua, a story he knew she'd shared with few others, he'd been so absorbed in his own world, that he'd tuned out her grief. A part of him hadn't wanted to share that hurt—and it almost killed him to admit that.

But Liza was an extremely perceptive woman,

and something told him that she knew. She knew he had refused to step up to the plate when he'd had the chance, and now, he'd lost her.

That pain started spreading in his chest again. He silently begged her to make eye contact with him. Give him something, anything, that might let him believe there was still a chance for them.

"And so," Liza was saying, "this is a sad night in some ways, because it marks the end of an incredible era at Breeland. But in other ways, I believe it is a new beginning for the school, for Anna Forian, and for the people she's loved." Applause roared through the room. Eli's ears were ringing.

Liza sent a signal to the wings, and a curtain lifted to reveal an orchestra of women, ages seventeen to indeterminable. Liza's dance students, still wearing their recital costumes, filed out from the wings and filled the front two rows of the auditorium. Bill Maxin ushered Anna on stage and seated her on a chair near the front of the orchestra. The audience responded with cheers and a standing ovation.

When the crowd finally quieted again, Liza continued, "So it is with great pride that I introduce to you, by exclusive arrangement with the board of visitors"—she gave Bill a slight smile— "the combined Breeland alumnae orchestra. And tonight, they'll be playing a piece that has great meaning to us all."

Rachel jabbed Eli in the ribs. "Now."

Martin shoved him into the center aisle. He walked quickly toward the stage, keeping a steady gaze on Liza. She still hadn't looked at him. "We couldn't have done this," she said into the mic, "without the generous help of so many friends of the academy. Anna didn't give us much time." The crowd laughed. "But I think we've come up with something that will begin to repay the tremendous debt we all owe her." Liza finally looked at Eli.

He held her gaze for long seconds, then handed her the box. Liza's fingers brushed his when she accepted it. He had to resist the urge to cling to her hand. She turned back to the audience. As many of you know, when Anna came to the United States, she was forced to leave her home in Austria, her husband, Rudolf, and her infant daughter. Despite the plans she'd made with her family, they were never reunited. For years, I know that she has struggled to find meaning in what had to be an immeasurably sad chapter in her life."

Liza paused, and Eli could almost feel the weight pressing in on her. He moved a step closer. She clutched the flat box to her chest. "She told me once that she found that meaning here, at Breeland, where she could share Rudolf's love of music with her students."

Indicating the orchestra behind her, she said, "some of these students. But what many of you don't know is that Rudolf not only played beautiful music, he wrote music." She gave Eli a grateful smile, "and thanks to our friend Dr. Liontakis, who enjoys significant contacts across international boundaries, we are able to present tonight something I don't think even Anna dreamed of."

Liza beckoned to Anna, whose eyes were gleaming with unshed tears. Bill led her forward to accept the box. To the accompaniment of a hushed audience, she peeled away the silver paper. Inside the flat box was a leather bound copy of the Dreamer's Waltz by Rudolf Forian—obtained after hundreds of phone calls from a library in Vienna, and preserved and bound by a friend of Eli's in Manhattan.

Anna, tears streaming down her weathered cheeks, clutched the manuscript to her chest and looked at Liza. "Thank you. Oh, thank you."

Liza embraced her, then turned back to the audience. Her voice was husky with unshed tears. "Tonight, the orchestra will present Rudolf Forian's Dreamer's Waltz." Liza met Eli's gaze. "And in recognition of the dreams Anna Forian gave us all, the dance department will interpret it."

Eli stilled. Vaguely, he remembered Martin's warning not to humiliate himself, but he couldn't make his lungs work. Somehow, he made it to the wings as the dancers filed on stage. He watched Liza take her place among them, and then felt himself fall completely under her spell as he watched the dance unfold.

He knew then that he had not given Liza the support she deserved. Just like her mother. Like her ex-husband. Like almost everyone else in her life. Her courage in dancing before them all tonight, despite her reservations, moved him.

He'd beg if he had to. If that's what it took for a second chance, he'd do it. He watched the dance, felt every step she took, and knew she'd wrapped herself so tightly around his heart that he'd never be the same after tonight.

When it ended, Anna was still crying. She wasn't alone. The audience surged to its feet and applauded. Tears flowed freely. Eli saw Liza duck quickly behind a curtain, then make her way off stage. He stood for a minute, struggling with indecision.

Something nudged his hand. He looked down to find Grace pressing a small box into his palm. "Go, Dad," she said. "Tell her now, before it's too late."

His fingers curled around the box. He paused to press a kiss to his daughter's forehead, then raced after Liza.

He found her in one of the dressing rooms, taking deep, calming breaths. He stopped at the doorway and allowed his eyes to feast on the sight of her. What a fool he'd been. How had he ever convinced himself that this woman wasn't an inseparable part of him. "You were beautiful," he said quietly.

With a startled gasp, Liza snapped her head around. "Eli." She stared at him for the span of three heartbeats. "You startled me."

"Sorry." He walked into the room. "I had to see you."

"I thought you'd still be backstage with everyone else. I—I didn't have time to thank you earlier for taking care of the manuscript. We couldn't have done this without you."

He paused to reach behind him and shut the door. "My pleasure. I was glad to do it for her."

Liza pressed back against the mirrored wall and watched him through wary eyes. "What did you want?"

That made him smile slightly. "You need to ask me that?"

"Eli—"

He held up a hand. "No, please let me finish. Here's the thing, Liza. I've had almost three weeks to think this through. And I know I haven't always been what you wanted. I know there were times—especially when it came to facing your memories of Joshua—that I was too wrapped up in myself to give you what you needed."

"I told you I understood."

"But you didn't," he said sadly. "And you shouldn't have had to." He paused. "I screwed up, just like I did with Mara."

"You had problems of your own to deal with. I know that."

His eyes drifted shut. "You did, too. But you made time for me."

"It's not the same," she said quietly.

He looked at her once more. "No, it's not. But that doesn't change what I came here to say." He crossed the final few steps to where she stood. It felt intoxicatingly good to be this close to her again. He had to fight the urge to take her in his arms. "I know I don't deserve it. And I know there are a thousand reasons why you should throw me out of your life, but my God, Liza, I love you. Doesn't that count for something?"

She studied his face with an inscrutable expression. "Everything's changing, Eli. The board has asked me to take on the administration of the summer program."

"Rachel told me."

"Without Anna," she shrugged, "it's a big job."

"You'll be great at it."

She fixed him with a pointed look. "I can't do it from Manhattan."

It took him a moment to absorb the fact that she hadn't said she couldn't do it with him, or with the responsibilities of a marriage or a family. She'd said she couldn't do it from New York. He wet his lips. "No. I'm sure you couldn't," he said carefully. "So I was thinking maybe Grace might like to live in Terrance. Permanently."

A tiny smile played on her lips. "You'd be bored stiff. What are you going to do, teach chemistry for the rest of your life?"

"If that's what it takes." He nodded his head. "If that's what I have to do to be with you, then yes, I will."

Liza shook her head. Amusement sparkled in her eyes, and Eli's ears were starting to ring. "I don't think it'll work," she said.

"It has to." He took a step closer. "Because I'm going to marry you, and this is where you belong. So if you're here, that means I'm here. For good."

"Who said anything about marriage?" she asked.

That made him frown. "Liza—"

"Though I suppose the board wouldn't really approve of their summer program director living in sin with one of their guest lecturers. It might not look good."

Eli wrapped his fingers around her shoulders. "Say, yes, Liza," he urged. "We'll work the rest out. I swear to you, we'll find a way to work it out."

"You'll stay here and teach?"

He thought of his research, of the groundbreaking strides they were making at the lab, of the very real possibility that within a year, two at most, he could play a role in finding a cure for cancer. Taking a deep breath, he nodded. "Yes."

Liza laid a hand against his face. "Oh, Eli. For a smart man, you can be a real idiot." He stared at her. She leaned forward to kiss the corner of his mouth. "The summer program only runs from May to August. I was thinking that, maybe, the rest of the year, I might like to give private lessons. In Manhattan. That is, of course, if you know someplace I can stay in the city. Teachers don't make much money, and the cost of living up there—"

He didn't let her finish. With a soft groan, he pulled her into his arms. "My God, I love you."

Liza sighed and wrapped her arms around his waist. "I love you, too, Eli. Enough to know you're worth a few risks."

He kissed her then, long and thoroughly, and didn't raise his head until they were both straining for breath. Liza dropped her head against his chest. "And while we're on the subject," she said quietly, "I think you should know that if you ever tell me again that you can't be what I need, I'm going to kick you in the shins."

Stroking her back, he put his chin on the top her head. "Really?"

"Yes, you dolt. I'm not a complete moron, you know. If I picked you to fall in love with, I'll thank you to credit me with enough insight to know what I was doing."

He choked out a laugh. "Just tell me you're going to marry me and I'll shut up."

"It's marriage or nothing?"

"It's marriage or nothing," he answered. "I want to make sure you wake up with me every morning. I want to go to sleep next to you, and share your dreams and your sorrows and your triumphs. I want to know that I have a home. I want us to have children—and if you don't want to, or you can't, or it doesn't work out—then I want us to lavish everything we have on Grace. Just let me love you." He swept her hair off her face. "You can't imagine how much I want that."

She smoothed her fingers over his shoulder. "Summers in Terrance, and the rest of the year in Manhattan?"

"Hell," he muttered, "the rest of the year in Timbuktu if that's what you want."

"No way. I'm marrying a Nobel prize nominee, I expect to at least have the trophy on my mantel." She tilted her head. "Do you get a trophy when you win one of those?"

He choked back a laugh. "Money. You get money."

"Oh, well, even better, although I think one of those big gaudy brass things would be nice. You know, like they give for softball tournaments."

"Liza." God, he was laughing again. How did she do this to him?

"Well, you have to admit, Eli. It's a real conversation starter. I mean, you can just sort of glance around in surprise and say, '*That* old thing? That's from the Nobel Prize Committee.' "

He kissed her because he couldn't help himself. "If it'll make you happy, I'll tattoo it on my forehead."

"Well, maybe someplace where no one can see it but me—"

"I love you," he said again.

"And I love you. And that's why if we're going anywhere, it's someplace where you can keep saving the world." Her expression turned serious. "It's part of who you are, Eli. And I love that part, too."

He could almost feel the blood filling his veins again. She'd finally done it—she'd managed to bring him back to life. What a fool he'd been not to realize that what he'd needed all along was to love and be loved. He kissed her again, more gently this time. "Thank you," he whispered.

Liza nodded. "How does Grace feel about this?"

With a smile, he reached into his pocket and

produced a flat ring box. "She was keeping this for me." He flipped it open so she could see the diamond solitaire. "On the off chance that her old man might manage to finally get it right."

Liza laughed. The sound set off sparks inside him. He took the ring from the box and would have slid it on her finger, except that the door burst open and Grace, flanked by Martin, Rachel, Anna, and Bill came streaming into the already crowded room.

"For God's sake, man," Martin said. "What did she say?"

Grace flew across the room and wrapped her arms around the two of them. "You have to do it, Liza. You *have* to. Even if Daddy didn't say it exactly like I told him to, you have to say yes."

Rachel looked at Eli, then at Liza. "Did we give you enough time?"

"Barely." He couldn't keep the surly note from his voice. If they'd given him just a few more minutes, he'd have had her right where he wanted her.

Anna laughed. "I have a feeling if we'd given you any more time, you might have created another Breeland scandal."

"And I," Bill said, "would have been stuck dealing with it." He looked at Liza. "Well, did you say yes, or not? Don't keep us in suspense."

Liza placed one hand on Grace's shoulder. She looked at Eli, pressed a kiss to the corner of his mouth, then faced the rest of the group. "You'll be happy to know that I can, on occasion, be smart enough to do the right thing. I said yes."

Grace squealed and hugged Liza fiercely. "Oh, good."

Eli slid the ring on her finger. "My thoughts exactly."

The other four occupants of the room rushed forward to offer their congratulations. Anna kissed him lightly on the cheek. "I'm so pleased, Eli. I couldn't have planned it better myself."

Liza gave her a mocking frown. "What are you talking about? You did plan it."

Everyone laughed. Rachel hugged them both, then started pushing Martin, Bill and Anna toward the door. "Let's go," she told them. "They can meet us at the reception."

"Five minutes," Martin warned as Rachel propelled him through the door, or I'm coming in after you."

When the door shut once more, Liza looked at Grace. "Are you sure you're all right with this?"

Grace nodded happily. "Oh, yes. I was the one who told Daddy to quit being such a jerk and do something about it. You should have *seen* the way he was acting, Liza. He was making me nuts."

"Pouting?"

"Cranky," Grace assured her. "Ever since you left him in New York he's been impossible."

"So you told him you thought we should get married?"

"Yes," Grace assured her. "I told him exactly what to say."

Liza gave Eli an amused look. "And what was that?"

"I told him to make sure he said that he knew he didn't want anyone else ever again."

"I don't," Eli said quietly. "I couldn't." He held Liza's gaze for a long second. "You're everything to me."

Liza's eyes misted. "I love you so much," she told him, then turned to Grace. "I love you, too."

Grace smiled at her. "I know. And that was why."

"Why what?" Liza asked.

"Why Daddy has to marry you." Grace slipped her hand into Eli's. "You made us love you, Liza. It had to be you."

Liza blinked back tears as she pressed a soft kiss to Eli's mouth. "I assure you, the feeling is mutual."

Curious minds want to know—is dashing millionaire Rory Kincaid about to resign as the sexiest man in town? Could his bride-to-be really be enchantingly infuriating Jilly Skye?

And if he steps down as one of the most eligible bachelors in America, what will happen to the millions of women he's left dreaming about . . .

This Perfect Kiss
by Christie Ridgway

**Coming in January from
Avon Contemporary Romance**

Christie Ridgway's star began to rise with her Avon debut, *Wish You Were Here*. Now, she's created her most captivating love story yet! Don't miss it!